The Poet and the Idiot

OTHER TITLES IN THE SERIES

Prague Tales
Jan Neruda

Skylark
Dezső Kosztolányi

Be Faithful Unto Death
Zsigmond Móricz

The Doll
Boleslav Prus

The Adventures of Sindbad
Gyula Krúdy

The Sorrowful Eyes of Hannah Karajich
Ivan Olbracht

The Birch Grove and Other Stories
Jaroslaw Iwaszkiewicz

The Coming Spring
Stefan Żeromski

The Poet and the Idiot

and other stories

Friedebert Tuglas

Translated by Eric Dickens

Central European University Press

Budapest • New York

Published in 2007 by

Central European University Press
An imprint of the
Central European University Share Company
Nádor utca 11, H-1051 Budapest, Hungary
Tel: +36-1-327-3138 or 327-3000
Fax: +36-1-327-3183
E-mail: ceupress@ceu.hu
Website: www.ceupress.com

400 West 59th Street, New York NY 10019, USA
Tel: +1-212-547-6932
Fax: +1-646-557-2416
E-mail: mgreenwald@sorosny.org

This translation was supported by a fellowship
from the National Endowment for the Humanities

ISBN 978-963-7326-88-2
ISSN 1418-0162

Library of Congress Cataloging in Publication Data

Tuglas, Friedebert, 1886-1971.
[Short stories. English. Selections]
The poet and the idiot : and other stories / Friedebert Tuglas ; translated by Eric Dickens.
p. cm. -- (Central European classics series)
Includes bibliographical references.
ISBN-13: 978-9637326882 (pbk.)
I. Dickens, Eric. II. Title.
PH665.T8A25 2007
894'.545--dc22

2007014653

Printed in Hungary

Contents

Introduction

Estonian literature in its written form is little more than a century old. While oral poetry dates back hundreds of years, and was avidly collected during the 19th century by enthusiasts who often spoke German at home, novels, poetry, essays and criticism written in the Estonian language did not begin to flower until the end of that century.

As Estonia was part of the Russian Empire, then of the Soviet Union, it is something of a miracle that the powerful presence of the Baltic Germans, the periods of Russification, and other more subtle forms of cultural pressure, have not eradicated Estonian as a serious literary language. Today, not only are many books written in Estonian, but most key works of world literature are translated into it, for a potential readership of no more than a million people. One of the central figures to encourage this development during the first half of the 20th century was Friedebert Tuglas.

THE AUTHOR

Friedebert Tuglas was born Friedebert Mihkelson on 18th February 1886 on the grounds of the Ahja manor where his father worked as a carpenter. The manor lay near the university city of Tartu (German: *Dorpat*; Russian *Yuryev*). His initial schooling occurred in the Russian language, but by 1901, Tuglas was being sent to schools where Estonian was the language of instruction. His childhood appears to have been a happy one and this is reflected in one of the sunniest of his works, the novel *Väike Illimar* (Little Illimar), which appeared in 1937, much later than the stories featured here. But at the age of nineteen, Tuglas fell foul of the Czarist authorities when he was caught up in the events of the 1905 revolution and spent three months in prison, in Toompea Gaol in Tallinn, right under what is now the Estonian Parliament.

For more than a decade after his release, Tuglas became a homeless wanderer, living in several European countries and visiting several more. By September 1906 he had established himself as a regular visitor to Finland, but his restless spirit meant that he spent five consecutive winters living in Paris at the Estonian artists' colony housed in a round building called *La Ruche*, and lived for much shorter periods in Germany, Belgium and Switzerland. He even visited Estonia on a number of occasions by using false passports he borrowed from literary friends for the purpose. But he could never stay long, afraid that the police would catch up with him.

During this period of exile, Tuglas also made longer visits to Italy (Rome, Genoa, Naples) and Spain (Madrid, Toledo, Seville, Granada, Barcelona), and his travel diaries from both those countries were later published and incorporated in his Collected Works. Being an Estonian, i.e. a citizen of a small nation, Friedebert Tuglas was always sensitive to the fate of other isolated peoples. His description of how the Catalonians fared with regard to the Castilians in Spain is as relevant today as it was in 1913 when he visited the Iberian Peninsula.

During the period of the First World War (1914–18), the author was busy writing some of the most memorable of his short-stories, several of which have been translated for this volume. He also wrote the summer novel, *Felix Ormusson* (which appeared in 1915), involving a love triangle. Like so many of Tuglas' works, this novel had a slow birth, being first thought about, then drafted, then revised and expanded, until a final version was arrived at. Also typical of Tuglas' working method is that parts and drafts of the novel were written in various countries, in this case near Helsinki and in Paris; Tuglas drew together the drafted fragments while on the shores of Lake Ladoga. A similar origin for each of the stories presented here can be gleaned from the notes at the end of this book.

When Estonia became independent after the First World War, the Russian Revolution, and the Estonian War of Independence, Tuglas returned home and joined various literary movements. In 1918, he married Elo Oinas, who was to remain his wife until her death in 1970, a year before Tuglas himself died.

During the 1920s, Tuglas settled down, became a literary critic, then Chairman of the Estonian Writers' Union and, in 1923, founded the literary monthly *Looming* (Creative Endeavour), which still appears today. On several occasions Tuglas was editor-in-chief of this publication. At about this time, Friedebert Mihkelson turned the nom-de-plume "Tuglas" into his official surname. The name is said to be *Douglas*—as in Alfred, Lord Douglas—pronounced in an Estonian manner. That same decade, Tuglas was made an honorary member of the Finnish Writers' Association.

During the 1920s and 1930s, Tuglas made two longer documented trips abroad, one to the Maghreb in 1928, another to the Scandinavian countries a decade later. His experiences in North Africa are recounted in an almost 300-page-long travelogue. Tuglas visited Tunisia, Algeria and Morocco (especially Marrakesh, Fez and Casablanca). As in the case of Spain some two decades earlier, Tuglas does not fail to mention smaller nations, such as the Berbers, and is aware of the history of North Africa during ancient times, also touching upon the subject of Islam and differences between that religion and Christianity.

In 1937, the same year that his novel *Little Illimar* appeared, Friedebert Tuglas was made an honorary member of the PEN Club in London at the same time a similar honor was bestowed on the leading Estonian woman poet of that epoch, Marie Under. The letter was signed by then PEN Chairman, Herman Ould, and there was even talk of setting up an Estonian branch of PEN.

A couple of years later, war broke out. The first Soviet occupation of Estonia lasted from the summer of 1940 to the summer of 1941. The German Nazis then invaded the country and stayed until the Red Army pushed them out in 1944. The rest of Tuglas' life was spent under the renewed Soviet occupation, which finally ended in 1991, two decades after his death.

Tuglas was leftist by instinct and had many friends among writers and artists with Communist sympathies. During the right-wing autocracy of the 1930s, such people had to tread carefully and remained more cultural figures than political ones. But once the Soviets arrived, things changed. Some left-wing intellectuals now occupied posts in the Soviet Estonian puppet governments, such as Johannes Semper, who served as Minister of Education during the government of 1940–41. In the 1930s Semper had been interested in aesthetics and philosophy, and wrote a dissertation on style and structure in the works of André Gide. An even more interesting, albeit tragic, example of political collaboration was that of the medical physician, expert on Modernist French poetry and later Soviet Estonian prime-minister, Johannes Vares (nom-de plume "Barbarus"), who committed suicide under suspicious circumstances in 1946, said to have been "persuaded" to go to his death by the Soviet secret police.

Tuglas himself miraculously avoided getting caught up in national politics in a fatal way during all three Estonian occupations, but he suffered as well. During the first Soviet occupation, Tuglas edited *Looming*, but then fled to the countryside during the ensuing German takeover of Estonia, when his Tartu home and several of his manuscripts were destroyed in 1944 during the bombing of the city. When the Soviets returned in that year, and the Estonian Soviet Socialist Republic was restored, a difficult period in Tuglas' life began. Accused, like Semper, of cosmopolitanism and harboring anti-Soviet sentiments, he was likewise expelled from the Writers' Union and forced to make his living by translating, having been banned from all publishing in his own name. After the death of Stalin, Tuglas and Semper were rehabilitated.

The only monograph biography of Tuglas to date appeared in 1968, written by the Communist Nigol Andresen, who had been the Estonian translator of the *Communist Manifesto* during the 1930s and still had good connections within the Party. But even Andresen had suffered during the post-WWII Stalinist purges in occupied Estonia and had spent time in prison, something Tuglas himself had managed to avoid after his sojourn in Toompea Gaol back in 1905–6.

When Friedebert Tuglas died in 1971, he had become revered as the grand old man of Estonian literature. His home, formerly that of the major Estonian woman poet Marie Under and her husband, who had fled to Sweden in 1944, was turned into the *Tuglas Museum* which, after renewed Estonian independence in 1991, was renamed the *Tuglas and Under Museum.*

THE STORIES

All the stories, and the essay, featured here were written during the First World War, 1914–1918, or in the first years of Estonian independence in the early 1920s. The style in which they are written can be termed Gothic Symbolist. They somehow reflect the troubled spirit of the times, but exhibit the influence of a wide selection of writers, ranging from J. P. Jacobsen, via Oscar Wilde and Maxim Gorky, to Friedrich Nietzsche and Georges Rodenbach, and Edgar Allan Poe—i.e. writers from Denmark, Ireland, Russia, Germany, Belgium and the United States.

Tuglas was interested in the visual arts, and this too can be sensed from the stories, which contain vivid, even garish, colors and descriptions of moods and landscapes that are sometimes heightened and distorted, as can be seen in paintings from that epoch.

The subject matter of Tuglas' stories represented here ranges from a starving prisoner, via a luckless pharmacist's hallucinations from childhood, a wandering soldier who encounters weird spirits, to a young man sitting in a park, accosted by a devilish lunatic who wants to introduce a new brand of devil worship to the world. Previously, between 1901 and the beginning of the First World War, Tuglas had written in a more realistic and romantic vein, but, perhaps on account of the mood of the war and his long wanderings in Western Europe, he began to write his core stories. Tuglas was always simultaneously working on several stories of rather different mood and subject matter, so that, within the general category of Gothic Symbolism, the results are interestingly varied.

The mentality of Friedebert Tuglas, as reflected in his works, has something of both the short-story writer Poe and the filmmaker Ingmar Bergman. Both of these artists oscillate between a pronounced morbidity and wacky, burlesque humor. Poe not only wrote "The Fall of the House of Usher" but also the spoof on the submission of works to various publications "The Literary Life of Thingum Bob, Esq." Bergman, whose black-and-white films of the 1950s were heavy, dark and sombre, and in which even clowns and circuses were redolent of depression and death, also made comedies and the epic "Fanny and Alexander," which is chiefly a work of sun and family, though still streaked with gloom. Bergman once said of himself in a TV interview: "At heart, I'm a jolly old man really." Such could also be said of Tuglas as he grew older, a man who, a decade or so after finishing his suite of Gothic Symbolist stories, ended up writing the delightful realist novel of childhood, *Little Illimar*, and who was always ready to turn his hand to hoaxes such as *Arthur Valdes* or write Whitmanèsque poems mocking Stalin.

*

The first story here, *Freedom and Death* (1915), already shows Tuglas' clear interest in hallucination and distorted reality. The protagonist is the starving prisoner, Rannus, who is filing away at the bars across a window facing the street. He is unable to emerge from his hiding place in the prison's firewood storeroom, where he can see, but not reach, city life below. The reader is never quite sure what he is seeing and what he is imagining. The building site across the street is described using starkly garish colors.

While Tuglas published very little poetry during his lifetime, there is often a poetic, even musical rhythm to his stories. The most well crafted example of this is perhaps *The Golden Hoop* (1916), which is divided into three parts where both the short paragraphs and interlude of the middle part of the story, give a feeling of tight composition. Once again, the theme of distorted reality and dreamlike landscapes is very clear, as is the vividness of the colors of faces, clothing and elements of nature. This particular story is based on a folk tale to which Tuglas added elements of his own.

One curious story is *Arthur Valdes* (1916), which is the fictional biography of a mythical Estonian writer, and also Tuglas' aesthetic credo. It is a partly autobiographical work from the time that Tuglas was living in Paris with a number of Estonian painters—Nikolai Triik, Konrad Mägi and Ado Vabbe—whom Tuglas had originally met on the Swedish-speaking Åland archipelago, between Finland and Sweden. This story has led various other Estonian writers, including August Gailit, Jaan Kross and Toomas Vint, to introduce the figure of Arthur Valdes, originally invented by Tuglas, into their stories and novels. Tuglas here in effect reviews a collection of stories he never wrote, using Valdes as his mouthpiece. Estonian academic and translator Mihkel Mõisnik examines the derivation of this style of fiction in detail in a dissertation.

Cannibals (1916) is a story of awakening sexuality and death. Three small children, two boys and a girl, are playing an innocent game of cannibals as they walk through the landscape near an old lime kiln. The sister of one of them has been missing for a couple of days. They then stumble upon her body in the kiln, where she has hanged herself on account of an unhappy love affair and pregnancy. The story examines the mood of the children and their growing awareness of adult sexuality.

Echo of the Epoch, written between 1914 and 1919, is not a story, but a series of short cultural observations, and is heavily influenced by the mood and events of the First World War. It is almost Gidean in its aphoristic quality. Tuglas made many such observations, which have been collected in a work entitled "Marginalia," the 96 short sections of which were collated from notes made between 1906 and 1936. It is clear that Tuglas employs a similar style in both his stories and short aphoristic pieces. But he was much less "literary" in the large body of critical works he produced over the years, with longer essays on, for example, William Shakespeare, Henrik Ibsen, Valeri Bryussov and Alexis Kivi.

The Wanderer (1919) is another of Tuglas' stories that was influenced by his sojourn in Paris. Again Tuglas divides the story into three parts, as he did with *The Golden Hoop*. It is a relatively bookish story, with Allan, the protagonist, reading everything from Flaubert's "Temptations of Saint Anthony" to the *Bhagavad-Gita*. The middle section involves a mysterious lady, while the final part blends themes from the first two: literary influences—this time Baudelaire, Nietzsche and Whitman—and the return of the lady.

The Mermaid (1920) is more of a modernized fairytale. It is the story of an outsider, Kurdis, a somewhat malformed trapper of frogs for the table of the island brigand leader Kaspar the Red. The local people worship Kaspar the Red, who bribes them with feasts and merriment. The all-powerful Kaspar bigamously marries a mermaid caught in his fishing net, wherefore the name of the story. In the end, the mermaid, when set free, does what all mermaids do, drawing the sad misfit down with her into the depths.

The Air is Full of Passion (1920) is said to have been influenced by Lafcadio Hearn, and tells the story of a cavalryman, the cynical Lieutenant Lorens, who chances upon a small house while out riding. The house is populated by rather sinister beings, including the young woman Mirandola. This story reminds one of the Weird Tales comics that had become popular in America at about the time Tuglas was writing it, and is perhaps the nearest Tuglas got to writing a horror tale.

The Poet and the Idiot (1920) is, by contrast, almost a philosophical tract. Tuglas originally wanted to include the story in his novel about a triangular love affair, *Felix Ormusson* (1915), but found that the subject matter and length of the section no longer fitted in. The main character here is still Ormusson himself, who is sitting in a park overlooking the city of Tartu. He is disturbed by a cranky figure whose pockets are stuffed with slips of paper, on which his madcap theory of converting the world to devil worship are written. The fifth and final section of the story involves a hallucinatory symposium including the "idiot" he meets in the park, a Dominican monk and various other figures, all of whom argue how a system of philosophy can be made attractive to the masses.

The last of the stories translated here, *The Day of the Androgyne* (1925), is somewhat lighter than the rest, perhaps reflecting the fact that Tuglas could relax, now that the Estonian Republic had come into being. What is intriguing about this short novella is the fact that it has the same style—*commedia dell'arte*—and subject matter—

sex change—as Virginia Woolf's novel *Orlando*, which appeared three years later. This story is said to have arisen from a jocular conversation at an authors meeting, where someone suggested Tuglas had published a (non-existent) collection of stories entitled "The Hermaphrodite's Trousers." The joke led to a well-crafted story, partly mood poem, partly spoof. In the space of one day, the Androgyne wakes up as a little Princess, ages years at a time, and turns into a man halfway through who, in turn, ages and becomes a cruel old Prince. The events are similar to those in *Orlando*, except that they occur in reverse; in the Woolf book, the Prince turns into a Princess. Whether both Tuglas and Woolf gathered their influences from similar Russian sources remains speculation. There are even echoes, in the opening passages, of Alexander Pope's "The Rape of the Lock." And Tuglas also manages to incorporate within the story a satire on the private squabbles of those in government.

ACKNOWLEDGEMENTS AND BIBLIOGRAPHY

I would like to thank Tiina Randviir of the Estonian Institute for her close reading of my translations of these stories and for rescuing me from the inevitable mistakes that a translator makes.

*

As search engines, the Wikipedia and other internet sources of information are so plentiful nowadays, I have not annotated the stories. I have often explained the few Estonian references by a word or two within the text. But the names of European and other artists, writers, composers and other cultural figures can easily be found on the internet.

*

Eight volumes of Friedebert Tuglas' Collected Works have been published to date as part of a project begun in 1986. Between 1957 and 1962, a set of eight volumes were published, covering largely the same works, but now that Estonia is independent and has shrugged off Soviet censorship, more of the previously suppressed or abridged material can be published. The new *Collected Works* will also include a good deal more of Tuglas' critical work.

*

The texts of all the stories and of the essay "Echo of the Epoch" (*Aja kaja*) have been translated from the Collected Works (*Kogutud Teosed*) of Friedebert Tuglas, as published between 1986 and 2001 by the Eesti Raamat publishing house in Tallinn. The notes on the individual stories that Tuglas himself wrote, and which are to be found at the end of the book, come from a volume entitled "Rahutu rada" (The Restless Path), published posthumously in 1973, where a number of supplementary notes are to be found that do not appear elsewhere. This volume has not yet been incorporated in the Collected Works.

*

When choosing which stories to translate, I have deliberately avoided some of Tuglas' most famous ones, e.g. *Popi and Huhu, The End of the World, The Last Greeting* and *Riders in the Sky,* as the volume *Riders in the Sky*, which includes these and other stories, can easily be obtained via on-line bookshops. These were translated by Oleg Mutt, an Estonian who spent his childhood years in New York and thus had a good command of English. To complete the circle, Oleg Mutt's son, Mihkel, is the present editor of the previously mentioned literary monthly *Looming*, which was started by Friedebert Tuglas.

Eric Dickens, July 2006

Freedom and Death

1.

The moon rose from behind the walls. Sharp black shadows cut the square stone yard in two. Between the round cobbles sprouted spring grass. The sickly green blades reached out above the cobbles still hot from day—as if extending welcoming healing fingers to their friends.

Rannus lay high up under the ceiling by the narrow window looking out. The milky light of the full moon shone in his face. He was a thin man with a straggly red beard, wearing a grey prison uniform. He inhaled the cool air from the large stones deeply, and watched the sky grow darker and the moon rise higher, turning pink.

He had been lying here the whole evening, hidden by birch logs, with his face turned to the yard, which he could see through the window as narrow as the slit of an arrow. He had seen himself being searched for, he had listened to the curses of the principal warder and watched the backs of the warders' heads, bowed in guilt.

They had strode around and quarreled until it had grown dark. They had opened the door of the firewood store and looked for him there. He had heard them rummaging among the logs and talking about him. His heart had been pounding with fear. He had stuffed his fist into his mouth, in order not to cry out. He was afraid his heartbeat would shift the whole pile of logs.

But they had not discovered him! They slammed the door shut and locked it again. He could see them standing helplessly in the yard in the evening light: to escape from the yard, surrounded on all four sides by stone walls like a well, and exit from which was only possible through a guarded passageway, would be something of a miracle!

He had risked everything, even his very life. Today or never! By tomorrow he would no longer have been lying here, his limbs free. Just before evening, he had seen the blacksmith crossing the yard with his tools. Tomorrow he would have been in irons with his fetters riveted. And the day after, he would be on his way to Siberia.

Because the local authorities had handed him over. Oh, how his doddering old mother had poked her fingers through the bars and whispered, how she had pleaded with the local council, had run alongside the judge's horse—her ancient hair flying and her hands stretched out! But they had brushed her aside.

Rannus lay there, his fist pressed to his teeth. He wanted to get out and avenge himself on them, to a man! He wanted to shoot the whole lot of them, burn down their houses, and gallop off to Pskov with their best horses!

He had never complained about his sentence. He had committed a crime and was being punished for it—that much he understood. But now an injustice had been committed. Was there any debt left for him to repay that justified this abuse? He had received more than his full measure! Quite enough, and more besides!

He would rather die than live forever without hope and remain in this pit they had pushed him into. He wanted to walk in the footsteps of that man whose deeds were spoken in a whisper from one generation of prisoners to the next, like memories from great epochs.

What was he compared with him! He had built a lighthouse on a high cliff. On stormy autumn nights it had cast its blood red light over the foamy waves, luring ships into its web like a spider. With a bloody sword in hand, his coal beard black fluttering in the wind, he had stood on the shore as the sea raged.

He had sat in the cell, and now in the woodshed, with an iron ring around his throat and his legs in irons. He had remained there for a long time, then he had escaped. He had broken his fetters like Samson and battered through the walls with his iron fists. Under the thin layer of limestone he had found an ancient secret tunnel. He had broken through to it and fled.

As they sat in their cell in the light of the yellow lamp, the prisoners fancied that they heard his chains jangling down in the cellar as they lay on their bunks. The autumn winds blew the ends of his long beard through the bars, and he seemed to be urging them on to great deeds there from beyond the cell, immortal for centuries, like the Wandering Jew.

And like this man, Rannus wanted to seek his fortune! The memory frightened and consoled him. He had wanted to walk in his footsteps, touch the same parts of the walls as the pirate had once done. This would have brought him—a wretched and crippled man—joy.

He watched the empty yard with feverish eyes. His thoughts raced at a crazy pace, his dreams were aflame. The moon crept higher and higher—it was as if someone were walking across the coal black night sky with a misty lantern.

As if in his sleep, Rannus counted the strokes of the clock. Then he gave a start: midnight already, and he was still here, at the start of his journey, anything but free! Was it not all the same whether you were lying on your bunk in your cell or hidden here under a pile of firewood, only to fall into their hands again the next morning?

He sat up, cautiously rolling the small logs off his body. The stack nearly reached up to the ceiling, so he couldn't stand up. He looked around him: the cellar was pitch dark. He could hardly see the faint glimmer of the birch bark of the tree outside the window. Everything was silent as the grave.

He began crawling on all fours, stopping every minute to listen. All he could hear was the way the dust fell down from the logs. Then all at once, his hands snatched at thin air. He turned around and sat on the edge of the pile, his legs dangling over the sides.

He listened again for a moment, but all was silent. Then he began to lower himself from the stack, feeling his way down with his feet. His toes touched the lower logs. He began descending, as if by a flight of stairs. The stack creaked and rocked under him.

Suddenly, he stumbled and fearfully grabbed the top of the stack. At that same moment, a log slipped out from under his feet and fell with a clatter onto the stone floor. Rannus crouched down, as if his legs had been hit, and put his hand, which had been bloodied by gripping the stack, into his mouth.

There he sat for a while, sucking his thumb, his eyes straining in the darkness. He was shaking all over with fear. He did not dare move an inch: how far might the clatter perhaps be heard! The warders would hear it through the open airing window of the corridor, and even in the guardroom they could be awakened by the noise.

He waited for a long time, motionless. But everything was still. Then he rose to his feet and began to feel his way over the piles of split logs, the ladders and planks. He moved like a poltergeist, secretly towards the door whose crosspieces he had once hacked through when he had been left alone for a while chopping wood.

He squeezed between the woodpile and the wall. His jacket scraped slightly against the plaster and the logs. He felt around the door, found the pile of sawdust, and dug into it. Then his hand eased the door open, so it stood ajar. Using all his force, he pressed his bony body through the crack.

He stopped just outside the door, struck by the endless darkness and icy cold. He found the stub of a candle in his shirt pocket and lit it: he was standing at the beginning of a narrow passage, his head touching the ceiling. Directly in front of him was a brick staircase whose crumbling steps led down into the darkness like an underground river in grey waves.

2.

Holding his candle close to him, Rannus walked down the steps. His hand was trembling and his knees shaking from fear, so he found it hard to walk. The air between the moldy walls grew even chillier. After several dozen meters, the staircase came abruptly to an end and a downward sloping passage began.

Rannus walked briskly downhill, like someone being pushed from behind. He took larger strides with his injured leg than with the healthy one. Blood began to drip again from his thumb and he stuck it in his mouth. In this way he loped forward, one hand to his mouth, the other holding the candle.

After some time, the passage changed. The downward slope grew less pronounced, the muddy floor almost leveled out. The walls, plastered at first, now became more uneven. The passage now was through limestone, and no attempt had been made to smooth the walls. Here and there, sharp stones jutted out, and he had to take care not to trip up on the uneven floor.

He walked for a long time and his pace slowed down. There were bends in the passage here and there and he had to sometimes make sharp turns. He stopped now and again, looking over his shoulder, but saw nothing: two or three weak rays from the candle were reflected by the walls, slightly illuminating the bumps on the walls.

Then the passage began to open out. A few steps later, Rannus was in a space the size of a small room, and before him lay the mouths of two passages. He came to a halt in dismay: which passage should he take? Which was shorter? And where did they emerge?

He stopped a moment to think. His indecision rose, and with it his agitation. Nevertheless, he could not spend much time deciding. He chose the right-hand passage, which seemed wider, and began proceeding along it. But his previous joy at being free was now ruined.

He only managed to walk for several dozen steps, when he suddenly stumbled over a pile of stones that had fallen from the ceiling. He scrambled over it and continued on his way. But the passage grew ever more irregular. All at once it ended in a confusion of higgledy-piggledy slabs of limestone, whose jagged edges were turned towards Rannus like the teeth of a saw.

He came to a halt for a moment at this rubble, and turned sadly on his heels. It was a dead end! He should have taken the other passage! He suddenly felt his exhaustion, his shirt grew wet despite the chill of the cellar and, on reaching the room again, he sank down wearily upon the pile of stones.

He wiped the dust from his pockmarked face. He wasn't used to exerting himself and grew tired so quickly! He looked around: curved black walls, a vault from which stones stuck out like claws, and the dusty floor, over which the candle cast a weak light.

Then his eyes fell on the candle. How rapidly it had burned! There was hardly half left. And yet he had a long way to go. But he could not set off now, he wanted to rest a while before setting off again. He raised the candle to his lips and blew it out.

He was instantly enveloped by pitch blackness. He stayed where he was without stirring, without even daring to lower the hand holding the candle. In the darkness, he now felt something else he had not noticed before, namely the silence. It was a dizzying lack of sound, which was tangible, painful to his skin.

He closed his eyes and tried to picture where he was. He felt as if he had left time and space and entered an underground realm of darkness and silence. He had abruptly left everything he was familiar with, daily life and human concerns, and felt as if he had been journeying for several days in a row.

His blood throbbed in his ears and fearful thoughts entered his brain. He suddenly felt himself to be shut in by the stone walls—around, above and below. He felt the ghastly stoniness, the sense of being underground, and that there was no way out. It sank over his being, he sensed it more with his body than his mind, began to bow under its burden.

Then a searing thought crossed his brain: what if neither passage led anywhere, neither the old nor the new? What if he had been destined to lose his way here? Being forced to wander around here for days on end, then collapse out of exhaustion onto the stone floor, his tongue parched in his mouth.

For there was another tale told about the pirate: that he did not escape. That he wandered through the cellar and remains there to this day. That he wanders down secret passages, muttering to himself, trying to find a way out. His black beard has grown so long that it trails along the ground, his eyes blazing out from out of his stiffened beard like those of a cat.

Perhaps he was waiting for Rannus round the next bend, would appear to him suddenly, hideous and unearthly. Perhaps he would all of a sudden place his iron hand on his shoulder, press his stiffened beard against his face, and whisper inconceivable words in a hoarse voice with his inconceivable tongue.

An unspeakable fear filled Rannus' heart. He snatched at the candle, but his hands were trembling so that he was unable to light it for several moments. He felt as if every instant of his life and death were predetermined—a more terrible death than human reason could imagine—the eternal night of a stone cellar.

He came to his senses when the weak candle flame lit up the grey room once more. He would almost have retraced his steps, given himself up to his captors. But this seemed as horrible as his escape.

Now he chose to go down the left-hand passage. It was much lower and even shorter than the other. He could hardly walk upright. The passage took countless turns with many cavities and niches. Rannus swerved between the walls, crept along on his knees over piles of stones, supported himself on ledges of limestone, clutching his flickering candle.

He tried in vain to judge where he was. Maybe under the castle; but perhaps he was already above the city itself. If only they knew, those who were now sleeping soundly in their warm beds! He was like a coal miner deep underground, wandering beneath their flowering dreamscapes through his cavern.

The passage grew ever narrower. Rannus now had to crawl on his knees. The air had grown stuffy, as if this were only some smoke duct and not an ancient secret passage. Nauseating, dizzying, unnamable odors entered his nostrils. His shoulders were covered with a thick layer of dust and his worn-down shoes slipped on the wet limestone slabs.

And if they knew! They wouldn't feel any mercy towards him! Not one of them! They would send hunting dogs to sniff him out. Set bloodhounds on him. They would rip him apart till he was bloody, tear at his flesh in their rage, throw him with limbs tied into a stone cell, and return to their warm beds.

Their most terrifying dreams, wherein they would see endless grey labyrinths and stone spiral staircases without end in horrible towers, were nothing compared with reality. The furthest huts in the wilderness were nearer than his lonely cave, which was only a few fathoms below their pleasant dwellings.

Rannus' bad leg began to ache. This old aching of the bone woke him amidst the damp cold. Shooting pains went through his limbs and he was now crawling, having been obliged to pull his leg towards him in this cramped space. With his face screwed up in pain and a cold sweat breaking out on his forehead, he crept onwards.

And it began to become clear to him: this was how the pirate had escaped. There must be another passage, one that he had found blocked up. Then the whole of the tale about the pirate began to seem quite improbable. Had he even managed to escape? In fact, had he ever really existed? Perhaps this was all a myth, and he himself was the first poor fool to try to escape by this route!

Now he felt a sharp pain in the finger that was holding the candle; the flame had reached his fingernail. Afraid, he stood the candle on the palm of his hand; it would only burn for a few more moments. The fiery wax was running into his palm, but he felt no pain. Then the wick drooped and went out in the pool of molten wax.

Pitch blackness surrounded Rannus. He tried to crawl on, but everything now seemed so narrow that he couldn't even move his elbows. He couldn't manage to move forwards or go back. His limbs began to shake. He fell over onto the floor, his body bathed in warm sweat.

Oh, if only he could return to his cell! But he was now separated from it, in a completely dark series of passages, foul-smelling and without a breath of fresh air. He could ramble about here for days on end without reaching anywhere. He was like a mummy in a stone coffin; no he was like someone buried alive who wakes and bangs his head against the coffin lid until he loses consciousness, before true death arrives!

He lay where he was for a long while. Then he felt a breath of air, coming from the smoke vent. He thought that this might be an indication of the end of the passage. He used his last strength to crawl a few feet further. The passage widened and suddenly he saw, just beyond a small turn and through thick bars, a patch of the city dawn.

For a long time Rannus did not move. All he did was look at the light at the end of the passage without turning away his eyes. It was the sky, a waft of mist, which seemed pink in the light of the electric street lamps, a point of boundless space after the phantoms of the blackness underground!

He approached the bars and tried them with his hand. They were the thickness of a bony wrist, riveted in place. He looked out. The passage led upwards for several feet before opening onto a wall with gaps. He could scarcely make out the sentry box on the earthen rampart and the dozing guard next to it.

3.

Daybreak. In the green sky a faint mist could be seen wafting in large patches; here and there, pinks and reds were beginning to spread across the clouds. The dark green trunks of trees stood in the chilly sunrise, as if coated with the greenish mists of dawn.

The sky grew more and more flushed. All at once the sun's rays fell on the clouds, of which light wispy ones hovered like towers above the still, dark blue curve of the sea. Mist rose from them in long swathes like watery hair.

Then black columns of smoke rose from the factory chimneys into the clean air, and hooters blew, long and low, like the first heavy stroke of the bow against the double-bass of the day, tossing watery grey spirals of steam into the air.

The day was awakening once more, a new day with people, horses and wagons on all the roads, with strings of carts, trains and ships. A new day over the factories, railway stations and ports, over the blazing chimneys, the thundering rails and the blood-red cranes in the soot-filled harbors.

How Rannus had longed for this day! How long he had imagined his freedom! He had imagined himself emerging in a meadow outside the city, surrounded by dew and a frolicking herd of horses. Or on the beach, where the gentle waves rolled onto the sand between the fishing boats. Or even in the dark of the forest, with cold stars winking through the treetops.

Instead of all this, he was still on the prison grounds. In several hours he had done no more than wander around the prison cellar. And there were bars across the windows and a guard on the rampart—he was almost as much a prisoner as before. In prison, where he would have to stay and die—within sight of boundless freedom!

He sat in the mouth of the passage, took hold of one bar, and began to file another, taking advantage of the growing noise from the street. He had a small three-faceted file used to sharpen saws. But the bars were thick and he would have to file through at least four of them. It was not going to be that easy to escape from here, and the work would take the whole day!

He filed away and at the same time watched everything happening outside. He watched the guard pacing the rampart. He knew this guard, he was number 13. He could imagine his mood from his posture. He followed him walking there and empathized with his boredom as he put his hand across his mouth and yawned.

As if the filing tired him, or he could not for some reason carry on, he sat cross-legged like a Turk at the mouth of the passage and watched life unfold before him. It was a long time since he had observed it: those people, vehicles and trees out there on the boulevard!

For him, someone used to tedium and stillness, the bustle out on the street seemed to go on for ever and was wearying to him. Weeks and months between four walls, with the same routine and the same people, had passed unnoticed. How long the hours seemed now!

He noticed the smallest things, becoming like a sleuth. He guessed at the nature of passers-by and their professions. He carried on his investigations even when they were out of sight. He attributed jobs, friends, wives and children to them. And he sat at the table that had been laid, eating lunch with them.

Then he turned his eyes to the street again. He saw large numbers of horses moving along, the color of chestnut, mouse grey and fawn. Wagoners, brewery dray horse drivers in leather aprons on carts stacked with beer barrels, and a whole string of carts, where blood red girders made an ear-splitting din.

Then he saw a peasant stop. He was wearing a grey jerkin, had burning eyes and a beard, and knee-length boots. He stopped his framed wagon in front of a shop, on whose door a shiny scythe was affixed. He knocked the dust off his clothes and entered the shop, staying a good while.

The horse scraped restlessly at the side of the road, froth coming from its mouth. What a stupid man, thought Rannus, going in there and leaving his horse unattended. Were there only so few thieves in town! But what a good horse, he then thought. The man himself was a churl, driving a wagon of manure, but the horse itself was worth a hundred rubles. Thank God Rannus understood the minds of horses!

The horse waited quietly, and the man did not emerge. Strange, thought Rannus, you can see but cannot touch. How many people are passing by, but no one touches it. It would be so easy: approach, take the reins, jump on board, and drive away. Pick the right moment or leave be—the art was in the timing.

His hands began to tremble. With one eye he looked at the guard, with the other at the countryman's horse. He was back once more stealing horses, trading them in exchange for those passing by on the street. And his heart pounded, as if he were really performing such perilous acts.

Then the countryman came out, got up on the wagon and drove away. Drove away! It had been such a good opportunity! But no one had taken advantage of it, neither he nor anyone else. Rannus grew sad and his excitement was snuffed out in an instant.

No, this was not really what he was thinking about. Each time he had left prison with the advice rather to die than to steal: but every time he had stolen again, as it was easier than dying. Now he was determined to pay back all his enemies; but when he thought about it, that too was pointless.

This was the reason, he thought to himself as if waking up, that he was neither a prisoner nor free. And he started to file away again. But his thoughts wandered hither and thither, confused and restless. His sight was broken up, as moonlight is broken up on the waves, and instead of one world, he saw several.

He saw the events on the street as if in a dream. A company of Cossacks rode slowly by, the irons of their horses jingled, the forest of grey spears swayed. Then he saw a beggar on crutches making his way over the rampart. And on the roof of the house opposite he saw a grimy man with a bundle of sooty rope, stooping again and again against the clear sky like a ghostly demon.

Then he heard a song, long-drawn-out and monotonous. The masons were singing as they placed their bricks on the top of walls. He saw how bricks were thrown from hand to hand from a yellow pile. The brick would rise as if borne on the crest of a wave, higher and higher, until it reached the hands of the master mason, who put it on the wall, adding it to the thousands of others.

It was like an ants' nest, like a hive of bees making honeycomb after honeycomb. The brick flew from hand to hand, thousands of bricks, until high walls had risen, the high ridges of roofs, by comparison to which people were tiny and ephemeral. Everything was happening in one mad rush, like the urge to travel to warmer climes, to which flocks of birds would wing their way in the autumn.

Only he was still here, behind bars, inside a rampart with a sword-wielding man on top—only he and the likes of him did not feel this urge. They were alien to the builders, to the construction workers who stacked brick upon brick, who hammered chains and built walls, in order to protect people from the likes of him.

Oh, those ants down there were merciless! They destroyed everyone that refused to build with them. Woe betides anyone that revolted against them! They would squeeze him out, just like pus was squeezed out of a good limb by exercise. They would put him in a cell, put up bars and nourish him with the points of their spears.

Rannus grew even more depressed. What had he fled from? From punishment, his sentence and Siberia? But were not his sentence and Siberia his only hope, and that of the likes of him? Because people have to be with people. If you are abandoned, you are even happy to see a prison guard.

Abandoned—thought Rannus, watching the evening sun over the rooftops. The air was gentle and blue. The rays of the sun fell like golden yarn across the sea. In the distance, church bells rang, announcing the approach of Sunday. Abandoned—a great longing welled up in Rannus.

How beautiful the world was, after all. Was this the same world he had lived in for so long? The breath of spring was everywhere. The trees were fragrant and the earth smelled different than before. Spring had opened its bounteous hands, and its gifts had become visible, even to Rannus there behind bars.

Rannus no longer wanted revenge! All he wanted was to be free, to savor all the joy that life offered. He wanted to be like those weary people, who were walking by, wearing coats and carrying their bundles. He wanted to be like these ants and bees.

Oh, to escape, to travel far away, with his ancient mother! To go far from himself and his past and start a new life. To mix with strangers. To be one of them who put brick upon brick on the walls or cast seed in the spring over the porous soil.

He had never thought any of this before. He was hungry, he was sick, and fever blew his thoughts about as if they were alien to him. They unraveled like spools of yarn above his head. For the first time, life was revealing itself in all its mysterious hues, with bells ringing and evening approaching.

He sat for a long time without moving. Endless numbers of lights appeared before him from the street lamps down below and the lamps of houses, until all the lights were reflected in the waters of the bay to the mistily twinkling stars of the heavens on the limitless horizon. It was like a cemetery of stars at Rannus' feet.

4.

Once again the horizon in the east began to redden, and the portal of the clouds opened up to the gem of the sun. A day was again awakening, a new day over the glassy windmill, whose rainbow penetrated the shower of sparks of the sun. A new day, a day of merry-go-rounds, of barrel-organs!

The church bells were ringing. Old ladies in black walked slowly over the ramparts, holding black books in their hands. Old maids from the kindergarten walked along with their troop of children: they swayed from side to side like an innocent gaggle of geese along the street, the children dressed in the white costumes of the poor. Clergymen rode in black gowns and velvet caps.

But Rannus was sitting where he had been all along. He had hoped to do a lot of filing today and finally make his escape. But now, on Sunday, filing would be perilous. He was tired and hunger gnawed at his insides, his mouth drooled and he had very little strength.

At midday music began to play on the ramparts by the blue pond. Men with round hats and gold braid stood on the round stage. Brass trumpets and brass instruments glittered in the sunshine. Drums and cymbals gave off a metallic sound.

At midday, people began to gather around the pond. Young men with high collars, canes and white summer boaters arrived. Young ladies in narrow velvet dresses and red parasols arrived as well. Town dignitaries in long black tailcoats came with their wives and children.

Along the boulevard under the trees was a ceaseless train of vehicles: red cars, well-groomed horses with carriages and caliches. In these sat officers in bright uniforms and gentlemen in top hats in the company of young ladies, buried in flowers, veils and colorful parasols.

This bustle on the ramparts buzzed, shouted, laughed and joked among the sweet waves of music and the spring-like wind. It was like a triumphal procession of spring and youth that reaped a harvest of flowers and smiles, proud and carefree, protected against worry and care.

Rannus watched all this, his eyes wide open, clutching the bars. This too was life—ah, he had forgotten it—this too was life! This multicolored carnival, this whirling roundabout—this too was the life of people. Yet he was lying here, behind bars, behind the guard by the moat with his sword, helpless, trapped!

Why did the others have to move about so well-fed, free, honored—with him lying here, his tongue parched and his innards wracked with hunger? Why did they have their own houses, horses and women—with him lying here, eternally homeless, loveless, joyless?

He turned his head aside in bitterness. It was impossible to think with an empty stomach. Proper thoughts only came with a full stomach. Everyone who had proper thoughts had their stomachs full. He too longed for such thoughts and a full stomach!

But he could not escape from his thoughts. Several thoughts sprang to mind as vividly as for someone nearing his end. Much the way that, before death, a consumptive nose grows sharper and the patient begins to think more clearly—his nose seemingly smelling goodness, righteousness and bliss. Yet these all had a very putrid smell.

Who was he? Had he shed human blood or entered the profession of a thief with a light heart? He had been a petty, timid thief. Had he not endured more hardship after stretching out his hand to take other people's property than those with a daily wage, slaving away in the fields? What was their work compared with the hardships he had endured?

Blessed are those who are higher up in society. Blessed are the rich, the proud and the respectable. Blessed are those who do nothing, yet eat; who live from the work of others and yet are always cared for. Blessed are those who live off violence, the word of God, and stupidity!

Blessed too are those who are lowest in society. Blessed are hunchbacks and orphans. What is wrong with a beggar? He holds out his hand and no one knocks it away. Blessed is he whose eyes are poked out, his legs chopped off, whose bones are broken—he has the right to hold out his hand!

But bloody abuse is the lot of those who cannot, are unable to, defend themselves—thieves, the condemned, fallen women—those who have walked out of paradise and can never find their way back. Bloody injustice is the lot of the wicked, the fallen, the depraved!

Rannus was listening in bitter pain: gentle music floated in the blue air as if on wings. Dancing oblivion and smiling grief blew him out above the festive crowds. Rannus' ear was struck by the despairing black and searing whine of the musical instruments: life is ghastly, human life is mad!

Oh, mother, mother, you who stooped wearily over the potato furrows of the manor, your body with child, your mind dulled by shame and pain, why did you not drown yourself in the retting pit cut out of the peat, under the swathes of linen, under the burden of stones! Why did you give birth to me on the tiers of a stranger's sauna, helpless and joyless!

Shame, sin and crime—there was no forgiveness ever for shame, sin and crime! For there is a special place reserved for the non-believer and the murderer, fallen women and their offspring, the sorcerer and the thief—a hell with its fire and brimstone. The sullying of the body, mockers and wanton people—oh, the sins of the fathers are visited upon the sons unto the third and fourth generation!

Rannus remembered his first communion and his first and last confession. That was in the prison—so long, long, ago! The Body of God sprang to mind, and the thought burned his mouth. The memory awakened his hunger, his mouth began to water. He would have eaten God only to still that hunger in his insides.

Once someone is fallen, there is no resurrection. There is no solace for him. Heaven says nothing to him. Even if he escaped there, his sin and shame from the past would stifle all his joy. He would not be able to look anyone in the eye. Everyone would wag his or her finger: Look, there goes the horse thief! What's a horse thief doing in heaven!

And Rannus wanted to flee to hell! There no one would see him, no one would notice him behind the backs of others and he would remain a shadow in a doorway. There were much greater thieves and scoundrels there, he would be among the most insignificant beings there. No one there would know his name and the Devil would step over him as he would over the tiniest maggot, without growing angry.

To whom else could he pray, if not to the Devil! He had no hope but in Evil. His belief in Good had died long ago. Have mercy on me, O Prince of Darkness! Help me, protect me from righteousness, goodness and bliss! Help your child! Protect your child!

And he lay there, his face an ashen grey, turned to the wall. He didn't move for a very long time. His mind was empty. Nothing but a brutish fear filled him. His hunger grew. He ground his teeth like an animal that chews its cud in its sleep.—Drums and trumpets resounded under the bright blue heavens!

5.

Evening fell over the city. Blue shadows slunk across the walls and houses. The sea of blackness spread. The electricity was switched on. A cloud of mist flushed like a painted lady, the trees on the boulevard looked like the silhouettes of black paper flowers.

At the edge of the black pond by a turn in the wall, the tents of the fairground could be seen. Black people were walking among them. Small lamps were lit in the tents. The lamps of the merry-go-round were lit too. They started to rotate like a fiery stove, a nest of fire, a wheel of fire—the fiery merry-go-round began to move with a roar.

Countless crowds of people were bustling within the city walls: urchins, whores and thieves, soldiers, beggars and sailors. Everything seethed and cried and boiled, and people thronged around the booths and the merry-go-round, whooping for joy, howling and jabbering, raising fumes and heat.

The crowd consisted of women with many-colored and bright red shawls round their necks. After them came the men with bagpipes, their hats on the backs of their heads, swaggering like sailors. Pickpockets, informers and scoundrels were yelling and running up and down through the crowd. Above the noise of this whole drunken mob, a barrel-organ could be heard and a clown staggered about on the steps to the show-booth.

The merry-go-round turned. Long serpentines could be seen flying through the air. Lanterns and mirrors turned. Varnished horses, cows and pigs turned, throwing hideous shadows over the thronging masses. Everything whirled, flew, everything was rushing along!

Painted ladies with large bosoms sat on the backs of pink, flesh-colored pigs. Behind them, excited men on red bulls and rearing horses ran, their arms outstretched, in the shrieking kermes of lights and mirrors.

Rannus looked on, his eyes wide, his nostrils enlarged. All this was life—he had forgotten it—this too was life! Red blotches appeared on his cheeks. His hungry eyes sought out the women on the merry-go-round as they flew along on the backs of pigs. All was a crazy whirl: fasting and feeding, hunger and satiety.

The merry-go-round whirled ever more crazily. The mirrors flashed by, showing glimpses of flushed faces in the crowd. Ever onwards! Ever crazier! And suddenly the whole whirling merry-go-round seemed to whirl up into the air, the horses after the pigs, and the whole ghastly thing seeming to turn upside down.

Rannus jumped up. He wanted to get out, enter this throng, or return to his cell! He was no longer afraid of anything. He stuck his head out through the bars and shouted. No one heard him! He gripped the bars with his bony hands and floundered like an animal in a cage. No one took any notice of him!

Boundless pain stabbed him like a piercing flame. The barrel-organ sprayed out fire, the merry-go-round sowed flames, large as sheets. The flames were over his head! His soul was being buried, buried!—He fell down, like a dead man.

*

He remembered:

They were running along, hunched forward, he and a grey-haired old man, across a heath strewn with junipers. Both of them had sheep thrown over their shoulders, hanging there alive with their feet tied together, their heads banging against the mens' legs. In the distance the barking of the dogs and the hoarse voices of human beings could be heard.—It was a dark autumn night.

The dogs approached. Their barking could be heard coming from both sides, the people were goading them on from behind, wanting to surround them. They ran downhill into a bog. The dogs followed them, baying forlornly, and they heard something in the darkness that almost sounded like the thudding of human feet.—It began to rain.

They wandered around on the boggy ground between the rotting, puny pine trees. They jumped onto hummocks and sloshed through the soggy ground, silently lugging their whimpering sheep. They heard their pursuers skirting the pitch black bog, crying out to one another as a signal.—The cold rain came down in torrents.

They stopped in the middle of the bog, shaking with fright and cold. He could hear how the old man was praying. His own young shoulders were aching. He lay down on the trembling sheep and cried along with it like a child.—Through the monotonous patter of the rain, they could hear voices coming from the edge like those of goblins.

*

He remembered:

A scorching summer's day with the sun blazing over the tents, booths and the merry-go-round, with the shafts of the carts sticking up into the air and people swarming all around. Horses were neighing, the cattle were mooing, and the sun looked like coagulated blood through a thick cloud of dust.—Then they managed to grab him.

"Thief, thief!" a shout went through the whole crowd. "We've caught a pickpocket!" And ten hands groped after him. Iron fingers held his chest and seized him by the throat, hundreds of red faces were all around, thousands of bloodshot eyes surrounded him, as far as the eye could see.—The sun blazed through the red dust.

He was pushed along, no one knew where to. He was dragged, shoved, thrown from one to the other, with dozens of hands grabbing hold of him. He was like an axle around which everyone rotated. The road led down to the circus green, further off was the stone-built inn, but they kept on moving—on both sides of the mob ran circus clowns, their tongues hanging out of their mouths.

Then the wave of people stumbled over a heap of stones and one of them had an idea: "Smash his fingers between two rocks, so that he'll never steal again!" They pushed him down onto his knees, spread his fingers out on a large rock. The rock could be heard falling and then the crack of bones. He fell unconscious to the ground from the terrible pain.—The neighing of horses and the clear sound of a flute could be heard from afar!

*

And he remembered:

They were rolling along in a blizzard of large snowflakes.—The heavens were grey.—He rose to his feet and lashed the horse with the ends of the reins. The carts jogged over the frozen acres. The horse's strength was ebbing away. It reared up onto its hind legs and looked back at Rannus with human eyes.—Night was falling.

They managed to corner him in a wide open space. They tied his two arms to the shafts instead of the horse and rushed over the frozen field. The wheels jumped on the bumpy earth. Many hands behind him held whips made from bull pizzles, like the hands of soldiers in a war wagon holding spears.—The snow kept falling in big, wet flakes. Night was falling.

They led him uphill. He was almost crawling on his chest, his toes pressing against the frozen hummocks. They wanted to dislocate his arms, blood seeped from under his fingernails. He could go on no longer. He fell down among the snowflakes.—Night had fallen.

"Brothers, I'm thirsty," said the lips of the dying man. "Oh, thirsty, eh?" they said, and one of them pissed onto his mitten and rubbed it over his lips.—Solitary flakes of wet snow fell in leisurely fashion from the heavens, the sky was a leaden grey. Night had fallen,—night...!

*

Late at night Rannus awoke. A drunk was waving his arms about by the city wall, treading the ground with his feet, talking to himself.—Infinite pain filled Rannus' breast: all is vanity! Everything is simply suffering! Even freedom is slavery!—The drunk unraveled in the moonlight like a coil of yarn—he unraveled the cobweb of the moon.

6.

An ear-splitting din filled the warm night. Cranes were winching up blood-colored girders at the building site. Granite-shattering hammers were falling with a heavy crash. Above all of this, above the scaffolding, the walls and the poles of bricks; above the vats of lime and the concrete moulds, the scorching sun rose through the fiery red of the brick dust.

Rannus was filing away in desperation. His hands worked like machine parts, but he no longer remembered anything—he had forgotten how he had gotten to where he was, and how long he had been there. An immeasurable amount of time had passed! The hunger, fever and phantasms had reached their climax.

He was by now more animal than human. He no longer wished for good or evil. All he wanted to do was live. To live—to get for himself one corner of the great tapestry that summoned one to life, to pull it towards him and lie on it, happily, eyes closed, his mouth full of bread!

Eyes glowing with fever, he stared fixedly through the red cloud in front of him: tilers were climbing up ladders with their loads, their legs muddy. Feeble little boys were treading their way up piles of lime, their heads hanging like those of weary horses. Bricklayers were dully placing brick upon brick.

Were they creators? Were they the masters of the world? No, they were machines, they were slaves, driven on by a thirst for life, urged on by hunger to climb the walls. All they wanted to do was exist, to stay alive. There was no collective effort like that which urges birds to fly to warmer climes. No creative ideal in the whole of their being.

Who knows why people need to suffer, struggle, die? Who is guiding the great building site of this world? Is there something up there that is unknown, unknowable, perhaps even non-existent? Or down here, horrible, black and maybe just as non-existent? But in the end, will they not fly, in one huge accident, into the jaws of death, while the whole edifice collapses around them?

Rannus sawed and sawed at the bars meanwhile. He used all his strength, while the noise of the building site continued. Finally, finally the fourth giant bar was filed through. Only a hair's breadth of metal kept it attached to the wall. Rannus was free, but he was unable to leave until nightfall, before darkness fell. This waiting was the worst. He remained motionless, his stomach hideously aching with hunger.

Now and again he lost consciousness and awoke with a start, only to find himself sitting there. His brain ached like smoldering charcoal. He saw dreams and visions, fragmentary and meaningless. Russet clouds sailed above him. Bluish globes swarmed, seethed and blazed, then burst apart in hideous pain. The pith of his brain boiled and bubbled.

He woke again suddenly and was astonished at the silence around him. He didn't know how long he had been unconscious. It seemed only a moment. The laborers were at lunch. They had eaten and were now sleeping on the ramparts on their backs, or on their stomachs.

Their bodies looked like sacks in the fiery sunshine. A boundless silence hung over the sleeping herd of slaves, whose limbs seemed rooted to the ground.

Warder 13 was again standing by the cell. He had red sideburns. The sun shone on his immobile face. He was wearing a scorched-grey uniform and a large cap. He was stiff and hard, as if made out of sheet metal, despite the burning heat. He was as motionless as a monument to the emperor.

Suddenly, a beggar on crutches appeared on the rampart from somewhere nearby. He bobbed along between his supports like a great big black cricket. He sat down on the rampart, took a loaf of bread shaped like a wheel from inside his coat and began to bite into it, clutching it in both hands. His whole body seemed to be eating, along with his toothless gums.

This scene made Rannus leap into action. He no longer knew what he was doing. He was like a wild animal. He gripped the crosspiece he had been filing at with both hands and flung it aside. He then jumped down and ran, stumbling, over towards the beggar. Warder 13 looked at what seemed like a ghost, his eyes wide open; although he was watching attentively, he saw nothing.

Rannus snatched at the loaf, but the beggar was holding it tight with both hands. He looked straight at Rannus with frenzied eyes, his mouth open wide, filled with dry bread so he was unable to yell. They dropped the loaf a couple of times, and it jumped from the one to the other, as if on springs. Then Rannus picked up a brick and struck the beggar full on the crown of the head. It cracked open like an earthenware pot.

Rannus snatched the bread and ran headlong between the two piles of yellow bricks, cramming the bread into his mouth. He swallowed the bone-dry crumbs, his eyes bulging, swallowed and fell down dead—in the fiery red brick dust.

1914

The Golden Hoop

1.

Jürgens stepped out through the cemetery portal. He stopped by the gates as if unsure in which direction to proceed. The evening street was deserted. No one stirred. All was still. Only the faint patter of rain on the sickly foliage of the avenue could be heard. Dusk had fallen.

At the gate two beggars were sitting. On one side was a blind woman, a shawl around her lemon-yellow face, deep depressions where her eyes should have been. On the other, an old man with no legs whatsoever, sitting in a low-sided crate like a trough with small wooden wheels underneath. In the hands of the old man, which touched the ground, were a couple of leather-covered wooden rings with whose assistance he could move along.

Jürgens thrust his hand into his pocket as if about to give the beggars something. But he found his gloves and started pulling them on. The gloves were damp. He brought both hands up to his face simultaneously: the gloves smelled of carbolic acid.

He could smell it everywhere. The pharmacy had poisoned him through and through. If he had a soul, even it would have smelled of medicaments.

With great effort he succeeded in sliding the gloves on over his emaciated fingers. He then turned up the collar of his overcoat and started walking. The ground was wet and soft. The drizzle seemed denser than before. Along both sides of the avenue stood one- or two-story houses. It was almost completely dark now, yet no lights could be seen in any of the windows.

Along the way stood one or two undertaker's and stonemason's. In the window, tiny children's coffins glinted along with the one or two silver tassels, wire wreaths, or an angel holding a palm branch.

The doors of the shops were still open, though inside they were dark and not a soul could be seen.

At the bend in the street, Jürgens glanced back: both beggars sat motionless in the rain. The old man had sunk back down onto his hands; he resembled a sitting dog.

The pavement consisted of large round flagstones and Jürgens stumbled at nearly every step. This only increased his sullen mood.

He felt that an injustice had been done to him, bringing him needlessly to this wretched placc to which he had no reason to come.

Naturally, the death of his mother had shaken him. He had left home twenty years before and had admittedly not seen her for the last seven. And he had rarely had the time to spare a thought for her. But she had been his mother, after all.

Now it was all over. Death had crossed out the past, as if with a black stroke of the pen.

He had received word of her illness when it was already too late. He found a short letter from his sister, an empty house and his mother's grave. He sent a postcard to his sister, bought a wreath for his mother's grave, and intended to stay no longer than it took him to sell the house, or at least rent it out at a good price.

This thought brought his feelings onto an even keel again. Death—it was inevitable, yet always made him anxious. He was not used to such thoughts, nor did he wish to become so. Life was, after all, something quite different.

He turned into the street, which led down to the town. A small dark man zigzagged from one pavement to the other and lit the gas lanterns with a long pole. From some way off the clatter of a cart could be heard. And this clattering finally woke Jürgens.

His fate and that of his sister came to mind: he standing behind the counter of the pharmacy from morning till night for twenty years amid the stale air of medicaments, and she in a small faraway provincial town, supporting her alcoholic husband, with her brood of children constantly growing. Such had been their lives.

One or two times a year they had written to their mother and to one another. He wrote about his salary increases, she about her latest child; their mother wrote that everything was as it always had been.

Perhaps they too had once had other ambitions in life. But life had not fulfilled its promise. And Jürgens had finally accepted life for what it was.

No, life had not been easy. And he had begun foolishly. He had gone to the big city like so many others from the provinces and found pleasure in his smart suit of clothes and in cavorting with the women there.

But thank heavens that was soon over. He simply didn't have the passion, at least not for sin.

Women—they required money, health and time. And he possessed very little of any of these.

First of all he had discovered the value of money and time. And his yellowish consumptive face did not bespeak the constitution of a lady-killer.

Then he understood what he needed was to lead a quiet life. A man had commitments and these commitments brought in money. Everything beyond this was sheer futility.

He had buried himself in the dust of the pharmacy.

At the end of every month he would accompany the other chemist's assistant to the tavern, order a bottle of beer, and talk about things they were both familiar with. And once a year, he would go out to the islands for the afternoon with his boss's family.

They would sit around the restaurant table, eat sandwiches and sip at their beers. The boss loved to tell stories about his schooldays. His wife dozed in the warmth of the spring sunshine.

Jürgens eyed the boss' daughter. She was thin and had a severe look about her. She was already over thirty and plain. But Jürgens didn't care.

He was no better off himself in this respect. His face was sallow, his short hair was graying at the temples and his hands were bony. But he hoped that the boss' daughter was equally indifferent.

For there was no question of feelings between them. They simply wished to put their lives in order—that was all—to put them in order more and more every day. That, after all, is the nature of every human being.

Now Jürgens regarded himself as being one step closer to putting his life in order.

This much he knew: Amalie Karlovna was waiting for him and maybe dreamed her dry, prudent dreams in her cramped spinster's bedroom between the parrot's cage and the narrow piano. He also knew that his father-in-law was waiting with his ledgers, his carafe of cumin brandy and his kindly advice.

Life had looked after him. He was not ungrateful.

He crossed the wooden bridge. Up and downstream, along the banks of the river, a few lights twinkled. Beyond the balustrade, the river's current flowed darkly, while, from afar, he could hear the obstinate clatter of a cart.

It was by this clatter that he recognized his home town.

Yes, everything was the same as it had always been: the same river, the same streets and stone walls around the gardens, and the dark tops of the trees as they hung over the walls. Everything was as it had always been!

The street lamps shone in the rain like dim globes of light. In the windows of the shops, lights gleamed. Water dripped from the thin shop signs. One or two solitary passers-by hurried past, shrouded in their coats. But nothing disturbed the all-embracing deadness.

That's what they were like back here at home, thought Jürgens, lagging behind the rest of the world, an unhappy and wretched people. Money, the only true value, and this they were incapable of making.

What were they worth, all their ideals and dreams, if they lacked money? What was the good of belonging to one or other nation if people in general are stupid, dirty and poor?

Oh no, he would not be taken in by such childish tricks. Adolf Ivanovich Jürgens knew what he was doing. He was sensible enough to look beyond all this.

What did he care about different nations! To Russians he was a Russian, to Jews a Jew, while at home they spoke nothing but German, since his landlord was a Baltic German.

If he felt anything at all, it was sorrow at the fact that he too had been born here. This fact had hampered him a great deal during the early part of his life. It was like a disease from which it took years to recover.

But now, the final bond had been broken. Now he wanted to be finished with his affairs here, so that he needn't be constantly reminded of them.

His destiny lay elsewhere, not in these muddy streets lined with decaying fencing made of wooden planks, at the end of which only a mournful paraffin lamp shone.

He came to a halt in a narrow side-street and stepped through a darkened wicker gate into a courtyard. The rain pattered unceasingly. He walked soundlessly over the stones overgrown with grass.

At the far end of the yard stood a dark, low wooden house. There was not a glimmer of light from any of its windows.

In front of the house stood a ghostly, leafless tree. A few sheets on the washing line shone whitely in the darkness.

Here, Jürgens had played as a child: below, the flower beds had bloomed; above, the burgeoning boughs had hung down. A bright-colored bird had sung in the foliage.

Now, the garden had long since gone to seed, the flower beds had been trampled, the trees cut down. Only the old apple tree still stretched out its decaying branches. Yellowed grass rose around him like tangled bristles.

Jürgens stopped for a moment in front of the house, but then he shrugged his shoulders irritably.

His heart was not rooted in these tree-stumps and stones. This heap of rubble was merely a means of sorting out his life, no more.

He entered by the open door and came into a large, low-ceilinged kitchen. His footsteps echoed thickly on the tiled floor. He groped his way forward.

Suddenly in the darkness, right by his ear, he heard a ghastly muttering, and someone seized his hand with cold fingers.

Jürgens froze for a moment in terror, his hair stood on end. But then he remembered: it was the old servant woman, Malle, who had been here since his birth. Now she was trying to console him with her toothless mumbling and her bony hands.

Trembling with disgust, Jürgens stepped into the next room.

He lit a candle and took off his wet outer garments. The room was unheated, so he could see his breath. He raised the candle. Everything was untidy and moldering.

It was obvious that old Malle could no longer cope. Like a cricket in the flue was how she now lived in the kitchen of the empty house!

Jürgens crossed the floor angrily a couple of times.

He looked at the walls, which were covered with faded wallpaper, the furniture whose upholstery the moth had attacked; he threw a glance into the filthy dining room where only the round table shone like a shield. Everything aroused feelings of horror in him.

Then he got undressed.

He lay down on the bed and closed his eyes. His smooth head lay heavy as a skittle on the pillow, his thin bony hands spread out on the white sheets. The candle burned without a flicker.

Then suddenly Jürgens felt the dampness of the bedclothes.

He opened his eyes, sat up and took a notebook out of his jacket pocket. He recalled the expenditures of that day and totaled them up. His lips stirred, now and again he wrote down some figures by the light of the candle, leaning on his elbow.

Then he let the hand holding the notebook sink and returned to his thoughts.

He was too tired and should really have gone to sleep. The sudden news, the journey, the distress here—they had all wearied him. He had not slept for three nights. He could feel the fever of fatigue in his limbs. Oh how heavy, how heavy was his head!

He opened his eyes once more.

He should never have undertaken the journey here, he thought to himself. Right now, life was demanding enough of him as it was. So much the more, as he had come too late to be able to change anything.

He dozed off for a moment, but woke up immediately with a start. He had managed to dream, but so confusedly that, on waking, he could remember nothing.

Things came to mind so abruptly that they frightened him. But then he grew calm again: he had gotten things under control.

He again began to estimate the value of the house, and his fever grew. This heap of rubble would hardly fetch much, even the plot of land itself would fetch more. And he made an attempt to calculate the price.

Then it struck him that he had not yet seen all the rooms. There had been a dining room, a living-room and a kitchen. But he clearly remembered that there had been yet another smaller room, whose two narrow windows and small door gave onto the garden. He had spent his childhood in that room.

He sat up on the bed and looked at the opposite wall. He remembered that there had once been a door there. But now the wall was completely smooth.

He jumped up quickly, picked up the candlestick, and ran over to the wall. He measured the floor in paces, felt the wall, and understood: the door had been wallpapered over.

Now he remembered back over the years as if in a dream: his mother had written how hard it was for her to get by; she had separated the children's room off from the rest of the house in order to rent it out; but no one had wanted to live there on account of the damp.

He wanted to see the room today—a strange fever seized Jürgens—immediately, now!

He rushed helplessly hither and thither, then Malle came to mind. He went to the kitchen door and demanded the key.

For a while, an incomprehensible muttering could be heard. Then a quaking hand was thrust out of the darkness. As Jürgens took the key, the icy hand tried again to stroke his, but it remained hanging in mid-air.

The key was large and rusty.

Groping his way, Jürgens found the lock and impetuously pushed the key through the wallpaper. The lock creaked, the wallpaper ripped away in long strips and the door opened.

2.

Immediately he stepped inside, Jürgens saw, to his amazement, that the room was lit up: bright sunlight shone in through the windows and the open door. He placed the candle back on the table in the first room and looked around him.

The room was long and narrow. The walls were covered with faded wallpaper. The old tulle curtains hung in the windows. A number of pictures in disintegrating frames hung above the tiny children's beds.

And yet the blinding brightness of the sunlight, which pushed through the branches and the tulle patterning as through a sieve, made everything new and radiant once more.

His sister Anna was sitting on the threshold, her feet in the garden, a doll in her lap. Her fair hair was tied in two narrow plaits with red bows at the ends.

They looked at the doll that lay in the girl's lap in silence. Its blue eyes were wide open, its rosy hands spread.

They then went into the garden.

The apple tree was in full bloom. The currant bushes were luxuriantly black. The soft soil of the flower beds steamed in the morning sunshine. Here and there apple blossoms fell like snow.

They sat under a tree and began playing:

The doll had just woken up. She washed it, combed its hair and received guests. First came an ant, then a ladybird, and finally a snail.

The doll sat on the dandelion sofa, drank morning coffee from an apple blossom cup, and conversed with the guests.

Then the guests went home: first the ant ran on its way, then the ladybird flew off and last of all the snail slithered off, its horns erect like small fists.

They grew tired of their game and sat there in silence.

A bird chirruped faintly in the shade of the leaves. The soil smelled good. It was so still that even the rays of the sun managed to peep through the leaves,—like a silver spider spinning its golden gossamer web.

Then, all of a sudden, they heard a strange noise: along the street a clear ringing sound could be heard, as if a wandering player were striking his instrument.

They both heard it almost simultaneously, raised their heads and listened. The sound drew near, sometimes ceasing for a moment, but then the gentle tinkling could be heard, nearer and clearer.

They jumped up together and ran to the gate, but the ringing had already passed them by. They ran into the street, but could only catch a glimpse of something glimmering as brightly as the sun: a large golden hoop, bouncing along over the cobbles. Then it vanished behind the corner of the fence.

Without saying a word, the children began to run after it.

They ran down small avenues past large gardens. The grass-covered lanes came to an end and the fields began—the children ran on.

They held each other by the hand. Anna had forgotten she was holding her doll; its hair fanned out and flowed behind her like a handful of flax.

They rushed after the sound of the golden hoop. At times they would hear it no longer, then they would stop for a moment and listen, panting for breath.

Sometimes it sounded like a street musician's triangle that he rang from garden to garden with a steel baton—and they were waiting for it to stop and for the red monkey to begin dancing beside a barrel organ.

At other times it seemed as if someone was jingling bells in the distance—and they expected to see a cartload of singing men approaching—with chimes, kerchiefs and pipes.

At times they thought they saw a little boy with glowing cheeks driving the golden hoop along with a silver cane. On his flowing shock of hair sat a golden helmet and on his feet there were tiny wings, as if he were flying along.

The road twisted and turned, up hill and down dale. The meadows greened. Here and there a copse of young birch shone blue. A snow-white cloud sailed over the flower-bedecked water meadow along with them.

Then they reached a large throng of people standing at the side of the highway. Dust rose from the stamping of feet. The sun glowed red. Everyone was chasing the golden hoop at once.

They tried to keep a hold of one another in the crowd. But the panting people forced their way between them, sweaty hands dragged them apart. They could no longer see one another, but ran on regardless.

The longer this chase lasted, the more madly everyone surged ahead. Their persistence infected others, they pressed on, fell over, and those who were stronger ran without looking back.

In the cloud of dust, the boy thought he could see the glint of the hoop and hear its ringing through the thunder of feet. It seemed to him that his life was rolling on along with the hoop ringing in the distance.

He would sometimes split off from the rest, take a short cut across the corner of a meadow and scramble abruptly up steep slopes. Then he got lost in a wood, all was still, he could hear the ringing no longer, the sun shone through the tops of the trees.

But then he rushed on again.

He trampled flowering shrubs underfoot, had no time to pick the flowers. He leapt like a hare over brooks, but had no time to stop and drink.

Here and there, the golden hoop shimmered close by. He snatched after it in the bushes, but hurt his hand. He heard its tinkling among the stumps of felled trees, but could not catch a glimpse of it. He looked for its traces in the ashes of the woodcutters' fires but could find none.

He left the darkness of the woods once again, finding the road and the people. The road ran dusty along a high bank. Below, a blue lake glittered. Triangular sails shone in the sunshine. But he ran on.

From time to time, his home, his mother and sister came to mind as if in a dream. It seemed he had been on his way for an endless period of time. Life seemed to have changed into a dream.

But once again the ringing of the golden hoop woke him. He saw it approaching, waiting for him around the next bend in the road. It seemed to be tired and resting on a rock by the roadside just as he was. One final effort and he would reach it.

His feet were cut, but he took no notice. He was deathly weary but kept on running!

The day drew to a close. He had run in one huge circle. The meadows were growing blue. He turned back in the direction of the town. Its windows gleamed.

He still could hear the sound of the hoop, faintly as if through a mist. There was no one around him anymore. He limped at a half-run beneath the trees. The street seemed filled with blue mist. Somewhere the hour struck. He felt a great weariness, as if he had been running for many years.

Then suddenly he realized he was back on a familiar street. Yes, here was the house of his parents.

He reached the gate and stood listening: somewhere in the distance the hoop still tinkled, but its ringing was becoming fainter and fainter, then it sounded as if it were right above his head, quivered and stopped as if dissolving into the evening.

He stepped into the garden.

Through the line of tall trees on the other side of the street, the low sun cast a broad swathe of light. The whole garden was full of its yellow glow.

He stopped in the middle of the garden and looked around him.

It seemed as if something had changed during the day:

The grass had grown long, wilted and was rotting in places. The trees, which had been blossoming that morning, were already full of apples that now and then fell all by themselves, bursting open and decaying in the lush grass. The whole garden was full of the odor of rotting trees and moldering grass.

It was all so strange!

The door to the room stood wide open as before. He stepped inside. The room was empty. But in through the lace curtains streamed a melancholy light. Everything was yellow, too yellow!

And in the yellow light everything seemed that much more sad and abandoned. The simple furniture had aged, the portraits on the walls had grown old, as if they were living people.

He stayed a few moments in the room. All was silent. All was so ghastly! Full of fear, he flung open the door to the other room and leapt inside.

3.

The room was black as pitch. It felt icy cold as the grave.

Jürgens was stunned with shock. Then he remembered: he had left a candle on the table. Groping about, he found the candlestick, but the candle had burned down and the wax had congealed long ago.

He called for Malle but no one answered. He called out a second time, a third, but all was silent.

Muttering angrily to himself, he stumbled into the kitchen. On a couple of occasions, cobwebs touched his face; he waved around haphazardly trying to brush them aside.

He reached the kitchen, but it was cold, as if no one had made a fire in the hearth in ages. The smell of clay was coming from the cold stove. In the darkness the narrow rectangle of the low window shone.

Jürgens listened. All was silent.

Fumbling his way forward, he approached the bed. His knees knocked against the bedboard, he stretched out his hand and groped about among the heap of rags.

His fingers touched a human throat, but it was icy cold. He pulled the bedclothes aside and placed his palm on the old woman's chest but it did not stir.

The old woman was dead. There was already the unmistakable smell of putrefaction.

Without thinking or hesitating any longer, Jürgens staggered back into his own room.

Only some dim shadow of a thought stirred in his head: just a few moments ago I was here in this room, the old woman gave me the key, I stepped outside for a moment, and now on coming back I find the candle burned down and the woman long since dead.

He did not think this thought through, but simply sat on the edge of the bed.

And once again the glimmer of a thought stirred in his brain: where was I just now—the apple trees were in blossom, my sister was playing—the golden hoop was tinkling, the highway was dusty, the sun was blazing down,—apples were falling from the trees and bursting open, the room was full of a yellow glow,—where was I just now?

But before he could think this thought through, he fell flat out on the bed, half-dressed as he was.

The grey veil of sleep settled upon his head.

But even in his sleep something ghostly hovered silently above him, retreating from time to time. Grey rays cut through the murky darkness, branched wheels whirled, fluffy feather pillows fell silently. He shrouded himself in sleep as in a sheet.

But through this veil of dreams a boundless melancholy took possession of him. His heart was on the point of bursting from infinite pain. He covered his eyes with his hands and the tears welled up through his fingers.

The sickly day broke through the low window. It was almost as dark as the night.

The decaying furniture shimmered through the twilight. Cloth was everywhere, discarded suits, unrolled lengths of material, rolled-up carpets—the clothes and material slept on the linoleum floor like sinister curled-up creatures.

Jürgens sat on the pile of cloth, his head in his hands.

Every corner was full of shadows. They came over the courtyard without ceasing. The shadows moved their heads, beckoning with their hands. Shadows were descending from the heavens as if down a ladder.

Jürgens heard their call. He put on his coat, pressed his hat low over his brow and went outside.

It was evening again. Rain was falling.

He wandered aimlessly through the streets, roving about between the trees and houses, lights and shadows. The town seemed unfamiliar to him. Perhaps he had seen these streets and gardens once in a dream. Then he found himself back in the courtyard under the ravaged apple tree.

He stood there a long while, lost in thought.

He had forgotten everything. Had forgotten the city and his waiting bride. Had forgotten why he had come here. Had forgotten that he should leave this place.

There was something else he was trying to remember. Something that was still surrounding him, like a fragrance, or merely a voice. As in a dream, he was pursuing the hazy, distant outlines of a second dream.

There was no longer any distinction between day and night. The light remained the same, the shadows were unchanged, the rain swished through the twilight—he had even seen this type of weather only in a dream.

Now, everything was only in a dream. Nothing was real any more. Reality had died out long ago.

Life had taken on a strange, ghastly appearance.

Sometimes in the course of an evening Jürgens would wander to the market place. He roved about between people and animals without seeing anything. Suddenly, he heard a tinkling sound through the buzz of market-goers and rushed towards it. But he then saw it was the bells round the neck of a horse and walked sadly away.

Then he found himself outside the town. There were open meadows on both sides of the road. A crow sat on the ridge of a haystack. The wind blew delicately through the bare branches of the trees, as if playing a musical instrument. He listened.

Then suddenly he saw something glinting beyond the trees. He began to run haphazardly across the meadow. The stubble was wet, his feet got stuck in the doughy earth.

All of a sudden he was standing in front of a windmill. It was turning its vanes sluggishly in the rain. His eyes followed the wet vanes for a while. Then he went on his way.

He strayed into the park. The bare branches there were full of strange surprises. It was a forest of unexpected opportunities. He walked on tiptoe and listened. But he could only hear the patter of rain on the quivering leaves.

He turned in the direction of the town. Looking back, he saw a black dog with a shiny collar following in his footsteps. He ran up to the dog, but it jumped in the air and disappeared in the treetops.

Towards evening the road took him to the riverbank. He could already hear its purling from afar and quickened his step. But when he reached the harbor he saw barges heaving chains. The cheap paint of the masts ran down the wood in the rain.

In the lower part of the town, which lay along the river, he wandered through courtyards. Two Jewish boys were playing on the steps with a small bell. They had curly hair, dark eyes and deep-red lips.

Jürgens snatched at the bell. But the child threw it in the air and jumped after it himself. The other boy caught it in mid-flight. And Jürgens saw how they tossed the bell to each other and vanished over the roof of the house.

He ran into the next yard to try to catch them up. But to his disgust he found a table in the middle of the yard and on it a blood-covered pig. A man with rolled-up sleeves, knife in hand, stood beside it.

But evening brought the greatest surprises of all.

Jürgens stumbled along by the planked fence, the branches along the avenue shook water down his collar. He meandered among the jumble of houses.

A bell struck in the tower, a street lamp lit up the red wall, water ran from a shop sign, lights shone through the huge red, blue and green eyes of the glass spheres in the pharmacy window.

Masked figures approached: a Buffoon, a Harlequin, a Columbine, a Moor, a Chimney Sweep and a Hurdy-Gurdy Man.

He heard the sound of a tambourine and went towards it.

But on a side street, a grey-haired old man passed by and threw confetti in his face. He then ran on, shaking a large sack. The water made the confetti soggy. Jürgens stood thinking.

This isn't it! he sighed and carried on walking. This is not it!

Then the shadows began to grow. Men in red cloaks were playing football. Large rings flew though the air. Jürgens snatched after them, his head bursting with pain.

What strange things he was seeing here on the street!

Soldiers from unknown states marched along in the pouring rain. A cart was moving in one direction, its horse in the other. People became giants for a moment only to shrink again to become tiny as beetles.

There were many shadows in the air now. The firmament was filled with phantasms.

Sometimes he noticed, on coming out onto the street, how a crowd of children would begin to follow him. They would point at him with their dirty hands and yell. Then they would begin to pelt him with stones and mud. He would break into a run, the children at his heels.

Immediately he felt how the children and he himself had remained where they were, while their surroundings were running along instead. Trees, houses, carts and churches were all running along. The red tower ran past too, its green roof flying like a kite!

He began to laugh, and laughed so hard that his eyes filled with tears. The children stopped in wonder and moved off. He was left alone in the middle of the street.

Then he suddenly felt a pang of melancholy in his heart. He walked along, his head bowed, crying. His heart was bursting with sorrow.

This isn't it! he murmured, wiping his eyes. This isn't it!

He tried to wake up, but didn't succeed.

Vaguely he remembered the bright children's room, the games in the garden and the chase after the golden hoop.

He wanted to return to that room! Back to that land of joy! Back under the blossoming apple tree!

Try as he might, he could no longer find the door. He knew it was hidden behind furniture and wallpaper. He shoved the cupboards and the bed into the middle of the room, but still he could not find it.

Then he began to rip the wallpaper from the walls. Here and there the wallpaper had been attacked by dampness and came away in large pieces. But in other places it was stuck fast and his work became exacting and painstaking.

It took some time for all the walls to be laid bare. And still the door was nowhere to be seen!

He looked at the ravaged walls in his befuddled state. In places they were green with mould, in others black with rot. In places old newspapers had been pasted up on the plaster under the wallpaper.

They were yellowed with age and printed in a script that had gone out of fashion. Lifting the candle, he tried to make out what was written there, those ancient events and distant happenings.

Then the hand holding the candle began to tremble.

He saw a black cross and under it his own name. He had died. An unknown hack had written a short obituary in the margin of the death notice.

What promise he had shown when young! But the beautiful blossoms had never born fruit. His was an unsuccessful, threadbare life.

He had chosen other goals and other surroundings for himself than those expected of him. He had been dead to all creative effort and activity. He had lived only for himself—and that was tantamount to never having lived at all!

And how appalling the end of his life had been!

After his mother's death, he had returned to his hometown after a long period of time. He had lived there alone, a stranger to everyone, until in the end he had vanished without a trace. Much later his corpse had been found in a peat bog beyond the town.

May God rest his soul!

Jürgens sat on the floor and placed the candle beside him. Its shadow fell large and black on walls and ceiling. He sat there a long while, his head raised.

Yes, perhaps, he thought. Perhaps that old obituary was right and it was he who was wrong. There lay the truth: he was a mere dream.

Must a dream necessarily be dreamed by someone? Can it not exist by itself, like a thought can exist in a book even when its thinker has long since been reduced to dust? Don't ghosts live their own lives without anyone seeing them or having an inkling of their existence?

Suddenly everything became clear to him.

He too was but a dream, a ghost!

He was now nothing but his own memory, nothing but a thought of himself. He was a belated dream, since the dreamer was already long dead. His suffering was but a sigh in the air like the rustle of leaves when the wind had already died down.

He felt himself changed into air, insubstantial as a shadow and weightless as a gleam of light. He no longer had the need nor the desire to change his image and fate. He was a mere presentiment, an idea.

That night, the sky had been strangely lit up. Wet clouds shone yellow as if by the light of some unseen glow. The earth had been covered with a dull veil.

Jürgens moved silently along the streets. Again he crossed the town, went down to the river, stopped on the bridge. For a long while he watched the current.

The water streamed on ceaselessly in the dusk. The formless substance below was like an image of all that was moving and transient: the myriads of water droplets in the yellow light of the clouds.

Some unknown force bore Jürgens on through the dark streets. He found himself once more up near the cemetery.

The large iron gates were closed but the two beggars were still sitting there: the eyeless woman and the man without legs in the crate. They sat there motionlessly, their heads bowed as if they were dead.

But as Jürgens passed them by the man sat up on his hands, leaned over to the blind woman and whispered in a ghastly voice:

"That man is dead!"

That, indeed, he had forgotten. He had read it and everyone else confirmed the fact. There could now be no shadow of a doubt, if even strangers noticed.

He walked on, trying to recall his past life. Perhaps he had been done an injustice, no outsider could understand his interior life. But what had happened to him on the outside had at least been accurately observed.

He remembered his own death quite vividly:

It had been a drizzly night, yellow clouds hung low, puddles shone phosphorescently.

He had, just like now, experienced strange moods. Many a profound truth had suddenly been revealed to him. And he had also been weary, just as he was now.

Remembering that time, he had arrived at the peat pits on the riverbank. In the light of the clouds he could see the large rectangular pits black around him. Between them were black pyramids of cut peat.

He walked along between two pits on a narrow strip of earth. It grew narrower and narrower. It swayed beneath him like a taut rope, so that he had to walk with his arms outstretched.

Ah, how well he remembered it all!

That time it had been like this too. The strip of earth had swayed in the same way and the smell of marsh gas and peat was as numbing as before. How everything repeated itself!

Suddenly the earth gave way beneath his feet.

He snatched at the air with his hands, his fingers gripped the steep bank, but it crumbled between his fingers. He reached out a couple of more times but again in vain. Then his head disappeared beneath the surface of the water. Thin hands floundered for some moments like the leafless branches of a tree, but then they too disappeared.

The clouds parted. Over the bleak landscape a bright yellow full moon appeared. In the moonlight two silver bubbles rose to the surface of the pitch black water.

1916

Arthur Valdes

1.

A few weeks ago, among the obituary notices, that of *Arthur Valdes* appeared in the press. The impatient reader will hardly have paused for thought at the words of condolence devoted to his memory. And yet these were respects paid to someone who, on dying, took a whole world with him. This world is all the more valuable in that we never managed to get to know it fully. We must again record the loss in the columns of history!

For a long while, I did not want to believe it. I consoled myself in the hope that this notice had sprung more from fear than reality. But now I have on my writing desk a letter from a companion of his, which was sent to me. And with these lines, written in the trenches, the last ray of hope vanished.

So, it is true, after all!

I remember the time I first met Valdes. It was in early 1905, or at the end of the previous year. What chaos there was within and all around us! What a conflagration of nerves and brains! In the same way as the consumption of mental and spiritual powers occurred during the war, so a similar crisis has occurred with us. We seared our nerves too much in these fireworks, our dreams were too bright, so that the reaction that followed could not fail to appear.

In those days I met, as I have indicated, Arthur Valdes for the first time. I remember his pale, narrow face, the thin, immobile lips at the corners of which lurked a mysterious smile, an unrevealed question with the answer twitching there. I remember his thin frame in the grey, unobtrusive suit he wore. I remember him from meetings of *Young Estonia,* where he would sit for hours without moving or saying anything, and his leaving, also without uttering a word.

But what I especially remember from those times is his manuscripts. It seemed as if they had nothing in common with their author. They were so full of consuming fire, hidden pathos, concentrated energy and were written in a firm and clear hand. The influence of Walt Whitman, whose works Valdes appeared to have read, could be felt, although he never spoke of that author. The influence of Whitman, and later Verhaeren, had engendered a certain element of *couleur locale* in Valdes. From them he had adopted a special freshness and sincerity when looking at the world around him.

I remember his beautiful descriptions of early spring, the bluish-green March evenings after a day of thaw, the intimate landscapes and the crusts of frozen snow, the bare trees, the pink sickle of the moon and a roaming dog that, its tail between its legs and its muzzle to the ground, would run timidly across the landscape. Or the picture of the warm April nights, the spring storms in the tall trees, a man and a woman holding hands as they ran along the darkened avenues, until a gust of wind lifted their garments and joy entered like a billow of warmth into their heads... But these idyllic images were abruptly followed by the horrible views of a forest of tall towers in the big city, the thickets of buildings and the mass of people crawling along like ants, awakening painful and irrational fears.

Some of these sketches appeared in the first *Young Estonia* publications and newssheets, but everything there was published under a pseudonym, so that their author never attracted any attention to himself. I only remember the late T. Sander praising him warmly. But that is no doubt the only recognition he received during his entire lifetime.

Nevertheless, in those drafts you could see the beginnings of Arthur Valdes' writing career: a rare modesty in all matters insignificant, and a remarkable persistence as to what was essential. It seemed as if he attached no importance to his writings at the time, as if they were mere exercises of youth. And yet he seemed to possess a self-assuredness, firm as a rock and unspoken, as to his future mission. When I suggested to him, later in life, that he collect and publish his youthful texts, he uttered the opinion that from them one could perhaps make a one-hundred page selection, entitled "A Rainbow", which would stand as a symbol of the fresh and colorful poetry of his youth.

2.

The years went by. Nothing was heard of Valdes, and I had almost forgotten him. Then suddenly, I chanced upon him in Paris. This was in the spring of the year war broke out. He had already spent several days in the metropolis, without seeking out the Estonian colony there or giving any sign of his arrival. Our first meeting occurred purely by chance.

The spring was very beautiful. After warm gentle days, mild nights would arrive when the air was so soft that you felt intoxicated from merely breathing it. We would often sit on an evening in front of the Closerie des Lilas on Boulevard Montparnasse under the chestnut trees on the corner of the rue d'Observatoire. Since the days of Strindberg and Edelfelt, this café had become the locale for Scandinavians. Trams would rattle past. Smoke and steam from the metro station would on occasions billow upwards. Otherwise the area was relatively quiet. Right across the street was the Bullier dance hall. Droves of people would enter through the low doors in the evenings. The Parisians would make haste to enjoy themselves, as if they intuited that within a few months this would no longer be possible. The later it was, the quieter it became. The fountain played barely audibly in front of us. The stars came out in a greenish-blue sky. Everything passed away in the soft dusk. There was something Oriental, moving and soothing, about this evening portrait.

But my memories of these moments are especially happy on account of the fact that they are inextricably linked with the name Arthur Valdes. It was in this environment that I got to know Valdes, and cast a glance at that valuable world in which the life of an extraordinary man was lived.

We often sat, late into the night, at a marble café table, listening to the voices slowly fading around us as the awkward Scandinavians left the building one by one to go home, and peering at the trembling leaves of the chestnut against the glassy depths of the sky, only occasionally exchanging a word or two.

Valdes had changed relatively little since I had last met him back home. His face simply seemed broader and longer than before, and I felt as if he were hiding his true face behind a mask. As with all people who live an intense inner life, his facial expression would change remarkably quickly. Sometimes it was apathetically blank, only to change, a moment later, on account of some fine thought or other, into a handsome, heroic one. And because of this surprising quality Valdes' face would change as Beethoven's was supposed to have done, influencing those around him.

Where Valdes had been all the intervening years is a mystery to me to this day. But he was said to have left his homeland and traveled to London where he earned his daily bread by way of all manner of employment, while mentally having undergone great changes. He now used his free time to travel to the South of France, stopping over for a couple of weeks in Paris. Earlier, he had also traveled a good deal. Although he tended to be rather reticent about his own life, he would talk with great enthusiasm about details of his journey. And so we freshened up our memories of life and art in Italy and Spain.

As we got to know one another better, I noticed that the author in Valdes had not died. In fact, he was now a more perfectly and genuinely writerly type than I had ever read about or met. Everything about him appeared aimed at one goal: to be creative. And this in such a discreet and unassuming guise that it was embarrassing for me to call to mind the noisy, but often spiritually impoverished, hand-to-mouth lifestyle that an author's career invited.

In the shadow of those days I spent with Valdes, a kind of wave of something chosen, sublime, something I cannot capture in words, would flow towards me, something whose existence nonetheless had something of the fragrance of flowers. The memory of him never fails to be a fertile source in me of feelings and thoughts. Remembering sometimes his words, sometimes his notions, but often simply his mere presence, I would be able to consolidate a description of a creative being.

3.

I was used to demanding of myself and others that a writer should primarily be an artist and a specialist. In opposition to this notion, Valdes would posit that a creative person could only be an amateur, a dilettante—in the most positive and attractive sense of the word.

Art as a profession is prostitution, he would say curtly. It awakens a measure of coquettishness in oneself, in one's entourage and audience. It gives rise to duties that cannot be fulfilled. It forces you to write, to produce, to create unceasingly. But this is the very opposite of creative endeavor. It leads to mannerism and "belles lettres." A writer ought to be like a Buddhist holy man who, by reining in his powers, increases them a hundredfold. Everything that is beautiful and powerful is born of chance, unintentionally, entering onto the scene by force. The best works are written when you have not yet become a specialist. The greatest ideas in literature are not discovered by artists.

And yet it would be a great mistake to claim that Valdes' ideas about literature could be embodied by the idea of banal leisure writing. Far from it! He placed the most stringent of demands on authors there ever could be. He demanded of an author a more boundless imagination and a greater amount of hard thinking than he would ever demand of anyone else. By narrowing down the field of writing, he wished to cleanse the activity of everything trivial, wrong and false.

People always feel instinctively, he claimed, that literature differs considerably from other art forms, that it contains something that fundamentally separates it from painting and music. You cannot learn the technique of writing or found academies or conservatoires for its sake. Literature can only be learned from life in all its fullness. And for that reason you cannot confine writers to some kind of caste, club or guild.

All art is based on simulation, but in simulation has its own premises. No writer can personally experience everything of life, every societal relation and state of mind, even if he were to live as long as Methuselah. But he can be in organic unity with society and mankind, so that, using this fact as a point of departure, he can truly understand other relations. The present-day guild of literature is, however, beyond society; it represents the bohemian spirit. Just in the same way as the plebs in Rome was unable to know anything of Rome's mission in the world, so the bohemian writer of today has no idea of the aims of society. He has a parasitical relation to culture and art.

An author should be an amateur! Literature should only be an ancillary activity for him! The further away his everyday profession is from writing, the better. Let him be a manufacturer, a farmer, a sailor, a huntsman. Let him do physical work, fell trees, dig the soil, make bricks: whatever he does teaches and shapes a sense of form. Let him see many landscapes and live simply among active people: that will sow the seeds of and deepen his imagination. How can we have an expansive and vivid imagination, if we see nothing expansive or imaginative in our everyday lives! We marvel at the visions of the Renaissance masters, but we forget that they were often in uniform or serving in the merchant navy, fighting against storms and pirates. Can we, in feebleness, create myths?

Paper eats up memory. Memory grows in an absence of paper. But memory is a prerequisite for imagination. Only an idea borne a long time in our memory can become an image.

Happy were the times when there was much thinking and little writing! When printing had not been invented, and parchment was expensive! Even happier were the times when thoughts were chiseled into stone: there were no pampered aesthetes then working with literature. How an economy of space in thought and word were taught!

It is necessary for us to act and not to vegetate. The desperate Sisyphean work of thinking will not help us—it is grinding with empty millstones. This has always been felt, but only vaguely and unscientifically. All those whose style embodied rhythm and energy have experienced bodily motion, even if only by walking. Nietzsche would walk briskly through the hills all day long while creating the verses of his "Zarathustra," noting them down in the evening on his arrival home. When we read Whitman, we feel that his lines were born amongst the thunder of wind and waves.

Mechanical production and travel by modern-day means of transport have distanced people from personal responsibility and direct contact with substance. Modern man has become an impotent fatalist. He produces by using machines and lives out his own tragedies by way of machines. He is no longer a fully human being. But it is necessary to *be*, so that nothing ever *repeats itself*. Not only in a spiritual, moral sense. All the more so in that composition depends to a large extent on the physical, elemental part.

The contemporary literary spirit is, in the negative sense of the word, superior and aloof from life. No ideal revolution can make it living and active while the writer is still part of a caste of writers until he becomes active, no longer fearing for his material existence. No aesthetes, but the "petty bourgeois"; no bohemians, but "heads of households"; no artists, but workers! That is what a future aesthetics needs.

4.

I remember how Valdes' thoughts at first seemed alien to me. But when I recall his mood and the environment that surrounded him during his years of development, I understand his paradoxes. It was a truth that had come to our Europe, a continent so eaten up by aestheticism, from without. I seem to remember having encountered similar thoughts in the work by Tolstoy entitled "What is Art?"—on different grounds, it is true. Through Valdes, an Anglo-Saxon creative spirit was speaking that would one day be heard here coming from America or Australia—kinetic aesthetics instead of our static, petrified aesthetics.

My text would, however, take on a too personal and limited importance if Valdes' literary thoughts had merely remained on a theoretical plane. Luckily, this is not the case. A large part of his aspirations vanished with him into the grave, but he nevertheless managed to give a mature glimpse of his talents. I am talking here of his collection of stories under the title of "Steps."

On trips to the Bois de Clamart, or sitting on the terrace at Bellevue, Valdes would correct the proofs of his long-term project. The book had been printed in the summer of 1914 and was to appear that autumn. But the Great War intervened, and, with a change in the exigencies of censorship, the collection remained on the publisher's shelf on account of the final story—to await better times.

It gives one a strange feeling to read a proof copy of this collection. The first impression is of a boundless compactness, which can be felt in a directly physical way. It struck me as something like a metal object, where you must exert yourself to pick it up. You didn't believe this to be ordinary paper and cardboard! I feared it would sink through the table!

I have to admit that I had been pretty skeptical on hearing Valdes' theoretical explanations. I had feared to encounter here in this book some kind of soulless positivism and utilitarian idealism. But instead I discovered a larger flow of stormy life energy than in any work of Romanticism. How much of the sufferings of that epoch had this seemingly cold man borne in his breast! How much bitter disappointment, how much acute vexation, and how desperate the fight against the pessimism of the age had been. This smallish book, born over the space of more than a decade, reflects all these steps taken towards Golgotha, along whose road our minds were led for years at a time. This is no result, but a road, and perhaps only in his last work, the story "Hot Springs," does the author utter his most recent thoughts.

Hopefully, the reader will soon have the opportunity of acquainting himself with this valuable book. But I do not wish to miss the happy opportunity to be the first to speak about it. I do this here with the kind permission of the publisher, especially with regard to quotes.

5.

The book begins with a prologue, "The Night Hour", which is written in rhymed prose. It reflects all those crises that the author lived through more clearly than the following stories, and, in order to understand him, we have cause to pause here and examine it.

The long poem is split into three parts. They describe three hours of the night, or rather three different nights of despair, between the damp, dark walls of Paris in winter. Into these parts are pressed all the despair born of loneliness and the individual's desperate longing: achieving reality, becoming something in time as it slips away, and rising for a moment to master this microcosm, which manifests itself as a murky ego.

The work begins with a description of night, pregnant with shadows:

"The night rain lashes silently against the grey glass and sadness seeps into the soul as through a light gauze. This is the moment that the monk sees Satan in the cavern of the monastery and sadness beats in the breast of the nun. It is the mood which Edvard Munch captured in some of his dreamlike interiors."

At that grim hour, Satan appears to the author. For the author is also a monk, who has made every sacrifice, and has fasted and prayed in order to attain his own bliss: the image and aim of his ego. But right now, the Tempter of formlessness and aimlessness surprises him. He *"approaches and moves away and comes again—in spirals, rings rising, falls, descends—and shadows move on the walls, like a flamingo's wings."*

The author is too weary to defend himself against the Tempter. He knows that the Great Twisted One is poisoning him with a lack of will, as in Ibsen's "Per Gynt." But at this moment he is powerless to fight against him.

"I have no power to enter the realm of silence and loneliness, I no longer have the strength to beat off this Satan. He comes like a thought, like an idea, as a last escape, a last way, when I am weary of all the landscapes I have seen."

In some verses the author then describes the apotheosis of formlessness, the Bacchanalia of aimlessness. The Tempter takes on thousands of forms, conceals himself in every object, without ever being anything himself, or revealing any concrete guise.

"And Satan peers from his hiding-place into the pictures: he buries himself in the negro procession's shields, as the wind stirs the growing grass—and tropical flowers nod their heads and the winds stir the ice at the South Pole—a black Satan dances on the walls!"

In the end, Satan's victory is complete. The author has laid down his arms. The first part of the Prologue ends with lines that demonstrate his total laxity, ghastly as an opium-smoker's dream:

"All voices die away and lights fade, only shadows fly and dreams approach. Night reveals the frightening spectral figures, night is filled with questioning, threatening eyes. The rain lashes, a grey mist covers the window panes, Satan turns, the leaden weight of the night hour rolls on."

The second part describes the author's peregrinations in the footsteps of the Tempter as he wanders the streets of Paris at night. Here, the tempo has changed, the beginning of a feverish impetus can be discerned:

"Oh nightly hour, oh murky wave of time, whose soul is seized by a fearful specter, where heaven is dulled and earth deteriorates and the mad whirl of shadows begins—oh nightly hour, yet blacker than death, whose dream seems more true than reality!"

It is a ghastly walk through the streets in the footsteps of the Great Specter, the Prince of Darkness. The city is shrouded in fog, the buildings loom like mountains and the crowds of people are horrifying. Somewhere, lights still pulsate like white balls, there is a carnival and the carousel horses whirl in the air, in a pink glow, as if naked. But the author rushes onwards, his fantasy grows ever more urgent, the rhythm ever more agitated.

Then he no longer recognizes the places where he is wandering. Endless districts open up in the night rain, endless boulevards stretch out. He crosses darkened parks, makes a detour up onto the city ramparts, dodges behind planked fences into gardens. All is dead. He no longer even knows why, but he keeps rushing on, his heart filled with anguish. Is he wandering in Cain's footsteps, is Cain wandering in his, or is he himself the accursed Cain? He breaks into a run, but there is no end to the streets, no end to this giant city. He longs for some border in this desert—an edge, a boundary! He staggers down into an embankment, the cobblestones are slippery with rain. Ever downwards, downwards, ever deeper, as if into a mine. Then suddenly he feels a breath of fresh air strike his face, and right before him looms a yellow line of phosphorescence. It is the Seine, still and horrible—the same line, no doubt, at which Maupassant stood in sadness." This is the only border for human beings: death. And the second part of this long poem ends with another variant:

"The rain lashes, a grey fog covers the Seine, Satan turns, the leaden weight of the night hour rolls again."

In the third section, the author has collected his final confessions and describes his last struggle with the Prince of Darkness. He leads him as if onto the ridge of the roof of a temple, to tempt him with the riches of the entire globe—over the tip of Montmartre, by the Sacré Coeur. This section begins:

"Oh whither, whither is Satan leading me? Before me the dark sleeping shadow of the Moulin Rouge. Below market squares fathomless as cemeteries, streets running from them like guillotines, the steeples above like crosiers of death.

I fall silent. Satan remains silent for an age."

Everything is covered with a grey veil, a kind of pristine mist confines him. *"Paris is in a fog, all of France is in a fog,"* the whole world has been transformed into a ball of fog, which runs its aimless course at the center of countless balls of fog. Everything has become spectral, there is no way forward or back. The Tempter, who at first was merely a disgusting, hunched spirit of evil, has turned into something like a symbol of boundlessness. And before this cosmic vision Man cowers. Who is he that can struggle against this Great Thing that corrupts the world, with its slack, warped, hazy misty Absolute! He wishes only to understand his role in this huge machine, his place in boundless space. And, growing tender like a child, he remembers his life, every suffering that the past has brought him: a hundred foreign cities, full of horror and pain, thousands of streets that captivated his lost soul, and the millions of houses that cast a shadow over his heart.

"Oh the past: thousand upon thousand minutes so painful, thousand upon thousand eyes pained by regret, thousand upon

thousand unforgiving lips, thousand upon thousand perished gods—as far as the eye can see.

Oh Satan, have pity, pity on me!

Oh the past: masses of people, books and countries, many tender, gentle, sweet dreams—but what remains are ways without aim and aims without a way and life as in a distant desert—as far as the eye can see!

Oh Satan, have pity, pity on me!"

But the Absolute, the Universe, has nothing to say to what is limited in scope, Totality cannot relate to the individual. There is no hope of understanding one another.

"All is so lonely, all so blind! All is so aimless, all without issue! Mana, the realm of the dead, still glows black, the Lethe still twinkles." One last time the despondent human being tries: *"I am not asking anything good of you, no miracle— oh tell me Satan, utter only your own name—even if it is as dark as a catacomb!"*

But there is no reply, even to this despairing plea! And the poem ends with yet another variant: *"The rain lashes, a grey mist covers the sky, Satan turns and the night hour rolls on like a leaden weight."*

Valdes does not, however, end his train of thought with this experience of hopelessness. Quite the opposite, this is his point of departure. Let it be that mankind will never reach the eternal truth only by way of mystical intuition—may he strive towards this in his own narrow area—it is nonetheless the prerequisite to all positive aims and images, to the combination of thoughts. In this sea of boundless pessimism, he wishes to light his own beacon, his own star, in this hideous space of the night.

6.

The book contains a further five stories, each about thirty pages in length. Although these have, as indicated, been written over many years, they nonetheless have a remarkably consolidated line of development. None of the stories repeat what is said in others, but each builds upon elements of the previous one. Each is a world in and of itself, and together they form a solar system.

The relationship between the thinking individual and form—that question appears in ever new guises and Valdes appears spellbound by it. The more an individual develops, the more conscious becomes the relationship between him and form. The more primitive the being, the more rudimentary the treatment of form. The shape of biological life that begins as a tiny formless and slimy cell and ends up as a symmetrical and noble human being—that is, at the same time, the yardstick of the intellectual development of these creatures. God became God only when He felt a yearning for form and created the world; with the birth of Man, the first awareness of form appeared. Valdes touches upon this notion in the prologue to "Steps." The first story of the book is also, in large measure, devoted to this theme.

How many naïve attempts have there been in people's imagination to build a bridge between living beings and lifeless objects! Without life, yet possessing it, living in an artificial, supernatural way—this thought is concealed behind the rough hewn and crude image of our *kratt*, i.e. a goblin. Medieval alchemists strove for this goal when they attempted to create a homunculus. But the most perfect of these creations, i.e. the Golem, was described in the manifold stories of the Jews.

A Golem can be created in a scientific manner, but can also be brought to life unwittingly. In the first case, he is the servant of his master, but in the second he becomes a fearful being, as no one possesses the means to rein him in. And so a leaf from God's secret "unutterable" name *(shem hamforásh)* fell onto a pile of clay and immediately a human being sprang up. He walked the streets of the city, and who knows what may have happened if someone hadn't taken it into his head to rip the secret letter from him—upon which the human being again reverted to being a pile of clay.

The Golem is closely related to our *kratt* but reveals a more profound imagination on the part of its creators. He is completely human to look at, but inside is coarsely material, lacking spiritual needs and sensations. He remains a lifeless body until one day his master breathes life into him for some particular task. He is a mere mechanical being who can, by way of strength obtained from without, take on the form of a living being by way of the "name of God" for a short while, only once again to revert to its constituent parts. What an analogy for human life itself!

Having an excellent knowledge of the Orient, Valdes used this motif in his story "The Golem." But he used this dry, bleak theme merely as a springboard for his own spiritual strivings and philosophical speculations. And what results he achieved!

A rich rabbi has a Golem. As the rabbi's servant, he cultivates the vineyard, guards the cattle and turns the quern. The rich rabbi has a twelve-year-old daughter, Lea. Sheltered completely from the outside world, she grows up within the walls of her home, accompanied by an old servant woman. But times of unrest break out in the town and the rabbi sends Lea and the old servant woman off into the countryside for protection.

One morning, as she is sitting on the roof of the house, Lea sees a young man in white robes driving a flock of goats up the hill. All day long he carries baskets of harvested grapes down from the vineyard. In the evening he turns the hand-cranked mill in the yard, later that night Lea hears, through her virginal sleep, how the wine trickles into vessels as he presses the grapes with his feet. She demands to know who this tireless servant is, but the deaf servant woman gives no reply.

So Lea makes a point of trying to see this marvelous servant from close up. What she sees is strange: a young man with a face, white as lime, a fixed gaze, skin that does not sweat, hair that does not curl. But he does work, endless amounts of work, he never seems tired, never rests, neither seems to speak nor laugh. It is horrible and pitiful!

And Lea makes a point of seeing him from even closer to. When windy days arrive, when the wine is stored and the corn ground, the servant is seldom to be seen. That day he performs a few tasks, then vanishes. Lea rushes after—and what does she see? The servant lies motionless for hours on end on the stone floor of the granary, gets up, does his few small jobs, and lies down again. Lea rushes up to him and puts hanks of wool under his head. The next day she sits by him and weeps. The third evening she sings to him from the roof of the house.

And here begins the most remarkable part of the story, where Valdes demonstrates his inner life and subtlety of style to us.

Human feeling and pity cannot evaporate or be lost. It is something essential, it affects through awakening, through creation. A gentle flush appears on the cheeks of the Golem when Lea is weeping beside him; his chest heaves when the girl touches him shyly. He possesses all the potential for human feelings, only his creator has not given him any of these qualities, neither joy nor sadness.

His countenance takes on the features of a human face, he begins to notice the beauty of things around him, and for the first time realizes he is tired after work. But all this does no more than awaken an inkling of something distant in him, no more than a dream does to a human being, and he falls back lifelessly onto the stone floor. Lea sits at his side, the tears run down her cheeks. Then she leans over and kisses him on the lips. What was that? A distant rumbling? A much greater foreboding? A memory? The Golem's heart quivers.

Every day he wakens a little more. It is fine weather again. The goats are in the hills, a new crop is ripening in the vineyard, new grain needs to be ground. With a vigor he has never experienced before, the Golem treads, light of step, he tarries when leaving, hurries home. Life becomes ever more marvelous. The two of them go into the hills to look at the ripening grapes. They rub the heads of corn and winnow them with their hands. In the evening they drive the cattle home hand in hand in silence, and the warmth of the sheep suddenly wakens the Golem from the long sleep that had seemed eternal.

So this is what the world is like! Such is life, such is Man, the king of nature! For the first time he sees the grassy knolls, the blue sky, the billowing grain and the pliant vines and Lea—Lea at his side!

But at the same time an awareness of his hideous secret awakens within him. He is not a human being! He is not even any kind of creature! The sheep are happier than he is, the pigeons on the roof as well. They are natural, but he is not. Every longing that something awakening to life could feel sprouts within the Golem: to be an individual, a human being, despite his few years and limited powers, however weak and suffering, but still a human being, whose breast quivers with joy and pain! What good is it to gold that it is valuable, or to the sun that it is hot, if they feel neither their own value nor their warmth?

And the Golem is joyful at the slightest sign that he is coming nearer to being a human being; he is joyful at the weariness he feels after the working day, he is joyful at the heat and cold he has to bear. They provide him with hope! He is no longer an insensate object! And he takes hold of Lea in full awareness of his awakening humanity. That is the source of his life and his joy. Like a flower in the sun, he opens his heart towards Lea, in order to burgeon in the warmth of the experience.

Now the grapes are ripe. They pick the bunches, carry them home, press the grapes in vats and taste the new wine. It is their first wine! Now the grain is ready. They go out into the fields, cut the stalks, tie them up, arranging them in sheaves. When they are weary at midday they lie in the shade of the sheaves, as a young man and woman, their lips pressed together, their arms around one another's hot necks.

One such day, the old rabbi returns home. As his daughter is not at home, he walks out into the fields where the Golem is supposed to be working, and finds Lea in his embrace. This is something ghastly for the old rabbi, even more ghastly than if it were an animal with which no human being should have any dealings. He is a mere object! And even before the startled couple can utter a word, the old man has raised his staff and cursed the Golem. The Golem collapses, his face white as lime, and dies. His development has not been brought to fruition, he is not free of the laws of nature. But if he cannot live as a human being, then at least he can die as one. Lea falls on her knees before her father.

"Kill me! Kill me!" she shrieks. "I, too, no longer wish to be human, if he is no more!"

This is where the story ends.

7.

Finding a point of contact between human beings and inert matter was the theme of the above story. Only one step forward has been made in the next story, to the world of zoology. And this once again occurs in a psychological and philosophical way, looking through his idiosyncratic prism the equivalent to which cannot be found in the whole world of literature.

This time, the place where the events take place is an aristocratic dwelling house near Trafalgar Square in London, and the only character is Sir Douglas, struck down by paralysis, sitting in his leather armchair near the fire. In actual fact, nothing happens in this story, all it does is present to us the memories of Sir Douglas from times long since past. While the framework of the story may be the only one possible, the inspiration for the theme came from a fragment of the Indian "Ramayana." It describes an episode in which Ravana abducts Rama's wife and flies with her through the air to the island of Lanka. A fight ensues between Ravana and Rama, the latter being supported by the King of the Apes, Hanuman, and his cohorts. Certain parallels can be found to the way Joseph Rosny depicts the life of gorillas in the story *Profondeurs de Kyamo* or even Jack London's novel *Before Adam*. But Valdes' point of departure is always of less consequence than his special manner of presentation.

What then is the theme of the story "In the Shadow of the Hill"?

Much as I would like to give a detailed account of the story, I also realize that, since the subject is completely different to what is normally considered to be literature, I would not succeed in conveying a great deal. It is but a dream at the fireside, a play of thought with the shadows dancing on the walls. But nonetheless!

Sir Douglas is old. Nothing is left of his former years: his youth, his health, his agility, even his memory, are gone. He now warms himself like a lizard at the hearth, until his manservant, who is nearly as old as he is, coaxes him to sleep. Only two monuments to the past remain, and still seem current: a clump of dried tropical grass and a gleaming skull by the fireside.

He allows the clump of grass to be handed to him, raises it before his face in his trembling hand, and imagines he still smells the fragrance of flowers. Then he is handed the skull and turns it over in his hands, with a malicious gleam in his eye. The manservant does not know what is causing this, no one does, nor does he himself as once was able to. And yet everything is still close to him, around him, in him. He again smells the fragrance of tropical vegetation, the odor of the stagnant water, hears the rattlesnake moving in the grass.

Sir Douglas rolls the skull in his shaking hands. It is too large to be a human head, its forehead is too narrow, its jaw too prominent, its fangs too savage. And indeed, this is the skull of the Great Hanuman, who was part of Sir Douglas' life. And the restless thoughts of the old man flicker like flames across the dead grass of the past.

The author uses sparse means to acquaint us with a more horrible drama than we can even imagine. It could be said that the subtlety he employs for this has no equivalent in literature. Like a vision, he conjures up before us a young woman with light hair, blue eyes and a slim waist. Then, by purely phonetic means, he offers us help in providing a feeling of the contrasting qualities, and suddenly changes scene. A succession of the most exotic landscapes appears: the white tent of the hunter on the ridge of a hill, a meadow filled with water on the banks of the river, the darkness of a tropical forest. Near the tent lies the blue-eyed woman in a hammock, dangling her leg over the edge. But how she has changed, this woman! How her eyes glitter, her nostrils quiver, her mouth twitches! Sir Douglas—it is he—is sitting in the doorway of the tent with a look of bitterness on his face, a rifle across his knees. Apes can be seen between the leaves of the trees. Sir Douglas snatches up his rifle and aims. The wounded and shrieking creatures hang from the branches by their hands and tails.

Then the décor nervously shifts a couple of times and the author demonstrates the revolting side of his vision. The situation we now see is so unusual that I no longer dare describe it. It might be compared to the episode from Voltaire's "Candide" which give a crude, yet lasting, depiction of the prior developments. The sixteenth chapter tells the story of Candide and of Cacambo's encounter with the apes.

What is it in Valdes' story that makes us feel somehow dizzy? No doubt the contrast between the development and the morality of the tale. We could perhaps be reconciled to the events if the protagonist were somehow a primitive creature at the mouth of his cave. But we are dealing with a son of culture here, a being whose appearance and inner being ought to have moved up to an entirely different level. Have not a thousand generations of culture tamed Wedekind's *Erdgeist*, his Lulu along with its instincts? Horrible!

Meanwhile, the fire at which Sir Douglas is sitting has gone out. The old man is bowed over Hanuman's skull. Two crowns of the skull gleam in the light of the embers, a red flicker lights up the carvings of the armchair, revealing them, concealing them. Trees sprout branches, branches sprout leaves, and, underneath, animals roam. Who is now sitting among the leaves, head white, cheeks sunken, with long-boned arms...?

8.

The story entitled "God of the Isle" takes its subject matter from the psychology of religion. It is the story of the Antichrist appearing on a small island populated by fisher folk, a society cut off from the rest of the world.

The aged pastor on the island dies and a young man comes in his stead. This young man has black hair, a beard, a swarthy face and dark eyes. His black suit is stretched over his thin, bony body, and on windy evenings he strides along the island's sandy beaches. He lives alone in the sparsely furnished presbytery, where the wind penetrating the cracks in the walls howls and rats run riot. He lives like a monk, devoted only to his books and his work. But his surroundings are utterly bleak, his life distressingly grey! In the evening, the pastor busies himself with the private distillery situated in the house, sits alone at the table and downs one glass after another. Red flecks flush his cheeks and brow, and the thin flames of the candle are reflected in his feverish eyes.

During those periods, his thoughts toss about from one extreme to the other. They graze the heights of the soul, sink into the strait paths of asceticism, and end up in nihilism. Vistas of emptiness are opened up: there is no aim or purpose, cause or effect. In this universal void, foolish planets wander blindly, shivering with cold. What does good or evil mean here, what is the point of ecstasy or anger?

The man grins through his black beard. A forgotten passion burns within him, and, with every quiver of joy, he feels how the Tempter's finger touches his heart. This is the same spirit that battled with Jehovah before the ages began. It is the same spirit that tempted mankind in the Garden of Eden and which has been falling through space in caustic despondency, right up to our day. Ah, on the Tree of Knowledge red apples still grow!

The pastor feels the Antichrist rise within him.

Each Sunday he preaches fiery sermons. He speaks of God's love in the homes of the sick and the unhappy. When spring arrives, he goes out under the open heavens and preaches among the flowers, as He who before him preached on the mount. On summer eves he stands on the deck of a ship and blesses the people on the shore across the silent waters. He begins performing miracles: by the laying on of hands he drives out the evil spirits, his touch restores sight to the blind. He waves his jacket over the waters, and the nets fill to their breaking point.

But then the nature of his communion service begins to change. It is as if the poison of evil seeps into goodness. He still reads the Bible, but his voice is like barbed wire, scratching the words of love until they are bloody. He presents the holy vessels at Communion, but the gold of the ciborium rusts and the outside of the chalice is coated with droplets of bloody sweat. He still utters the old prayers and blessings, but he turns them inside out, reads the prayers backwards, reads prayers of requiem at christenings, says prayers for the sick at the marriage service. So in the end he has exchanged good for evil, abusing the sacrament and blessing sin, and the mass has become a mockery of God.

Over time, suspicions are aroused among the congregation. There are those who were already shaking their heads at his miracles. And a rumor passes among the people. Here and there heads are put together and grow flushed. Then the wise elders of the congregation meet to discuss the matter. They talk of the preacher in a dejected manner. The spiritual life of such uneducated people, including the old parish clerk, is extremely well depicted. They have nothing to base their ideas on, they can hardly formulate in words the thoughts that move through their grey brains. In his vaulted room, the pastor strides back and forth in agitation, wearing his chasuble, his black beard bristling, and watches the visitors with penetrating eyes—until they retreat back over the threshold.

But at the same time those who are for the pastor group together: to some he has restored sight, others he has made rich, has ensnared yet others with his red tongue. Many of these are women. Discord erupts in families, wives divorce husbands, children shrug off parents.

A confusion of thought takes hold of the congregation, as if their heads were full of lice instead of thoughts. People see visions in broad daylight. Women give birth prematurely, children are born with teeth and long hair. One old crone falls senselessly to the floor during Communion when she suddenly sees tiny horns growing amid the pastor's hair. Then one Sunday the whole congregation sees a figure whose face is like that of an ape standing beside the pastor at the pulpit—words move from the tip of its tongue to that of the pastor.

The fear of the people knows no bounds. They storm out, run rings round the church, not knowing what to do. Then they seize ice picks and harpoons, surround the church, stuff the windows and doors full of bundles of faggots and set light to them! What a crackling, what a blaze! Evening arrives, the sky grows dark, the sea is black. Then, through the flames, they hear a howling and a grunting sound, and a red pig charges out of the flames, along with a herd of red piglets. They rush towards the shore at great speed and vanish over the cliff into the darkening sea.

The grim symbolism of the story would still have been obscure if the author had ended it at this point. But instead he ends with a spectral vision:

A spring wind is blowing across the stretch of water, the waves billow, the foam flies—from the pink foam, delicate beings with transparent wings and pink faces rise. The autumn evening shrouds the waters, the brassy face of the chill moon rises over the swishing waves—a herd of heavy beings with dull faces rides through their crests, then sinks back into the depths with a death rattle.

With this symbolic image, the author has rounded off his final dream of the hideous struggle between Ormuzd and Ahriman. But can this story be grasped in one single reading, one review, even less by one image? In it are contained so many thoughts and feelings, it is as light and as heavy as are the allegorical beings at the end of it.

9.

Valdes should not be thought of as one of those people who fantasize and are divorced from reality, who conjure up horrors for purely literary purposes, people who produce art for art's sake. People who mystify, magicians holding sway over their phantasmagorical world. But they are divorced from life, asocial, and therefore not really people of the mind.

Valdes was too much of a social animal for this, too strongly linked to contemporary spiritual and material welfare. To a certain extent, he was also political. This may explain, on one hand, his sudden disappearance from his native land; on the other, his aesthetic views, influenced by social points of view.

The best proof of this is his short-story "Antoninus." But at the same time, one should emphasize the fact that Valdes was too subtle an artist to expose his views openly or promote them.

"Antoninus" depicts events from our recent past. It is a look at a shattering tragedy, as if taking place on stage. It is a succinct piece, but what words there are fall with a swish, like swords, through the air. It has few characters or events, but the tread of Fate can be felt in the movements of the characters. Not even in the silent dramas of Maeterlinck or Crommelynck was such a fateful atmosphere created.

One of Valdes' most specific qualities was his unerring instinct when searching for form. The ideas contained in his works always came together in his head simultaneously with their literary form. They are organically linked, the bark has grown into the tree, they are impossible to separate. And the story "Antoninus" is really a play, a tragedy in one act, only the stage and the descriptions of the characters are richer than usual. The theme required a particular form.

I would have to quote for pages on end, if I wanted to give Valdes the opportunity to demonstrate the spirit of the action in his own words. So please allow me merely to summarize the plot here, and add a few remarks.

There is in a muddy little town in our country, an even muddier yard that the events take place in. It is the year of the first Russian Revolution. The town is under martial law, the punishment squad has marched in. While elsewhere the revolution has flared up and enthusiasm and passions are running high, here all you feel is the fear and cowardice of the local inhabitants. There is nothing bold or proud about their behavior, just the cautious peering out of slaves from under a low brow!

A stranger has fled here to hide away—neither a revolutionary nor a political activist, simply an unobtrusive scholar who has gotten caught up in the fateful events. He has never before noticed what was happening beyond the windows of his library. He used to pass by the masses cautiously, like a total stranger. His gaze was fixed on the past instead of the present, and some inscription on a stone would be of more interest to him than the entire year's issues of the contemporary press.

But he is now here, in a strange town, living in a tiny room in a shabby boarding house, his beard unshaven, his passport a forgery. He suffers from the ignorance, from the cold, from everything surrounding him. The story begins with this bleak picture.

A candle is burning on the table. On the other side of the planked wall, rowdy peasants, visitors to the fair, are drinking. When the man presses his face to the window pane, he sees the grey yard, and people and horses bustling about. The ground is covered with a muddy slush, and sleet is falling from the sky. The horses neigh amid the gloom.

The scholar turns his back to the window and takes out a volume of Marcus Aurelius, which has by some miracle lain forgotten in his pocket. He wants to wipe everything around him from his consciousness. This philosophy of resignation has always been an oasis to him, somewhere to flee to, when life presses in too closely. Here he can find the equilibrium of the mind, *galene*, which he seeks.

But everything disturbs him in these surroundings. The din from the yard increases, as does the drunken yelling from the other side of the wall, and he is forced to hear all this alongside the wise thoughts of Antoninus. But what is even more ghastly is an ominous whispering, from the next room, the corridor behind his door. Hoarse voices speak of revolt, escape, bloody deeds. And these sounds around him pain him physically.

All he can do is hold out and wait until he can flee these horrible circumstances! They represent nothing more than an incomprehensible false step in his life, a side step into an alien world. Somewhere, the life in which he feels at home has been preserved: clarity of thought, the lofty achievements of art, a quiet study to work in, devoted students. He just has to bear it for a few more days—and he will be himself again, freed from oppressive inaction.

These grim thoughts are interrupted by an unexpected visitor, who pokes her head around the door. It is the little daughter of the boarding house landlord. She has curly hair, bright eyes, dimpled cheeks. There she stands, rooted to the spot, a doll in her arms. The scholar has never been close to, or liked, children. They have simply served to disturb the rational course of his life. But now the child is like a ray of sunshine between the clouds. He makes a move towards her, but she shies away and disappears. With the shutting of the door something innocent and unblemished is shut out.

His loathsome situation continues, entangling the refugee like a spider's web.

Then the landlord himself comes to see him. The scholar is startled at this unexpected arrival. No, he hasn't come for any particular reason. He just wanted to see whether his lodger was all right. He is the soul of kindness and politeness. But the landlord doesn't leave; he complains at being dead tired from the day's confusion, sits down uninvited on a chair, pulls off his muddy boots, wipes the sweat from his forehead, and looks around the room. *Oi, oi,* he moans, what times are these, what agitated and difficult times! He falls silent and peers at the open book on the table. What language is that, he asks, such a strange language—he lists the languages he has heard of. Oh, I see, Greek, never heard that spoken. But in these hard and troubled times you hear all sorts of languages. He falls silent, then talks about the country fair—is the stranger here for the fair? Then he talks about languages again, and the troubled times. Finally, he gets up and bows his way out, his obtuse face turned towards the stranger all the while.

When he has gone, the scholar jumps up and paces the room nervously. Then he sits down resolutely at the table. No, it was nothing. Just an idea brought on by nerves. He sinks back into thought.

Marcus Aurelius wrote his *Tà eis heautón* in a distant barbarian country, among rough soldiers in an army camp, in the forests of the Marcomans on the banks of the Danube. He battled against his environment, was a superior being, asserting himself in spite of the travails of the world around him. He succeeded in being emperor and philosopher at one and the same time.

Emperor and philosopher, the scholar suddenly asks himself. Was he a philosopher when he was acting as an emperor and an emperor when philosophizing? Did he practice what he preached when speaking of humanity and tolerance? When pursuing the Quadi, Suebians, Bessians, Bastars, Sarmatians and others, was this in order to teach them humane values? Or when he had shut himself in the silence of his residence in resignation, was he not carrying out the same grim duties within the empire he led as the leader of any superpower in the world today? Was it not Governor Cassius who nailed prisoners to the cross or smashed the bones of deserters, making sure they stayed alive "as a warning to others"?

The scholar's eyes look down at the book where it says: "We are all thieves; in the way that the spider lures flies into its web, and the farmer rabbits, the fisherman sardines, the huntsman bears, so I am hunting the tribes of Germania or Sarmatia. I am no better than them."

What is an individual, if he cannot assert himself, the scholar thinks, gazing into the darkness. If he cannot defend himself, cannot keep his borders clear of attack. But self-assertion requires war, violence, assaults. It is easy to philosophize when superior and aloof. A philosopher must have power, employ violence, make war. What good is the philosophy of a prisoner, a refugee or one of the masses, people who suffer nothing but the burden of keeping themselves alive? A powerless individual and the masses are nothing but refugees and prisoners. They are governed by fatalism.

During this train of thought, the child appears again. Now she dares enter the room. She approaches, looks around, and shows the stranger her doll. And the stranger expresses an interest in the doll. What is her name? Margarethe.—I see, so she's called Margarethe.—Does she talk?—Yes, she does, but others don't hear her, only she, the child, hears.—And the stranger takes the little girl onto his knee and talks with her. He too can hear the doll speak, really.—At that, his little guest bursts into laughter.

But while talking with her, the scholar remembers that he too has a similar little daughter somewhere. He rarely thinks of this fact, nor of his family and his private life. This thought saddens him, feelings of regret swelling in his heart. Life should have been different...

But the child chatters away about her small observations. A lot of strangers have arrived today.—Oh really, says the thinker indifferently, what sort of people? Many soldiers, policemen and gendarmes. They have beautiful uniforms and proud swords.—The thinker suddenly gives a start and grows pale. With one ear, he is still listening to the child's innocent chatter, with the other, to sounds coming from outside. People are driving carriages, people are walking about the house, whispering in the entrance hall. The child looks fearfully at the stranger's face, then slips back onto the floor and retreats, her doll in her arms. Her eyes are full of fear and diffidence.

No sooner has the child left, but the landlord returns. He apologizes for the intrusion, but isn't the stranger bored. Wouldn't he like to have company for a short while? He sits on the chair and looks at the stranger. Oh, what horrible times, he says. All sorts of people wandering around, and you haven't a clue who they really are. Carrying arms, entering buildings, they are driven back, flee... The landlord's voice becomes a hoarse whisper: has the stranger heard what is happening in the town and around? A dialogue ensues:

"No, I'm a stranger here, I don't know."

"Horrible, *horrible* things." (Footsteps in the entrance hall.)

"What sort of things?"

"People are being killed, *killed*." (Running in the entrance hall.) Three people have been shot on the town square. I was there." (Whispering in the entrance hall.) "They were lying there in the snow. Their eyes were open. I've never seen dead people before. It was terrible." (Several voices whispering in the entrance hall.) "And at the time of the shooting, several people in the crowd were arrested. I took to my heels!" (Hissing voices in the entrance hall, like a nest of rats scattering in all directions.)

The landlord's eyes have bored into the face of the stranger, his voice is so low it is almost inaudible. He is no longer so much talking with his mouth as with his deeply set eyes. It is the voice of a dumb animal. His blue-veined hands hang as if broken. Suddenly a memory flashes through the mind of the thinker: Marcus Aurelius smashing the bones of deserters—as a warning to others. A momentary fear crosses his face.

Meanwhile, something has happened that the thinker does not understand. The landlord has left the room. He did not see when that happened. He tiptoes to the door and bolts it. Then he glances swiftly behind him. The room is empty. The candle is burning. The window is black.

He rushes through the room. Everything is as before. He listens. Suddenly the whole house is silent as the grave. Not a single sound. Only the beating of his heart. Then, like a specter, he sees someone's face outside the window. He rushes over. But outside it is night, black as pitch. His heart misses a beat.

What now happens is described in the story with frightful simplicity and concision.

It is if someone is whispering somewhere, but the stranger cannot determine whether behind the wall, above the ceiling, or under the floor. The horrible whispering is hemming him in from all directions. He flounders around, looks under the furniture, tries the door. The whispering increases. It is as if the walls are moving, bulging, coming apart at the corners. He stops in the center of the room.

Then very faint footsteps are heard approaching the door. His eyes are fixed on it unblinkingly. He sees how the door handle is slowly being depressed and rises again, slowly and silently. Only now does he hear knocking. He makes no move, nor does he reply. Another knock. Then a shaky voice from outside: "Open the door. It's me—your landlord." But at the same time he hears another voice from beyond the door, which reminds him of the jangling of spurs or chains. He remains silent. Then a sudden loud knock, unknown voices yelling: "Open up! Open up! We order you to open up!" The door shakes, cracks, bulges inwards. The thinker remains motionless. Everything in him has turned to stone. He sees how the crack around the door begins to grow black, yawning wider and wider. The walls begin to fall in, moving from their places, cracks appear at every corner. The room changes shape, becomes a void, a parallelogram, like a cardboard box crushed underfoot. And among all this cracking and crashing he hears the endless cry issuing from many throats: "Open up! Open up!"

Then suddenly, from beyond the door, he hears a child's high cry of despair: "Don't let them in! Don't let them in! They'll kill you!" The cry is smothered by a hand.

The thinker's hand moves instinctively to his pocket. He seizes his revolver, raises it to his temple and fires. There is but one memory in his dying brain: Avidius Cassius, Marcus Aurelius' governor... Then that, too, is cut short.

I have hardly been able to convey any idea of the story here. I have hardly been able to give an idea of the social and philosophical profundity that emanates from it. It is the tragedy of an individual who has accidentally found himself in the vortex of time without realizing its full significance. All that is left for him is to kill or be killed. But if the heart is not up to it, you have to exit from life. This would be the final dead end for him.

But Valdes did not become petrified in this kind of pessimism.

10.

The only story left to review is the final one, "Hot Springs." But it is on account of precisely this story that we are unable to read the collection with full understanding. For that same reason, I will have to abandon the idea of a more detailed description of it. Let it merely be said that Valdes provided a serious and thoughtful description of a utopia, set in the future. The book ends with lines that are an incomparable surge of victory, and there is nothing in Estonian literature to match its power.

After reading the last few stories the reader will have felt a natural urge to seek fresh air and sunshine. Here everything has become so hemmed in, so oppressive! It would seem that even Valdes himself suffered on its account. These stories seem to be the fruits of his most difficult years, and so the memories involved appear to have affected him like a glimpse into the abyss. "I have suffered too much, to again become optimistic and lyrical," he once said, adding: "And yet I am not sure for which hours of my life I should be more grateful for increasing my sense of life: the ones of suffering or the ones of joy."

Evidence of Valdes' life at the time, and of his desperate urge to penetrate the depths of life and existence, can be found in the scraps of diaries he left behind. When read, they provide more than hieroglyphic hints. "This is no longer thought," he repeats, "but boundless pain. These are no stairs but a series of descending steps into the abyss." And again: "Can the intensity of human thought increase to such an extent that it can burn through the human organism like too powerful an electric lamp?" Valdes too is among the sort of people who "could not imagine that, if others had not thought unceasingly, the world would not have survived to his days".

It is without a doubt that this deeper immersion in life on Valdes' part represented his final "steps." In them, the purely decorative tendency disappears more and more, giving rise to more of a spiritual space. He moves away from fantasy and approaches a realistic manner of depiction—so that he is more able to abandon the former and give himself over completely to the latter. For while fantasy is, after all, an important prerequisite of art, this is sometimes only revealed in the linguistic material.

While I have demonstrated above that changes occurred in Valdes' work over time, these are not of a sudden or unexpected nature. But his investigative mind, which constantly touches on questions concerning the relationship between an individual and his surroundings, grows more flexible. He no longer uses the word "form" in such a material sense as in his earlier works. The eternal struggle between substance and spirit no longer appears in such concrete guise.

These works are realistic, but only to Valdes' way of thinking. His entire life, he wrestled with one technical question: to try to learn the *rules of fantasy*, to master the logic of unreality and achieve psychological credibility in his most fantasy-filled themes. That is why his thought and feeling attained such a weight of seriousness. He always hits the nail on the head. He needs no more than a single word to conjure up an image or portray the nature of something, so that unexpected vistas open before us. At first reading, this feels like a physical burden, which cannot be borne lightly. If we are to compare his style to anything in literature, then perhaps there is only Flaubert's *Salammbô* and *La temptation de Saint Antoine.* But while Flaubert's works are stylistic, Valdes' are psychological extracts.

Leafing through Valdes' book of stories again and again, I have tried to find an answer to the question: what distinguishes this work from thousands of others sewn together to form small booklets? Without a doubt, his special appeal lies partly in the fact that he offers us pure content— mental, "substantive" literature— after an epoch when a literature devoted to the cult of form held sway. But the main focus is nonetheless that the content is seen from an entirely new angle than had been achieved heretofore. He represents an entirely new aesthetic.

The limits of literature, as with any art form, are the limits of the individual himself. No one can reach beyond the boundaries of the individual. But, of late, the limits of art have undoubtedly been narrower than the limits of human beings. Thinkers have invested an incredible amount of energy in the expansion of science, while artists have yet to catch up. Human thought has expanded to form a wide circle, but no space has been afforded for aesthetic activity.

Science has opened up boundless vistas. On the one hand, astronomy, geology and evolutionary science have substantially expanded man's grasp of both himself and the world around him. On the other, biology and chemistry have examined the very smallest particles of life. The macrocosmos and the microcosmos have been brought much closer to us.

But this progress is not to a large extent reflected in literature. Naturalism is too narrow and superficial a concept: it keeps on revealing the same ant-like view of society, without its idealist horizons ever opening up to a cosmic breadth. When natural science is palely reflected in literature (e.g. Wells, Rosny), it is in the guise of scientific dreams, the scientific imagination, the depiction of bizarre utopias. But a new aesthetics, a new spiritual breakthrough across the board—these have not been achieved.

Valdes offers us some efforts in this direction. But right from the start, he has been aware of the dangers lurking here. It is not sufficient for art to merely popularize science, art must also be able to tackle any subject using its achievements. No pathos for outer space à la Flammarion or a novel covering the progress of science like Bölsche! However philosophical Valdes' works may be, they have nothing in common with the literary puppet theatre created for didactic reasons. He is, first and foremost, an artist, with strongly accentuated psychological abilities.

And for this reason he is not really the author of fantasy or the imagination he at first seems to be. Despite all the differences, I would like to compare Valdes with Wells. Their works contain much imagination, but the work of E. T. A. Hoffmann, Poe or de Quincey is alien to them. Both their methods of creation contain an element of speculation. They are both realists to the full extent, but realists of a completely new order. That which may at times seem to be fantasy is only so in that we lack an understanding of the underlying science. While Hoffmann's fantasies tend to have sprouted wings, so to speak, and he frees himself from all the fruits of human experience, Wells' or Valdes' fantasies require the achievements of present-day science. Nothing supernatural, but nature to the very end! This is how their basic aim can be put into words.

11.

O Lebensmittag, feierliche Zeit!
O Sommergarten!

These words by Nietzsche were written on the cover of Valdes' surviving booklets. He was 30 years of age when the dark clouds of his life parted and he was liberated from the caustic pessimism of his youth. He felt, for the first time, the joy and passion of creation—and at one such joyous moment, Nietzsche's beautiful words about the great noon of life sprang to mind.

Valdes' surviving literary drafts and sketches can be retraced back to that time as well. It is to be hoped that a portion of these will appear in print quite soon, so that it is unnecessary to describe them here in any great detail. From them, we can follow Valdes' development after "Steps." In these short pieces, aphorisms and mood portraits, sometimes only written in the margins while sitting at a *bonfire* after a long day's march, he approaches once again the freshness and joy of life of the poems of his youth. You can feel the sun shining in the noon of his life.

But he, who spoke of the value of a career as a soldier, was, in his daily worldview, an enemy of war and violence; it must be that he had contact with that profession earlier in life than was generally realized. All his life he had written about the opposition of spirit and matter, form and chaos—now he himself was swallowed by matter and chaos.

In the light of this opposition, Valdes becomes even greater to my way of thinking. I can see his optimistic attempt at leading a living life: his thoughts concerning man give matter form, his feelings provide it with life. Just as Solveig's song saves Per Gynt from the Button-Maker when his "raw material" is destined for recasting, Lea is trying to save the Golem. Lea did not succeed, nor did Valdes, but the spirit grows ever stronger, greater, more beautiful, and one day its golden reign will commence.

This beautiful optimism was what we inherited when Valdes perished.

12.

Finally, a few biographical details about Arthur Valdes. He was born on March 2, 1886 in Tartu Province, attended the Hugo Treffner private grammar school, graduated from the Davis & Harrison Technical College in London, then went into business. Shortly after the outbreak of war, he volunteered to join the British forces and was killed on the 20th of January of that year at the Battle of Ypres. I received the details of the last days of Valdes' life, as well as his papers, from the Estonian seaman Kusta Toomingas, who had joined him in battle.

1916

Cannibals

Three lakes glittered in a row like three oval mirrors. Their surfaces rose in tiers. The reverse image of the clouds rose like glassy steps as they rushed across the cold autumn sky.

On the banks of the topmost lake under tall trees, the red tiled roofs of the manor house rose. Its straight pillars peeped over the framework of the bushes, supporting the high attics with their long windows, upon their snow-white hands.

The lakes were bounded on two sides by russet and grey hills. Rising and falling cold springs were drawn and purled down from ridges that hid the horizon. Then they withdrew again and opened up into the blue distance of late autumn.

Along the shore of the lowest lake, the cannibals moved.

They had been marching for a long time through the autumn landscape. Their legs were tired from the hummocks, their eyes from the bare trees and the leaden grey clouds. But now and again, their minds flared up like juniper wood.

Whooping to one another, they rustled through the clumps of yellow flag. Cursing the cannibal's heavy labor, they stamped their way along the soggy bank. With a long knife they cut human flesh from the bushes and gnawed the bones of poor Christians, until their faces were yellow with alder juice, and they swore:

"There's so much blood! A hell of a lot of blood!"

Up in front was the redheaded son of the farmhand, Jürna. In his hand he carried the spiked club of a savage, the tops of his yellow calfskin boots were rolled down like a funnel, revealing a glittering knife.

He swore, spat and whistled in turn, pressing his muddy hands to his mouth. He rolled his eyes and, on hearing a sound in the reeds, his ears pricked up like a horse's.

Behind him peeped the son of the blacksmith, Jaan, a small boy with fair hair. His grey eyes sometimes stared as if in a dream, blood covered his pale face—then he would hear Jürna mysteriously hissing, and come to.

Behind both of them came the carpenter's daughter, Miili, who had a button head, slit eyes and a yellow skirt. She cried out shrilly from fear and laughter in turn, leading her little brother Jass by the hand.

Jass had a round belly, a thin neck and big eyes. He stumbled over the stalks of plants, and seemed unable to hold himself upright. All he could do was cry.

Last of all, the dachshund Sami trudged along, waddling from one leg to the other with effort, knees splayed, claws bunched. He was a brownish yellow all over, as if wearing an autumn coat, along its belly were two rows of nipples.

Cannibals made their way through the irises up to the bridgehead, where they went down through a hatch.

Here it was dark, you could smell the damp, the planked walls were covered with moss, but half the floor was dry.

How far away everything seemed!

A thin stream, through which a yellow glow could be seen, trickled above their heads, but at the other end of the bridge the pale yonder of the sky opened up, dissected by a number of bare branches.

Jaan stopped in the middle of the bridgehead and listened to the purling of the water. He thought he had heard a voice crying from the far end of the bridge, one he had heard many times before, and ran towards it, slipping as he did so.

Yellow bubbles whirled on the black surface of the water, dead matted grass covered the bank. A limitless hayfield stretched beyond, with the forks of streams curling round the tree trunks. By hopping from stone to stone, the cannibals reached the island, where tall alders grew. The grass rotted between the lush blackcurrant bushes. Large water rats hopped around among the brown leaves.

The bare branches of the trees stretched forth like a crisscross of arms. Cool patches of sky shone through the grey fingers of the forest. The watercourses carried fallen leaves like tiny black boats.

Then the cannibals crossed the barren marshland, moving in the direction of the beach. The ground swayed beneath them, they shrieked in fear, Jass was crying, Sami waddled into the bog pools before they managed to reach the beach.

Suddenly, a juniper heath rose out of the bog. The children ran from one juniper to the next, the dog barked at the rocks—and suddenly they were on an open hillside.

Right in the middle of a knoll, like a scalp, stood two midsummer night bonfire pillars, turned to charcoal. The grass was blackened by ashes and cinders, as if scarred. Melted glass glittered in the ashes like the eyes of the earth.

How wide the view was from here: on one side, the distant azure of the forest; on the other, the red roofs of the manor through the trees, below the leaden grey surface of the lake.

Ahead of the children several hillocks rose, reaching out like waves toward the horizon. On a hillside on the other side of the valley stood the old lime kiln, its high tiled roof supported by low walls, like a pyramid.

The late autumn sky with its ashen clouds stretched above this grey landscape. The clouds came in clumps from the southwest, rushing across the windless sky. Their silhouettes melted like smoke in the cool haze of the evening.

Jaan lay down in the grass and put his hands behind his head. A cloud crossed above him, throwing a pale shadow onto his face. The wind puffed through the bonfire posts—again this sounded as if his sister were calling from afar.

"No one has seen Juuli," he said grimly, closing his eyes. "She's been gone for three days, and no one knows where she is."

"I do," said Jürna hitting a nail with his club. "She's been locked up in the distiller's room."

"What would she be doing there?" said Jaan, raising his head.

"Don't ask me!" replied Jürna, hitting his finger at that moment. "I've seen them myself, sitting on a malt crate," he continued, putting his fingers to his lips. "I'd wandered into the steam room and I saw them sitting on the crate dangling their legs and laughing."

"But nobody's seen her for three days now," said Jaan again, sadly. "They've looked for her everywhere, but she's nowhere to be found."

"Your father went and looked at the distillery," said Jürna, drawing traces in blood along the shaft of his boot. "But he didn't find her. I heard him ask the distiller. 'Where's my daughter?' was what he said. 'Am I your daughter's keeper?' was what he replied. 'What have you done with her?' shouted the old man. But the distiller released some steam which filled the room, and jumped out of the window."

Jaan lay there in silence. Oh, how sad, how sad was his mood!

He had never seen his sister the way he did now, lying there. He could see her eyes in the air, her hair and skirt fluttering in the very slight breeze. The air around him was full of his sister.

He could see her, arranging her hair every morning in the tiny mirror in the back room of the blacksmith's house, how she would walk through the house and how the boys would be hammering the glowing iron so hard that a sea of sparks flew around her legs. Then she would seize her skirt with both hands and run shrieking outside. The assistants would merely laugh into their grimy beards.

She entered the carpenter's house, where the men were planing shavings of the best wood imaginable for her alone. Her apron filled with wood shavings that smelt of resin, she would run home across the main road, the carpenters shouting wisecracks after her.

Then she would knead the dough in an earthenware bowl, blow on the fire so that her face grew flushed, bake cakes and sprinkle sugar icing over them. Jaan would read a book by the window, with one eye on the flames, one ear on the sizzle of the fat on the iron.

When evening fell, Juuli would tie a headscarf over her hair and disappear, while the old blacksmith grumbled and cursed her. Down in the distillery, the steam would be let out of the boiler, rising in a cloud over the building, and from the cloud the sound of music could be heard.

One summer's night, the nightingale sang on the manor grounds and the scent of roses wafted over the wall. On waking, Jaan watched in the moonlight as Juuli silently freed herself of her clothes, sat for a long time on the edge of the bed, and listened to the nightingale.

It was thus that Jaan still saw her sitting, her hair spread out in the silver flush of the moon, her lips opened towards the scent of roses, the nightingales singing unceasingly.

But what had happened to her in reality? Why did everyone grow so agitated when people spoke of her?

Her father spent the whole of Sunday looking for her with his assistants around the manor and in the woods. At night they dragged the lake with a net by the light of lanterns and, in the morning, quizzed the fairgoers on the road. But no one knew anything.

As in a dream Jaan had an inkling of some secret everyone understood. He again saw his father's angry face and could hear how the women put their heads together in the manor yard and whispered. Through the clouds of distillery steam her effervescent life floated like a mirage.

Oh, how sad, as sad could be, was his mood!

Meanwhile Jürna had patched up his bloody hand and started all over again. The blood clotted in the wound, but he squeezed it out and drew horrible pictures on the tops of his boots.

"That's how the Indians do it," he said. "One day I'll open my veins and paint myself red all over with blood. Then they'll bury me as an Indian."

As no one answered, he continued:

"When the Indians have no salt, they open a vein in their arm and drink the salty blood. They can live for weeks on end in the forest on their own blood."

But now his wound had finally dried up and not a drop more oozed from it. He looked at the masterpiece on his boot and said:

"When the Indians are on the move, they carry blood bags on their backs. At the campfire they pour the blood from a skull into a cup and sip it. Then they pull their cloaks of red feather over their shoulders and begin to snore."

Jaan raised his head in Jürna's direction and Miili looked at him with fear, her mouth open.

"But at midnight an Indian in a black cloak on a white horse arrives at the edge of the woods, puts his fingers to his lips and whistles—like this!"

All at once, Jürna put his fingers to his lips and whistled with a noise so penetrating that their hair stood on end.

The cannibals jumped up and looked around them in trepidation. Meanwhile, evening had fallen. Ashen clouds flew across the grey landscape, piling up as they did so. They rushed like sinister beasts, rapidly changing shape. Now they were horses with flying manes, riders with flying cloaks, flags fluttered—a cold wind gusted through the clouds.

The junipers stood black on the slope of the hill, the manor house was far off on the horizon, the hillocks receded in waves, the limekiln crouched in the middle.

The faces of the children grew pale—it was all so horrible.

Suddenly Jürna pointed towards the limekiln and yelled throatily: "There! There!" Then he put his thumbs into his mouth, whistled loudly, and began to run along the hillside in front of the others.

They dodged about through the junipers, the water purled under their feet, then the bushes ended and the ploughed fields began.

They crawled along the hillside through the stalks on all fours, as if through the spines of a hedgehog, with Jürna in front, a knife between his teeth, Sami bringing up the rear, curved like a maggot and staying close to the ground.

Now and again, Jürna would lie dog-like and let out a hissing sound to warn the others, then he would rise on all fours and carry on crawling. All the while he cursed silently to himself, spittle dripping past the knife and his bloody boots scraping through the stalks.

Now the limekiln towered black several dozen meters away. The ground was white with lime, the bushes pushed up through burst sacks of fiber. A broken wheelbarrow lay turned over, its legs in the air; fragments of mashing tuns writhed upwards like snakes.

Jürna whistled again and motioned with his bloody hands, the knife still between his teeth. They split up into two groups: Jürna went alone, the others entered the other end of the building.

It was a square construction, the walls hardly rising above the ground. On all fours sides loomed the abrupt and equal triangles of the roof.

His back curved, a knife in his hand and his eyes wide with fright, Jürna rounded the corner. Then he stopped in amazement: thieves had stripped the entire side that could not be seen from the manor house of its roofing tiles. The naked rafters resembled the ribs of an animal.

The cannibals cautiously approached the wall and looked inside. The kiln looked like a pitch-black ravine. The wind barely stirred the laths.

Then something so ghostly began to take shape before their eyes that they did not at first perceive what it was. A black curtain in front of them began to move in the breeze, miraculous and quietly. A moment later, a human face, eyes wide open, stared at them at the level of their own heads.

They started, but before any one of them had understood, the face disappeared as silently as it had come.

They retreated in horror, not grasping what they had seen, eyes peering into the darkness.

Now they did see as, from that same black curtain, a large and serious human face, surrounded by flowing hair, came into view.

Someone had hanged themselves, the body now stirred in the wind!

The knife fell from Jürna's hand, he seized his bloody boot tops so that it would be easier to run, and staggered towards the manor, howling. Only for a few moments could his stooped figure still be seen and the scraping of his boots against the stubble be heard.

Jaan and Miili tried to follow him, but their legs were shaking so violently that they became rooted to the spot. Suddenly they realized that night had fallen. The ground was covered with an impenetrable darkness, nothing could be seen of the manor. Fear so intense they thought they would be choked by it arose within them.

Then Jaan managed to regain enough strength to whisper in a hoarse voice: "That was Juuli."

Miili replied, barely audibly: "Yes."

They turned back, their legs still shaking, and returned to the kiln. Now it seemed so ghastly to them, that they stayed a few paces away. But their eyes could clearly see Juuli's flowing hair and face shining in the darkness.

"Shout something to her," whispered Miili, "maybe she's still alive."

But Jaan's mouth could hardly utter a croak, not even a whisper. He summoned all his strength, but the words would not come. He swayed on his feet and took hold of Miili's shoulders with both hands in order not to fall over. There they stood, the three of them, before the corpse, the girl between the two little boys.

"Juuli?" said Jaan, finally finding his voice. "Juuli?"

On hearing his own voice, his courage returned. He stepped up to the wall, his eyes bulging, then pressed his face against the laths, his gaze boring into the darkness.

The dead girl's face was raised slightly over one shoulder, a coal-black strand of hair hanging limply down. She moved continuously, so that now her face, then her neck faced the onlooker.

"Juuli, can you hear me, Juuli?" cried Jaan. He spoke a couple of phrases more, even though he himself realized it was futile. Then he turned to Miili, who was standing behind him: "She's dead." For some strange reason, no tears came, and instead he said: "I'll take her down."

"No, no!" groaned Miili. "Don't touch her, don't touch her! I'm so scared!"

But Jaan had already approached the wall and was attempting to remove the roofing laths. He had suddenly grown strangely calm and determined. In the darkness he seemed so big and strong.

He found a narrow space between the laths and wriggled his way inside. But he now realized that the dead girl was not hanging from the laths or rafters, but from a beam that ran along the entire space under the roof. He fumbled in her direction, but the dead girl was out of reach.

Then he dragged himself onto the beam and sat astride it, beginning to move forwards. He soon found the noose, but the knot was tight and he couldn't undo it.

He sat there for a moment in the darkness, feeling fear again, and saw what looked like a shower of sparks flying before his eyes. He turned his head and looked over his shoulder. It was already so dark outside he could hardly make out the roofing laths and Miili's face dark between them.

"Give me Jürna's knife," he cried to Miili and began to edge his way backwards, pulling the rope along the beam with him. But the dangling of the dead body and the touch of the hair made him feel sick.

Finally he reached the laths and stretched out his hand, but couldn't reach the knife. Then he climbed down from the beam and took a few steps towards the inner edge of the kiln, his arm stretched out all the while.

All of a sudden Miili saw the arm disappear in the darkness. Then she heard a cry, and all she heard after that was the soft thud of a body bouncing from stone to stone.

Jaan lay motionless for a moment or two, dizzied by the pain of the fall. He sat up and groped around him. He was sitting on a flattened pile of lime, from which some stalks were growing. He stood up and extended his arms. All around him the walls were slippery as glass.

Then he heard Miili's and Jass' cries and looked upwards.

High above him, the darkening sky could be seen through the laths and above him hung the black lump of his sister's corpse. Then he suddenly felt the rush of manly courage he had felt when trying to untie the knot above.

"Don't cry up there!" he yelled. "I'm quite alright."

Then he saw Miili's head between the laths and heard her asking something up there in a frightened voice.

Jaan began to feel his way around the bottom of the pit. It was round and full of stones and piles of lime. The walls were slippery as ice in places from the caked lime; here and there they contained holes or were lumpy.

Then Jaan tried to climb upwards, but fell on his back onto a pile of lime. He made several attempts, but failed each time.

Then he remembered that there may have been a door on the side of the kiln that opened onto the valley side. He felt around for quite some time and finally found it. But it was blocked by stones, lime and earth and he realized a few moments later that he would not be able to open it with his bare hands.

"I'm not going to get out of here," he said to himself, sitting wearily on the floor.

"My God, what are we going to do now!" he heard Miili saying with a sob, along with Jass' sniffing.

But their crying emboldened him.

"Don't cry," he said again. "Run home and tell them that Juuli and I are here."

"I'm not going anywhere!" moaned Miili. "I daren't leave. And how could you stay here alone?"

"But I just can't get out," replied the boy from the pit.

"Then I'm going to stay here the whole night long," gulped Miili. "If you're staying, I'm staying," she repeated choking. "And maybe Jürna will tell them at home, and they'll all come here during the night anyway."

Talking like this, they again became fully aware of what had happened. They turned their gaze silently toward Juuli's dead body, but no longer saw anything through their tears.

They sank to the ground and gave themselves over to their flowing tears. Their hearts were bursting with boundless pain and their thin bodies were shaken by groans.

It was not the horrible night around them, the dreadful place, or the bleak corpse. What affected them was the fact that their mutual friend, older playmate and sister was dead.

The terrible way she died meant nothing to them. All they thought of were the sufferings of the dead girl, and her eternal loss. No power on Earth could undo what had been done. A black shroud of death had been cast over all chances.

"Never again!" wept Jaan. "Never again!"

At length his tears dried and he sat up shaking. His head was ringing and his eyes could no longer make out even the grimness of the dark. He could hear Miili sobbing as if through a thick cloud.

He looked around him, but the velvety darkness hid everything. Then he began to detect the odor of wet lime and of some plant or other he hadn't noticed before.

He looked up: the sky had grown lighter, stars were shimmering through the laths, and he felt the chill.

"Miili," he cried. "Miili."

A faint sob was the only answer.

"Is Jass with you?" asked the boy. "And Sami?"

"Yes," replied the girl, barely audibly.

"That's good," said the boy and fell silent.

He sat there thinking and looking upwards. How time dragged on! What time could it be? The stars became clearer. And the boy began to shiver with cold.

"I'm cold," he said and his teeth began to chatter.

"Cold?" asked Miili groping around her. "Hang on." She undid the bands of her skirt and pushed the garment through the laths. "Take hold of this!" she cried. "Cover your legs with it."

The skirt fell onto the boy's head like a bag.

Miili sat there in her thin petticoat. Jass sniffed and was dozing off. Miili took him onto her lap and began to sing a lullaby. He was soon asleep, still hiccupping now and again in his sleep. Sami rolled up into a ball at the girls' feet and also fell asleep. Miili swayed backwards and forwards to ward off the cold and felt how both the baby and the dog warmed her. She was no longer crying.

Then from the depths she heard the voice of the little boy:

"I've been thinking: Why did Juuli kill herself, what made her do it?"

"You don't know?" replied the girl, rocking the child. "She didn't want to live," she said. "The man at the distillery had dumped her."

"Yes," replied the boy thoughtfully. "But she didn't have to die because of that?"

"My mother said that she was expecting a baby," said the girl.

"A baby?" said the little boy, surprised. This came so unexpectedly that he remained silent. "What d'you mean a baby?" he asked.

"I mean she'd been making love to the distillery man," replied the girl.

Making love—Jaan had heard the expression often enough, just like he had heard about having babies. But did babies come from love and were children born after death?

"Why did she love, when it all ended so badly?" he asked.

"You can't do anything against love," replied the girl. "When it comes, no one can resist it." She rocked the child back and forth. "It's like a dream, like sleeping on a feather pillow and seeing endless numbers of sweets in your dreams." She sighed. "And after that the children get born."

Both of them had heard this before and taken note of what they had heard. Even having children was not entirely a closed book to them. And yet how strange everything was! How full of mystery even the tiniest thing was! It was as if they saw this for the first time that evening.

They both sat there, their faces pale and pain filling their breast, as if the sorrow of the world had put its cold hand between their hearts. The night constantly gusted strange thoughts and feelings, threatening to bury the children in them—the starry, cool night.

Jaan looked up: more and more stars were lighting up the sky. Out of the depths of darkness they looked large and fiery. The earth down there was cold and clear, but the heavens seemed filled with the fire of exuberant stars.

And now, in the starlight, the walls of the kiln could be made out. Their glassy edges glittered in the green and blue light, like ice flowers bursting into flower above his head, rays refracted by the colored stones—Jaan was sitting there as if looking for a signet stone in the well.

Love—? he thought, surveying the corpse of his sister. Is this love? And he remembered everything he had ever heard and read on the subject. He knew it to be a sweet pain, something to be desired, a happy madness that forced you to do what you did not want to, and leave undone that which you wished to do. And in the end, the fiery flames of love reached right up to the edge of death!

Jaan got up and examined his aching limbs. How his arms and legs and his heart were throbbing! He wanted to start crying again because of the pain, cry for a long time and in a manly way. But then he felt the skirt wrapped around his legs.

"Miili!" he shouted. "Miili!"

"Shut up," she replied softly. "The baby's asleep."

And again she rocked the baby on her knee. She was like a young mother there in the dead of night, among the deserted hillocks. For miles around, near and far, there was no one except the three of them, forgotten in the limekiln. Only darkness amidst the emptiness of the fallow fields!

Suddenly she saw a swaying light on the horizon, then a second and a third. She jumped up and a moment later shouted with joy:

"They're coming, they're coming!"

"Who's coming?" asked the boy from the pit.

"They're coming to take us home!"

She could no longer sit still or stay where she was, but hopped from one foot to the other, holding the heavy child in her arms.

And the lights got nearer and larger all the time. They rose onto a hill and descended into a valley, without showing any sign of those carrying them. It was like a procession of yellow balls of fire across the night fields.

"They're going down into the valley," cried Miili every time. "Now you can't see them any more," she informed him. "Now they're climbing up the hill again," she shrieked.

But at length human shapes could be made out in the darkness. Jürna was running ahead, his hair blood red in the light of the lanterns. After him rushed the blacksmiths, stumbling along in their large leather aprons, their clogs clacking on the stones, their sooty faces black as coal in the light of the huge lanterns.

"Where are they now?" asked thc little boy hopping from foot to foot.

"They've just reached the ridge," then said suddenly "Don't show them where we are, don't let them see my skirt!"

Her voice was gentle as the virginal blush of dawn on the coy horizon.

1916

Echo of the Epoch

Notes from the period of the Great War, 1914–1918

1.

Once again the spirit of the times has surprised me... I was sitting in the dark, weary after a long journey, in a cold railway carriage. The train stopped at a station whose windows had been smashed. In the waiting room weary soldiers dozed, sitting around a smoking carbide lamp. Another train came in the opposite direction. In the darkness, the wounded were carried across the rails. Someone ran onto the platform in front of the station with a red lamp. Then everything fell silent again.

Only one traveler had entered our carriage at that station. His spurs rattled, he poked me in the side in the dark with his scabbard, threw his rifle up onto the baggage rack, and went and sat down opposite me, saying nothing.

I felt a certain unease, as if someone were staring at me. In the darkness all I could hear was the deep breathing and snoring of those sitting on the benches as they slept. I turned restlessly from side to side, as if seeking relief from some impending disaster.

Then I suddenly heard the sinister voice of the man opposite:

"It's all pretty horrible, isn't it? Everything you see, hear and feel—? Both what you see at night in your dreams and the visions of the day—?"

The stranger stopped, but before I had a chance to recover enough to reply, he continued in a hoarse whisper:

"It's like that, isn't it: you can complain about your small troubles. But isn't the pain of the world so immeasurably greater? Doesn't it wash over your head like the waves of the ocean, drowning you and all your petty sufferings?"

Who was this ghastly stranger? What did he want of me?

Again, before I had the opportunity to open my mouth to reply, the stranger put his hand, heavy as iron, on my knee, placed his mouth near my ear and said in a voice, husky and sepulchral:

"You have had two great passions in life: art and women. But you have gotten over these passions. Time has destroyed the most important part of you. All that remains is the animal instinct for survival.

You have been living weeks and months like a savage, without seeing one single book, without writing a single line—and yet you are not dead!

You once imagined yourself as Don Juan, blazing like a torch—but are you not now writing up all your memories like that cynic Swift: *Only a woman's hair?*

Maybe you have only managed to cling to one dream; instead of your *Ars amandi* all you have retained to keep you awake at night in the depths of your soul is—*Ars moriendi.*

But you will not speak of it, will you? You don't even say much any more, do you?"

At that moment I ceased to be tongue-tied and shouted, jumping up from my seat:

"Who are you, satanic stranger, that you can read all my most secret, most painful thoughts like a book?!"

But he did not answer. I could only pick up his chortle.

He took his spur off of his right foot with a jingle, pulled a pipe out of his pocket, and stopped it with tobacco. Then he took off his left spur with a similar jangle, pulled a cigarette lighter from his pocket, struck it, and raised it to his face.

Then I saw: it was the skeleton of a dead man, wearing a helmet from the trenches and a soldier's uniform!

2.

The world was ripe for such a terrible catastrophe. It had neither the material, nor the spiritual strength to live on. Its dreams were sentimental and delicate, its reality rough and ruthless. Every kind of equilibrium of spiritual and material values had fallen away long ago.

We had accepted too much of the oppressive heritage of the previous century.

The atmosphere of *fin de siècle* continued. Those whose souls were of brittle material, could not stand reality. They writhed in a fever of Weltschmerz, in what Sigbjørn Obstfelder termed *angst for livet og angst for døden*, fear of life and fear of death. Nietzsche was also doubting by this time that he was alive, that he had not been turned into sheer prejudice.

Greater spirits had also been poisoned by this plague. Even though they were preaching an affirmation of life and the joys of existence, behind their words a *horror vacui*—the fear of emptiness that had already appalled those weary in the Ancient World—could be sensed.

Mankind was sick. Everything we loved had been poisoned. Even the medicines with which people hoped to cure the world were poisonous. They would go to people's heads like intoxicants, filling their hearts and minds with sweet pain. That poison was Flaubert, Beardsley, Debussy. The great poisoned chalice was Nietzsche.

The tragedy of the situation lay in the fact that the mental illness of mankind was also represented by the highest level of human culture. Recovery from this sickness in these circumstances meant actually descending from this level. One would have to have desisted from everything that had been conquered by way of desperate exertions, it would have meant fleeing downwards from the heights of philosophy and aesthctics—downwards—towards the level of the masses.

And what awaited one there?

A dull *haute* and *petite bourgeoisie* with all its privileges: capitalism, militarism and clericalism. And the proletariat, which had exerted itself unceasingly for decades, without managing to break out of its steel cage, since the large majority could neither be educated nor organized.

Roman Rolland says in the introduction to his "Beethoven" in the year 1903:

"The air is heavy around us. Old Europe grows weary in its fusty and putrid climate. A mundane and stifling materialism burdens thought and fetters the powers of action of both governments and individuals. The world is suffocated by caution and petty egotism. Human kind is growing weak."

Ten years later, there occurred an attempt to escape from this airlessness. We have seen the fruitless fissuring of great, unforeseen egotism that has torn history to shreds with the blood of history, and with tears.

3.

Not only ourselves, but several generations to come, will bear the stamp of the events of the present. We are from the old school, were born, grew up, received our education and opinions during the *ancien régime.* This storm hit us as adults, it has shaken us, but on account of our age, it has not shaken us to the roots. But what is the state of the lives of Europeans who are still in the cradle? What kind of memories will remain in the minds of a ten-year-old Belgian, Pole or Serb? Will there not arise a generation similar to those whose fathers once fell at the barricades in Paris, or died during the hopeless struggle in the catacombs of the Communards, a generation whose first experience of life is that it is illiterate?

But maybe such a generation, brought up in improved circumstances, does not even notice the feeling of change that will for ever overshadow our consciousness.

4.

During the first months of the European war, the time of the massive battles of the Marne, the following comparison could be found in the newspapers: the French soldiers were reading Henri Bergson during their free moments in the trenches, while the Germans would carry books by Nietzsche in their knapsacks during attacks. During the first stage of the war, while national passions were aflame, Nietzsche's name was mentioned as an apostle of war, someone to fan the flames of the German conquest of the world. As they had not forgotten during the 45 years previous, Nietzsche had himself stood at the walls of Metz, a Prussian officer's helmet on his head.

Poor old Nietzsche! The "last apolitical German" as he called himself! He who hated the Prussian spirit and belief, its militarism and its society, above all! He who never ceased saying that his forefathers were in fact Poles and that their surname had been Nicki (a supposition lacking any foundation)! I remember seeing a picture of him as a soldier in the Franco-Prussian War: how helpless and ridiculous he looked with his sword and helmet, as if a muzzle had been put on a lion pup. Now he has to carry the standard of his chauvinism, on which is written: *Deutschland über alles!*

Many paths have been trodden, it is as if the tanks of war have trundled over the past. Museums have been burned down, libraries thrown to the flames, nor has the mental life of mankind fared any better. When we awaken from this madness in a year's, two years' or ten years' time, we will at least be different from what we are now. The epoch following the bloody days of Napoleon has already been historically termed "the newest times." What will be the name of the era following the European war? At present, all we can unfortunately call it is: the future.

And that future, with its barely discernable content, we will leave to those who, in their blindness, are incapable of understanding national passions. We know that this future will never live up to our dreams, but hopefully its shortcomings will be closer to the truth than those of our time.

Until that time, let us judge the German Kaiser, Wilhelm II, as being *Übermensch* Number One. Until that time, may the distant relation of Friedrich Nietzsche, the shoemaker Nietzsche (his shop sign can actually be viewed in Berlin Steglitz!), know that his "eminent learning" has been implemented by means of the Romanian bayonet, the dum-dum bullet and poison gas. And every pilot who steers his zeppelin in the direction of Albion feels the same surge of ethics as did Zarathustra in the greatest moment of his life.

But for all that, this fiery abstainer from human passions and pride in the future has not yet been discredited.

5.

Rousseau is wrong when he claims that all the ills experienced by mankind of late are to be attributed to cultural development. Whatever the culture, it at least tames people, teaching them to at least feel ashamed of their brutality.

There are epochs, however, when, by general consent, the masks are down and people say: "Let us be open about our lack of shame! Let us kill, rob, do violence. We have revalued our evil and found it to be good!"

Then mankind is again thrown back decades, downwards into the depths, into the darkness.

It is therefore inappropriate to talk of the economics of history. History tells of mad squandering. How much must be paid for the evils of mankind: wars, religious strife, alcohol. How much spiritual and physical energy is lost by way of them!

But it would seem that the larger the economy, the worse the budget. And the bookkeeper, who is assumed to be above and beyond the clouds, has already discredited himself.

6.

We have no overview of history. We remain surprised that, in the days of Louis XVI, when the people were attacking the Bastille, he noted in his diary: "Nothing at all!" (He had not shot one hare that day, and what he wanted to say was: everything else left him cold!) Do we not ourselves write a hare-hunting diary, leaving out events whose consequences are inestimably greater so that they go unnoticed?

7.

I saw Nicholas II only once. When the huge empire was beginning to unravel at the seams, he felt the necessity to enhance his authority as ruler by appearing in person. He undertook a round trip to the peripheral parts of the Empire. He was a pathetic little man with eternal fear and caution written all over his face, surrounded by uniformed and plain-clothed bodyguards, in whom could he inspire an understanding of his power and authority?!

I also saw Kerensky on the street in Helsinki. He was at the height of his power, but his face was chalk-white on account of the strain, and he had sprained his wrist by shaking so many hands, his ears were deaf from the ovations. What was this man thinking? Had he any inkling of his humiliating fall from power?

There is something dangerous in power. Neither physical strength nor mental attachment can guarantee it forever. Power can be turned against its embodiment overnight, turning it into the most wretched plaything. It only takes one step to move from the throne to the guillotine, as was said long ago.

But those thirsting for power have not yet grasped this truth, judging by the human psyche. History always manages to find willing victims. It finds a surfeit of them—and their mutual struggles give rise to the most grievous tragedies.

8.

Lermontov says somewhere: "Passions are nothing more than ideals in the bud." Passions have indeed been turned into ideals in our times, but some of them have been translated back into passions. Herein lies the tragedy of the present age.

Beethoven says in a letter: "Power is the morality of those who are different from the masses." But power is interpreted as morality all the more when it is a matter of unlike individuals.

Brandes says that Balzac was not so much a historian of human society as a naturalist. To describe present-day society you would, above all, need to be a zoologist.

Caligula loved his horse so much that he intended to build a house for it and appoint it consul of Rome. How many "consuls" nowadays should not be reduced to the level of a horse instead and put in a stable!

Has Prometheus not been seen girding his loins and asking for a light for his pipe? That is how Prometheus' fire mission can be understood. That is how the greatest ideals can be understood, with which people were supposed to light up the world like a sun!

The world is an island now, where Caliban holds sway. Is Ariel still alive? Has he not died of despair and been buried in the desolation of the desert?

9.

I have recently been busy reading the history of the French Revolution. In order to obtain an objective understanding of the passions of the present, I submerged myself in the details of past passions. History increases one's feeling of relativity only as little as it is an amusing pastime.

I have again read the history of the Terror. How many crazy passions, misunderstood ideas, and dreams of a better world there were that then turned into acts of criminality! And alongside all these, the anguish of death, despair, curses... It is like opening up the mass grave of history.

One of the apostles of terror, Saint-Just, proclaimed as the ultimate truth: "those who show mercy to prisoners deserve punishment; those who do not wish for bliss deserve punishment; those who do not want the reign of terror deserve punishment!" And Robespierre explained that the revolutionary government signified the despotism of liberty against tyranny.

And so the "despotism of liberty" then exerted itself. But that despotism was blind, as despotism always is. All logic was lost, the Terror swallowed up both enemies and friends, rich and poor, republicans and royalists, in the end it swallowed itself.

The Terror of the age of Robespierre is an interesting episode in history, in that there appears to be no social class logic among the reasons for killing people. From a general to a doorman, a banker to a washerwoman, from a renowned scientist to an idiot—all of these had to place their necks under the guillotine. Marshal Nicolas Luckner died alongside a soap-boiler; Father Eulogius Schneider died alongside a haberdasher. But in general, the victims stemmed from precisely those circles that could be termed educated, and for whom the Revolution was supposed to have been staged, i.e. petit bourgeois elements, craftsmen and farmers. History tells us: of the 2,750 victims of the Parisian death machine, 650 were wealthy and important, the other 2,100, poor people.

The Procrustean bed of the Terror united all classes. And the leaders of the Terror imagined that with the falling of heads the last vestiges of difference would disappear. When the famous chemist Lavoisier asked for a stay of execution of four weeks on account of an important discovery he was about to make, the President of the Tribunal answered him by saying, in the sincere belief that he was uttering the greatest truth of the Revolution, "The Revolution is in no need of scientists!" So the scientist in question, like the others, was subjected to what was termed "the people's razor," as the guillotine was popularly dubbed as a joke.

It is not our task here to pass judgment on the past. Even less does it arouse passions within us. Only one feeling arises within us, and that is a feeling of amazed sympathy.

It is like the powerful *bas relief* of Danton going to his doom as he gives his name, age and place of residence before the Tribunal:

"I am Danton, an adequately well-known revolutionary, 35 years of age; soon, I will no longer be residing anywhere and my name will live on in the Pantheon of history."

When, during the epoch of bourgeois reaction, six Jacobin commissars were sentenced to death, they managed to die like the heroes of a folk tale. As soon as the death sentence was read out, one of the six pulled out a knife and stabbed himself in the heart. Dying, he handed the knife on to the next man, who immediately plunged it into his breast and handed it on again. So within a brief space of time the knife had passed from hand to hand, until all six condemned men lay in a pool of blood.

10.

The last time I traveled abroad in the late spring of the year war broke out, I traveled via Wierzbowa. There I was stopped by a colonel of the gendarmes, one Myasoyedov. I myself was a fake, but my papers were in order. Only one small mistake had been made when the document was stamped. I explained to Myasoyedov that the pass was valid, and the pointless nature of the fact he had kept me half under arrest for the whole of twenty-four hours. But the gentleman replied cynically: "You might be in the right, but what do I care about rights?" And he pointed to a couple of old German ladies who had missed some train or other: "Do you imagine that they're anarchists? Of course not. But do you think I'm going to let them through? Don't let the idea even enter your head!"

I read recently in the newspaper that Myasoyedov had been hanged as a traitor to his nation. Something frightening and terrible.

I can still see his face now, full of pride and cynicism. But I cannot imagine him during his last moments. Would he still have that cynical smile on his face when the hideousness of the epoch dragged him by the neck into the realm of death, would he still be saying: what do I care about rights?

11.

Jonathan Swift tells in "A Voyage to Laputa..." about the island of Laputa, how civilization has reached its apogee, and, in "A Voyage to the Country of the Houyhnhnms," how mankind has degenerated to such an extent that cultured horses use men as draught animals.

It would seem that the author wanted to allegorize the future of mankind by way of such grotesque caricatures.

Civilization grows ever more powerful in its triumphal march along the path of development. This must result in mankind descending to the level of the two-footed Yahoos. With what should the growing gap between culture and civilization be filled? How can mankind be saved from becoming more and more brutalized? At any rate, a satisfactory answer cannot be found in the cynicism of the likes of Swift.

Nor does the following passage from the diaries of the Goncourt brothers foster optimism:

"Sometimes, it strikes me that the day will come when our contemporary peoples will create for themselves an American-style God—a God whose existence will be confirmed by the newspapers; such a God will be present in the churches, his image will not spread the light very far, nor will it be the fruit of an artistic imagination... but proof of his existence will be captured on film… Yes, I can imagine a God who has been photographed and wears glasses. In those days civilization will have reached its apogee and steam gondolas will sail through Venice."

If such is the "apogee of civilization," I hope that we may not live to see it!

12.

A foggy, cold and moonlit night in February. The Moon is shining through the clouds, now brightly, now dully. The shadows of houses fall black across the snow; the streets glitter as if covered with ground glass.

I have to walk across town. But this route is more dangerous than if I had to cross a desert.

It is strange that such horror can arise on brightly lit streets. It is strange that no one is about, and all the windows are unlit. So strange, that you could imagine that only dead people live in this town…

But the town is not dead after all. The icy air is filled with the endless sound of rifle fire. To the right and to the left, from south and north, there are volleys of shots, in bursts still more volleys, but no one firing a rifle is to be seen. All you hear is the whine of bullets above your head.

This town is being fought over by three armies: one wants to leave, the other to stay, and a third is advancing. And the martial laws of all three are valid in their own way.

A senseless fear has gripped the town. Everything is heedless and senseless, such as the hail of bullets in the night sky. No one any longer knows anything. But the rifles continue to fire, as if of their own accord.

I stay in the lee of the houses, I run from doorway to doorway and from one street corner to the next. I carry no weapon, nor should anyone be my enemy. But death lies in wait for me as for any other mortal.

Then three or four cars drive out of a side street and rush ahead at a crazy speed. At the same time, twenty to thirty men appear from another side street, running after the cars. In the moonlight an indescribable battle commences.

I have found myself between the warring factions, pressing my body into a depression in the wall. The bullets whine past. I am shaking from cold and fear.

Beyond the corner of the roof, I can see a piece of iron-grey sky. Across it a bunch of silver grey clouds are sailing. Ah, clouds, the Moon, the stars. I am looking at them as if up from the depths of a dungeon…

13.

Autumn is here again—cold and bleak. Like the blind King Lear with his hair blowing in the wind, a helpless tree stands out in the open. The clouds are many, watery grey, leaden grey, the grey of rotting wood. The rain lashes like a lazy whip through the dark air.

As a child, I would always hear the evil spirits howling outside in the autumn. They came from the fields of the manor, vanished behind the ancient threshing barn, would move in procession across the stubbled fields, moaning all the while. Then I would be afraid of the dead, of death and the realm of death.

Why, now that autumn has arrived, do I hear ever more evil spirits out abroad in the open spaces of my native land?…

14.

There is a grim rule: *quae medicamenta non sanant, ferrum sanat, quae ferrum non sanat, ignis sanat*—what medicine does not cure, iron will cure, what iron will not cure, fire will cure.

But in the end, habit cures all. Where fire and sword no longer hold sway, all that is left is weariness and oblivion.

If someone has a splinter under their fingernail, he will cry out, pull out the splinter and live on as before. If you chop off a finger, a hand, an arm, both legs, both arms—he will remain the same. He grows used to his misfortune—and he lives on. A legless man strokes a dog in the warm sunshine and is happy. Everything is a question of growing accustomed. But before this familiarity arrives, fire and sword must be employed, the cup of protest and subjugation must be drunk down to the last dregs.

The leaves have fallen from the weeping willows along the banks of the canals in Bruges this year and on the shores of Lac d'Amour the young grass has sprouted. Even now young girls have fallen in love and even now the young men of Rheims have kissed their loved ones in the shade of the trees in the dusk of the evening.

Life is not yet at an end—this wordless, unconscious, sweet life.

15.

Our lives are full of paradoxes and we are often in conflict with our own convictions. Nevertheless, despite everything, the pessimism of experience does not in the end poison everything. Our convictions always drive us on to a new struggle, where we seek the way out of the cul-de-sac of the present.

If we ask anything of fate, then above all we ask that it will preserve in us a sense of truth. That it will preserve our optimism for the future, despite moments of pessimism. That it will allow us to retain the steadfast conviction of the necessity of a social revolution, among all the moods of bankruptcy.

The world has to be created anew, after all! The old one has failed, is full of fissures, it does not chime, merely clangs like a cracked bell. Better metals, clearer fire, finer form!

1914–1919

The Wanderer

1.

Allan awoke in a broad soft bed, supported by four pillared feet. The sun was shining from the rue Monsieur le Prince and glittered in the mirror over the mantelpiece and the glass cupola of the Rococo clock that stood in front.

Allan stretched and yawned wearily. The Rococo clock had stopped, but, judging by the sun, he guessed it was around ten.

The sound of footsteps and carts could be heard from the street. From the direction of the Odéon, there was the noise of omnibuses and some other vague rumbling sound. Then Allan saw the marble plaque on the wall of the building opposite as he did every morning when he awoke; in that building the philosopher and sociologist Auguste Comte had lived.

Allan felt the warmth of the sun and the lightness of the air outside the window, but was surprised by how unaccountably depressed he felt. The previous day, he had spared himself, like Cervantes' famous protagonist of the story "Graduate of Glass," only viewing wallpaper patterns in Cluny and settling down at the small English café near the Luxembourg Gardens towards evening. And yet he had the feeling that he had experienced the most unimaginable events, whose ghosts were still there in his sleepy head.

He had seen wanderings and peregrinations in faraway lands back in time, in another world. But these events, in which only the shade of a dreamlike sylph enticed, had melted into a single mood of despondency and listlessness in his memory. He could not catch her outline, much less her face, but her eyes afforded a soothing tranquility. The being merged with airy veils that floated through space like soft clouds, then vanished.

Allan yawned again, rose and got dressed, feeling neuralgic pains throughout his body all the while. Then he read one of the newspapers from his native land, which the post had brought, then wrote a letter, trying by doing so to keep in touch with the outside world. On sealing the long aesthetically wrought envelope, he again sank into a dreamy mood. He put the letter aside and leaned back in his chair.

How quiet and peaceful it was in this flat! How numerous were the objects that awakened reverie or helped one forget the outside world!

On a low shelf stood a row of books, whose mere appearance quickened his heartbeat. He stretched out his hand, took his beloved "Temptations of Saint Anthony" by Flaubert, in the grandiose Alphonse Lamerre edition, and began leafing through it. One passage caught his attention, for the umpteenth time. He read it slowly a couple of times, in a quiet voice:

Je peux faire se mouvoir des serpents de bronze, rire des statues de marbre, parler des chiens. Je te montrerai une immense quantité d'or; j'établirai des rois; tu verras des peuples m'adorant! Je peux marcher sur les nuages et sur les flots, passer à travers les montagnes, apparaître en jeun homme, en veillard, en tigre et en fourmi, prendre ton visage, te donner le mien, conduire le foudre. L'entends-tu?

At that moment, a strip of paper fell out of the book onto the floor. Allan bent down, picked it up and read the following lines, written in his own handwriting, from a year or so ago:

But he who is born will surely die and the dead will be born again. For this reason do not mourn that which can never return.

All beings are invisible, unseen, in their pristine state, appearing during their intermediate state, o Bhârata! And in death they once again achieve invisibility. What is there to fear?

These were two sutras from the Bhagavad-Gita, which had captivated him once upon a time.

Allan suddenly felt a pain in the region of his temples. No, not that! He swiftly slid the slip back into the book and put it aside. Not that again! It was too powerful for him. It was poison, absinth, he feared it. He shut his eyes.

But all the world was full of it, in each book he read, in each work of art he looked at, he felt its presence. Yet it was the only thing in life that still interested him. He felt himself inclined towards it like an alcoholic, despite the futile resistance of reason. His whole life was immersed in it.

And since when? he asked himself. Could this be pinned down to any specific period? Had it not stolen up on him, quietly and imperceptibly, until ultimately, it had overcome him, just as Maupassant was overcome by his Horla? Where did real life end, and that for which even the term dream was too clear, too rational, begin?

And yet he felt completely normal. He perceived his surroundings quite objectively. Nothing had changed in his consciousness, except himself. And, up to now, no one had noticed!

Occasionally, he bumped into old friends. He met them at Bernheim's, at concerts or in the Luxembourg Gardens. He sometimes visited them at home. Then they would talk a lot, disputing matters of art, drinking wine, and no one would notice anything.

On coming home, his mood would be light, boundlessly light. He had again brushed against real life, his soul had pressed the joy of life and its healthy aspects against his cheek. He could still feel its sweet warmth. And he sank into a restful sleep on his broad bed.

Once asleep, he was carried by his dreams into weird worlds, where not even the planets of our solar system were visible; instead, spectral moons would shine into ghastly cellars... And there was so much of Gustave Moreau's grim beauty... Or where fragmentary landscapes arose, as in old masters, obelisk-shaped hills, with windmills on top and blue horizons beyond, but ah such strange, strange blue! Or he would see nothing that touched his mind, merely feel a musical mood, a melodious image from Florent Schmitt or Ducasse: a swamp with miniature palm trees, ibises in the dusk, and he himself alone, disembodied, a shade, almost a musical chord... He shuddered as he sat up in horror.

But this much he knew: dreams furnished no proof. Dreams were empty, shadows that did not suffer a breath of wind. He could summon them as much as he liked. He knew their logic and held sway over them, as did every imaginative sleeper. By dreaming he had, in his time, fooled around, revolted, tried a thousand different things. Like a drunkard he had been a wastrel, setting in motion the most terrible orgies of dreams. And now he had grown weary of them.

But there was something that was even weirder than dreams. They were visions, in the middle of the day, on a bright street, with your eyes open, right in front of you. He wished to blend them to his memory with dreams, or, even better, with things he had read. And he believed he had once read about a Hindu who, while walking along the street, tried to adjust his turban, but had only succeeded in removing his head instead. On another occasion, on emerging from a metro station at the Place de la Bastille, he had wandered through the ruins of a prehistoric city at whose one edge were carved Schliemann's day laborers, jackals at the other. He wandered far and wide through Paris until, with a half-eaten mandarin in his hand, he had found the Place de la Révolution. And one day he saw, in the Tuilerie Gardens, nothing but black people and heard a strange language...

But usually, the visions were only momentary: the unnatural movements of a passer-by, a sudden change of light, or simply a thought of his own that lacked a solid rational base, while the thought itself was entirely logical. And this mental mirage threw him instantly from one extreme of existence to the other, ever further away, severing every link with reality for minutes at a time.

But although he feared these visions, he was at the same time tempted to play with them. He would stop at the banks of the Seine, lean over the stone parapet, standing next to a dozen other people and looking down at the chocolate surface of the river. But presently the color of the object he was viewing would change: the river turned a leaden grey, then dark green, then rays emanated from it as from radium and he felt himself penetrated by them, not only he himself, but those standing around him! He could see through all of them! For a split second, an indescribable joy would seize him, that none of those around him had any inkling of this. The Seine rolled along in its yellow waves...

On other occasions, in between the legible text, strange passages would appear in long swathes, passages that were intoxicatingly beautiful. He could be reading the most banal newssheet for this pleasure to occur. Sometimes he would recognize the strange text, sometimes it would be surprisingly new. He once found a passage from "Tuti-Nameh" or from Sa'adi's "Orchard," or a piece in some contemporary novel or a travelogue. Then he would put aside the book and continue to follow what his reading had caused him to break off. Around him would be the buzz of the café, or shrill children would be playing diabolo and the sun shining.

In museums, he would indulge in orgies of the imagination. He feared them and yearned for them at the same time. One such self-indulgence he especially liked was the Trocadéro with its Negro art and sections displaying art from Mexico and Indochina. He mobilized the wooden and tin sculptures of the Negroes as if for large-scale military operations. Red plumes fluttered, tin shields rattled, and Allan saw mummies from the Yucatan moving all on their own, opening their mouths and rushing down the hillside, while metal rhinoceroses dozed by fountains or pools. Down in the basement his attention was especially drawn to a seven-headed and ten-tailed stone snake; he placed his hand on it and felt its coils rising and falling. It was so horrific and sweet he would have liked to tell someone about it.

But he was afraid to reveal his secret. He feared that, in doing so, his retreat would be cut off and he would be burning his last bridge. Up to now, it had all been for himself only, everything had remained hidden in his brain, and the outside world had no inkling of it.

How much was real in all this? he asked himself. Where was the boundary between reality and the imagination? He himself felt a clear distinction between the two worlds, but the moment of transition was unclear, misty and unprovable. Was it not possible to nudge this boundary back and forth, was it not variable, and would it not be possible to confuse the two worlds at some time or other?

Allan opened his eyes with a start. At least one and a half minutes, which he had devoted to these thoughts, had passed. He wiped his brow with a trembling hand.

How bright the room was! Specks of dust whirled in the flood of light. Down on the street, a barrowman with a clear voice was offering his customers tomatoes and parsley.

Now all that enveloped Allan was a dreamlike sadness. It was like a substance, a fluid, which seeped in from the world, and, even if not very substantial, held the scent of flowers. And it was invincible, in that it had no reason to be there and did not rely on external factors for its existence. It brought a physical pain with it, his head and chest burning with a nameless fire.

Allan pressed his hat down onto his head, left the flat, and descended the creaking stairway. His landlady greeted him and a gentleman passed. Allan stopped at the front door, a bit surprised at seeing this stranger. He had an athletic appearance, a brutish and rough face, and was wearing a top hat. He gave Allan a disgusting smirk as he passed. From his movements and his wooden face, Allan could see that this was no Frenchman. He could have been an American half-blood, almost a boxer.

Suddenly, Allan felt a wave of warmth go through his body: his landlady smiled at the strange gentleman as she would at every occupant of the house, and asked in her throaty voice: "Back again, monsieur—?" She uttered Allan's name and handed the stranger the room key Allan had just left with her.

For an instant, Allan wanted to turn back and explain the mistake, but something glued his feet to the ground. "What, again?" uttered his bloodless lips, and he looked around him with the glance of a dead man.

It was a clear, cold September morning. The city buzzed all around, people were hurrying along, wheels were turning. At the end of the street, the Eiffel Tower rose, like a giraffe above the city.

2.

Allan stood at the prow of the ship looking at the water.

The sea was blue and lilac in shades of mother-of-pearl. The flecks of sunlight broadened, bent and fell apart as the ship cut through them. Silence was all around. All that could be heard was the distant chug of the ship's engines.

Then the islands approached again. One or two isolated villas with red towers rose above the foliage, their windows wide open and, in them, people looking at the ship. Then the people and the villas disappeared. The islands continued with their black and green evergreen trees, red and white rocks like the teeth of the sea, between which the ship cruised slowly.

Allan yawned deeply: what peace—for once!

He had fled the metropolis on the Seine. Now he had left behind Charles XII's capital city. The ship was carrying him into the bleak expanse of the North. He felt freedom in all his being. And end had been put to appalling temptation, ahead there lay only freedom and peace!

He watched the water as it rose at ship's bows and ran away in two wings, as if bewitched. It was no longer water, but gelatin, pliant glass, liquid silver. Neither bubbles nor foam, just two slender folds that ran through this remarkable mirror. It seemed as if the ship were not moving, only those two waves. They ran through the water, gliding towards the rocks; the wind bore the white clouds, but the ship was motionless.

Allan thought:

Does not the hypothesis exist, that all material phenomena are manifestations of different states of movement? It is a question of speed. He had seen the huge power involved in a waterspout. It had lost all the qualities of water, color, weight and moisture. It was as hard as some metal or other. When you hit it with a stick, it bounced off without making any impression. You could only cut off a chip, which would then regain its qualities as water, with a sword. So all your feelings came only from movement that had been, or was, present now.

And did not the differences between people lie only in their mental movements? Some moved sluggishly and aimlessly. Others would rush, swift as the wind, like meteorites, and sometimes you could cut off a sliver with a steel sword. But weren't there even more powerful spirits possible, from which you could cut nothing, not even with a diamond? These would be the souls of the *Übermenschen.*

He looked behind him along the length of the ship. The freshly painted lifeboats gleamed. Above the white handrail of the captain's bridge, the red face of the helmsman could be seen and, from time to time, the clang of the marker bell could be heard, like large beakers being clanged together. Smoke rose in black streams from the funnel and wafted over the archipelago. In its snow-white purity, the ship looked like a large creature tranquilly and consciously plying its route.

Allan then recalled the mechanical and artificial culture of mankind! Just like the lone ship here, thousands of keels were cutting through the water all around the globe. Express trains, metro engines and cars thundered along. Zeppelins were launched into the sky like huge cigars, planes rose from land and sea in order to fly over Gaurisankar or Mount Ararat. What did one more flood mean to them! The Flood would not wash away those who moved like sea snakes along the ocean floor or rose like dragons into the clouds. What was the ebb and flow of the sea to those steel-bodied and diamond-spirited ones whose thought moved a thousand times faster than Noah is his old ark!

There was a healthy and intoxicating joy in this thought. Allan nursed it as you would a child that was noticeably growing. And he felt himself growing along with it.

Ah, he too would like to be steel-spirited! Would like to cast off every torpid dream, turn his back on those tempters that had surrounded him. He would like to rise out of the neurasthenic spleen like a sea eagle, his breast bursting with power!

He took his light sports hat off, wiped his forehead, and felt how softly the wind stirred his hair. It was so good, so good to feel the brush of the air, in which could be detected the crispness of salt and the smell of iodine. The billowing air penetrated his white suit, touching his limbs like the caress of space surrounding him...

Suddenly he sensed the presence of someone near him and abruptly turned his head.

Right beside him, a young woman was standing, in a light-colored costume, one elbow resting on the gunwale, the other arm hanging down alongside her body. She was wearing an English hat, from which a long blue veil, in which she had entwined the hand that hung down, hung.

Allan made a startled movement because the woman was so very close to him. Otherwise, there were few travelers aboard ship: one clergyman, returning from a congress, a couple of old ladies with a lapdog, a few German tourists, three commercial travelers who played cards, and, down below, a handful of immigrants sailing back from America. But he had not seen this young woman. Their close proximity had something uncomfortable and discourteous about it. But he pulled himself together and stayed where he was.

The woman had a narrow face, a supple neck, half hidden by her veil, and a slender body. Her complexion was clear to the point of transparency and her expression animated in an unhealthy way. Allan had seen such typically English young girls in Dieppe and Ostend, where they dreamed their melancholy dreams and rode on horseback with a passion. But what captured his attention were her eyes.

These were elongated and narrow, hidden by long lashes, beneath which what looked like violet-grey oval gems shimmered. The woman was standing in three-quarter profile to Allan and he could nearly see both her eyes simultaneously. They were so penetrating that they almost seemed fixed. And now Allan noticed the unusual curve of her nose and brow, which he thought he had never seen in any living being.

The woman was standing so close to him she must have been able to hear his wheezy breathing, but she seemed to be paying him no attention. And Allan lost all reserve. Out of a sick curiosity, he moved even closer to the woman. His eyes sucked onto hers.

Now he saw the reflection in her violet eyes: the mother-of-pearl sea, an island with a couple of palms, under the palms an athletic looking man wearing a red turban. But beyond the island a ship with a maroon sail was receding, and at the prow stood a woman in a blue veil.

Allan looked up in agitation. Before him stretched the smooth sea, a few rocky islets could be seen in the distance. The sun was beginning to set and the sea was growing dark.

Again he saw the image in the woman's eyes: the turbaned man jumped up, stretched out his athletic hands in the direction of the ship, ran towards it with a look of horror on his face, wrung his hands, opened his mouth, and one could imagine a cry of despair, so that a couple of blue birds rose from the palms into the air... and all around, the yellow sand of the island, the dazzling sea like a shell.

Allan's brain throbbed like the onset of a bad headache. His knees began to shake, his hands to perspire, and he was panting. Then he muttered, using his last strength, trying to rouse himself and his companion:

"My lady...! My lady...!"

But she hardly turned her face towards him, made an indeterminate gesture in the direction of the setting sun, and whispered something in what could have been an unknown language. While her words seemed so unclear and distant, her eyes glittered with an inexplicable intimacy and proximity. Never had Allan seen such a gaze, in comparison to which those of his mother and mistress seemed cool and stern. There was something like the friendship of millennia in that gaze, a painful empathy and commiseration that seemed to physically penetrate everything and understand everything.

Then she turned and walked with even steps towards the stairs, turned once more and looked at Allan, one arm still raised and the other hanging down, entwined in her veil. Then she vanished below deck.

Allan was rooted to the spot. He hardly managed to turn his head and see that the sun had now descended to the sea surface, which was growing rapidly redder, the ship itself casting violet shadows. Allan took a few steps, came to a halt and wiped his forehead. It had all been as in a dream.

He did not even notice how he climbed up onto the bridge, approached the old sailor, casually asking to where the young English lady was traveling. The captain turned towards him and said:

"What lady?"

"The one who was standing next to me in the bow."

"There's no young lady on this ship," replied the captain, turning his gaze again towards the sea.

That too, thought Allan, stumbling absent-mindedly down the steps, that too has happened before. After all, it was the great bard himself who had told the story of Faust, Cagliostro and the Wandering Jew as he returns to his native land. How far away the coast of Norway now seemed, a storm arose over the sea. Gynt again asked the unknown gentleman and the captain answered in the same words: we don't have someone like that on board.

Allan leaned on the rail and looked out over the sea. The ship seemed to be moving faster. The water rubbed against its side, the bubbles whirled, pink and red in the sunset. The spectacle opened up a tiny crack in Allan's thoughts. The bubbles of the foam whirled, a single, secret thought whirled:

Ever faster, ever faster moves the soul of the *Übermensch*. Does it not in the end pick up speed so that its material embodiment is no longer visible? Does it not become transparent as glass and so hard that a diamond is soft as lead by comparison, making no impression on it?

He knew there existed transparent fish that could not be seen in the water and that could be felt to be in the nets only on account of their weight. Could there, then, not exist invisible human beings? Yes, people! In the way that there were invisible salamanders that could only be detected by the wind passing round them, could there not also be superior beings among mankind, which couldn't be detected unless they passed through a certain flame of thought? For one swift moment, when all the power of thought had been concentrated as in the brain's magnifying glass, focusing into one single thought?

Allan gasped for air. In the twilight that surrounded him, he more strongly smelled the sea air and felt the rhythmical rocking of the ship. The ship was rushing into the distant night. Could not a long strip of grey land already be seen on the horizon—the distant shore of the North? Ah, that was what Allan was racing towards in order to forget and rest up from his somber dreams! But was he not also transporting his thoughts and dreams there? Was there anywhere on this small globe they would not reach, where he could escape their intoxicating and appalling poisons?...

Now Allan understood: he could not savor the physical qualities of the *Übermensch* and the technical progress of mankind without seeing an inkling of more profound perspectives beyond. When a pilot rises into a thundercloud, his thoughts rise with him. When the mechanical side of an airplane has been refined to perfection, then the mind of its inventor, too, must be refined. A diamond spirit becomes refined in a body of steel!

He was a poor experimenter. He tried to capture with his brain those radio messages that were being sent from other planets into space by perfect beings. This was so painful, so limitlessly painful! He was a progon who had to suffer all the pains of presentiment until one day some genius invented the right equipment. He was the forebear of the *Übermensch* and in his brain the fire for which others would employ the coal reserves of Britain and America, solar energy, lunar orbital force, the ebb and flow of the sea and the Earth's gravity, maybe even Man's egotistic and erotic energies, was ignited. All of this could perhaps be captured by machines, just like the air's electricity, and be put to use in a previously unknown manner. It was now merely concentrated in his brain, his poor, aching brain...

It had now grown completely dark. Allan descended the steps into the interior of the vessel. Through a gap in the walls, machines were revealed, huge crankshafts rose and fell rhythmically, in the half light a half-naked man was flexing his muscles as if he himself were part of the engines, a volcanic heat wafted in his face and he could smell the sour odor of oil. Allan swayed along the long corridor, found his cabin, and opened the door.

An electric crystal lamp was burning near the mirror, the porthole seemed black, the red furniture and carpet on the floor, russet. On a folding chair sat the woman from a short while ago in her blue veil, her hands resting in her lap, her eyes raised, the penetrating atmosphere even more intense.

Allan stopped in the middle of the cabin, unsure what to do.

"Do not address me," was what he heard, as if in answer to his own thoughts, in a language that vaguely resembled the language of human beings. "Do not ask me my name. Call me, whatever you wish. Or do not call me anything. Because I am greater than any name. You cannot tell others about me. You can merely feel my presence. Look at me for an instant, someone no one has ever seen before."

3.

Allan threw a glance across the circus arena.

A woman wearing a green body stocking was swinging high up under the big top on a thin rope that looked like gossamer. A blue kerchief was tied around her body. Its points flew out behind her head like small wings. The light fell on her from above and her arms and legs gleamed in the slight glow. But, while her body moved rhythmically, her face was immobile and deathly pale. Only her eyes seemed alive. Her gaze was turned at Allan alone, as if lamenting and pleading for help. It was as if they were spreading phosphorescence, lighting up the vault of the circus tent.

Down below him on a mat sat an athlete in a black body stocking, over which a blood-red cloak had been thrown. His conical head was raised, his grey bull-like eyes were turned towards the swaying woman, and he was gesturing with his huge arm as if lending strength to the tightrope walker. His five spread out fingers cast a shadow across the sand. He was as terrifying as an executioner.

At the edge of the arena stood a trio in yellow suits, who played while dozing. The theme was melancholy, the flute bleated sorrowfully, the oboe prated, and after it the drum. The audience was dozing on a half-empty bench, their faces yellow with boredom.

Then Allan got up and left. The woman under the big top nodded very slightly in his direction, as if saying goodbye.

Allan stopped by the show booth. Its pyramidal outline stood black and, from within, a monotonous sound could still be heard. From somewhere beyond the woods, the chug of a departing train could also be heard. The quivering light of the large Lux lamps rose from behind the station building, whose black-winged roof cut sharply through the light. The signal glowed red like a bloody eye, the rails glinted. It was a warm night.

This view was strange, as if Allan had never seen it ever before. He looked around, not knowing in which direction to go. In front of him loomed the station warehouses, a few wagons stood like ghosts on the rails and further off were some dark houses, but the whole of this panorama was ringed in by the woods. Someone put out the lights in the station, also the Lux lamps beyond it. All that was left alive was the noisy circus, and from chinks in the tent a ray of light would appear, with Allan in its path.

He was thinking absent-mindedly. His whole life had vanished somewhere, receded into the distance, he had been left up in the air. And he simply submitted to the image he saw, without considering the framework of space and time in which it found itself. In it, eternity and space were blended.

Only thoughts of home awakened him from this mood. He began to walk slowly in the darkness, accompanied by the deep beats of a drum like the sound of a Negro's gong. He turned off the road and walked along a path. Tall bent grass brushed against his knees, somewhere fruit was rotting. Then he began to walk uphill between two stone walls. The ground was bumpy, stones slid away from under his feet, he stumbled over large tree roots and touched the cold, damp stone with his shoulders. Then the walls receded and on either side only tall rocks and the outlines of pine trees now towered. Beneath his feet, the smooth stone resounded like a floor.

Allan raised his head. Against the low roof of the cliff, the narrow black silhouette of a house could be seen. Around it stood slender pines, stone pines, with sparse branches near the bottom. Above the house a constellation of bright stars moved in the cooling night.

Allan regarded them for a moment with a deep feeling of sadness, then ascended the stairs, above which the roof stretched out, supported on four tall pillars. He could smell the scent of wet autumn flowers, cloying like rotting grass. He opened the front door, walked through the entrance hall whose floorboards creaked, and entered the room.

Through the window, whose rectangle was halved by a lone tree branch and cut off at the bottom by birch saplings, shone a murky light. The flowers in the vase were outlined in black against it. A few small portraits could be seen above the bed with their white *passepartouts.* He could make out the profiles of Nietzsche and Whitman, between them one of somebody unknown, but perhaps greater than both. The yellow net curtains hanging from the brass rail were pulled back to the sides of the window in bows.

Allan lay down on the bed as he was, in his clothes. The pillow under his head felt marvelously soft, the entire bed seemed to be rocking beneath him, as if he had lain down above the water on a bending willow branch. He looked up at the ceiling, where a soft light shimmered. Beneath it were dark and light patches of wallpaper. The whole of the opposite wall was filled with low bookshelves, containing hardly discernible volumes. Above them drooped a few flowers in a vase, black as coal in the darkness.

Allan felt quite lightheaded. His breathing rocked the bedsprings as if he were on a swing. His sick heart beat slowly. He shut his eyes. Where was he now? In the beautiful landscape of Kemi, in the pretty Jaro fells? It didn't matter. The blood buzzed in his veins, his limbs felt light as a feather, as if he were slowly evaporating into these strange surroundings.

He suddenly felt that right now he was living through the greatest and most significant moment of his life. He had descended into a valley full of foreboding and horror, but was now beginning to climb out. He had now climbed up onto the watershed, hurrying and panting, and could see a new world from the hill at Nebo: fairy-tale castles in a forest of palms, above which shone the rainbows of fountains. He had climbed up onto the Chinvat Bridge, where souls are judged. Tiger-headed orderlies weighed them in huge dishes with their ochre hands, adorned them with the ostrich feathers, and sent them to the gods who were eternally playing handball with soft red balls in green meadows...

Earthly passions had vanished. Thoughts, so black and heavy had fallen into oblivion. Feelings, so black and heavy, had fallen into oblivion. Everything that came when waking, that the hot sun would bring, and the gusty winds, the bursting forth of the Earth into bloom and the ripening of crops in the autumn, had fallen into oblivion. All that was left was being, silent and profound.

He stretched out on the bed. It was as if his organism had been transformed in the same mysterious way as a leaf does when its green chlorophyll changes to yellow xantophyll in autumn. The Earth lives its own dream life, hardly breathing, but its hair withers and falls out, only to burst into bloom again the next spring. It is like a plant, which only flowers once every hundred years. It had now lived a century in his feelings, and the bud was beginning to open.

And in his ears the music of the spheres rang through the darkness, far off and indistinct:

Je ne vois plus rien.
Je perds le mémoire
Du mal et du bien.
O la triste histoire!

It thrummed like a string, spanning from space to space; plucked by an invisible finger on the kannel of the planets, it rang again, the singer from Sagesse, with this sad, sweet refrain:

Je suis un berceau,
Qu'une main balance
Au fond d'un caveau.
Silence, silence!

Some of his dreams were only voices, the fragrance of flowers, a flash of light. He saw nothing concrete, no events, figures or outlines, only the change of light—green, pink and ultramarine waves that rose and fell. Soft sounds like organs, harps, bird song, sighs like the soughing of the woods and the rush of the sea, were heard. Then the fragrance of the flowers would change, hardly perceptibly, the mignonette attaining a dark, discreet fragrance, the honey grass could be smelled, garlands and wreaths of tea roses fell through the air.

Out of these dreams of light, sound and smell, riverbanks and the arches of bridges began to be visible. The water flowed heavy as lead, the banks were unscalable cliffs. Bleak bulrushes grew on this side of the bridge; beyond, couch grass, above which humming-birds and warblers flew in a rainbow arc.

Allan tossed in bed, stretched his arms and yawned. His brain was quivering in a fever of thought. His dreamy eyes widened like abysses.

Then the dreams suddenly changed, becoming stormy and painful: sea reeds of aluminum swished, a large red tiger was leaping through the reeds with eyes ablaze, roaring its metallic roar. Jackal pups rushed behind it through the forest of steel, the brass earth resounded as the tiger moved along. And then, suddenly, a strange sound could be heard, the sound of a bassoon of brass, the hunt for prey in the reeds!

Allan opened his eyes and shuddered. The room was bathed in the greenish light of dawn. The fearful dream dissipated in the green air. Beyond the crystal panes of the window, yellow birch trees swayed.

Again, around his bed the aluminum reeds of his dreams grew, driving their steel roots into the folds of his mattress with white swallows swaying in their tops. Allan stretched out his hand and stroked the sleeping birds. All at once the wind rushed through the reeds and the swallows fell into the open mouths of the jackals. The cotton of their nests floated to the ground like snowflakes. Then great despair tightened its hold on Allan, his pain grew like a liana, his love and pity shed petals and sprouted buds, until the reeds blossomed as couch grass. All of a sudden the birds flew out of the dying jackals' mouths as a pillar of multicolored humming-birds, ranging through the air like a singing rainbow.

He had crossed the bridge and was beyond the high arches, which rose out of the leaden depths of the river.

Then he heard a cry from afar. It could be heard several times, low and soft.

He opened his eyes and saw the darkish morning green of the room. He sat up, leaning on his elbows, and took a deep breath. Outside the window, snow was falling in large flakes, like wool. The air was filled with invitation.

Allan stepped outside. On the stair stood the woman, one hand raised, one in her veil. The snow was falling over her, but she did not seem to feel this. Her eyes smiled through the snowfall, which seemed soft and caressing, like a white veil over the blue one.

"Come!" said the woman.

Allan walked behind her, bareheaded, into the soft realm of snow. It covered the entire ground, the trees were bent under its flaxen bunches, the stones bore it like white turbans. The whole world was like one huge feather bed.

Before them were someone's large footprints in the deep snow. The walker had staggered from side to side as if drunk; there were the traces of fingerprints in the snow-covered stones as he had stumbled. Then Allan saw the person they were following.

It was a large man, in a black bodystocking, a red cloak over his shoulders. It seemed he had fallen between two rocks while running and his cloak had spread out. His face was contorted from his tribulations and a trickle of blood had fallen from his mouth onto the snow. It was bright red, a beautiful color. The man was dead.

"Who is that?" asked Allan, as a strange tremor passed through his body.

"Don't ask," replied the woman. "It is no longer anyone. If he had still been alive, he would have felt pain. That has passed. He is no longer."

Allan looked up. A great peace held sway over him. He felt a wonderful lightness. He felt it made no difference whether he walked on the ground or rose into the air. All the laws of matter seemed light as bubbles, whirling in spirals.

Around him, the forest loomed, higher than he had ever seen it. The branches of tall fir trees drooped like white wings. Between them, the road rose gradually to higher ground. Then the trees took on strange shapes, as if bowing their branches downwards, they broadened out like hands carrying something, and the clumps of snow on them changed to form some kind of foliage.

Then a small temple could be seen through the trees. It had crenellated towers at the edges and cupolas grew like flower buds.

They stopped on the steps, and the woman looked Allan in the eye with a kind of forlorn sadness. And Allan saw that this was no longer a human face, but purified, like that of a spirit.

"Are you afraid?" asked the woman. "But this is your fate. You will go on, you will turn back. You are over the bridge, you are still on this side of it. You are aware, you have lost all consciousness, only to discover it again. And so on, to infinity. That is your fate."

Allan stepped inside the temple. Its gilded cupola rose into the heights, descending to carved flowers and birds. In this dimly lit golden room a ring of huge candles and torches burned, emanating light and fragrance. Between the candles a small child with a smiling face sat on a giant lotus flower, its hands stretched out towards the circles of lights that flickered around it like bright petals.

1921

The Mermaid

1.

A strange murmur filled the crisp air of late autumn, as if an invisible bird were fluttering its wings. The restless sea rushed, beyond the dunes the reddish dead grass rustled. A slight breeze ruffled the surface of the endless stretch of ocean, crossing the grim sands of the island.

Kurdis was standing in the dunes. Before him, on one side, the grey sea merged with the leaden clouds; on the other, the winding horizon of hills of sand joined the ashen colored sky. A windy space bordered the world.

With eyes the color of water, Kurdis surveyed the splashing of the sea, above which a number of gulls cut slowly through the air. The pupils of his eyes dilated and contracted, as they sought the moving line of the horizon. A painful sadness quivered on his thin lips.

His was a strange face, not human: an endlessly high and empty brow, and a tiny rounded chin. On his large skull grey bristles stood erect, the wind stirred a few white wisps on his chin. His mouth was filled with large horse's teeth for which there was no room; they bunched forward, giving him the face of a bird.

He was a strange monstrosity, a figure seen in a distorting mirror, like something exhibited to the world in a murky jar, a horrible creature from the depths of the ocean.

And yet his heart was childishly pure and gentle. His mind was like a bulrush, bent hither and thither by a thousand winds. He let his eyes wander sadly over the expanse of land and water.

The island rose out of the bluish depths of the ocean like the back of a whale. In the middle of the hump of the island stood a pyramidal church, sinking in the sand. The huge stones of the walls stood out black against white circles of cement. And in the middle of the hump of the island seven storm-swept pine trees grew, pronged like tritons. Their bare-branched skeletons stood darkly against the firmament. In the flames of the summer sun, the hills stood yellow as brick.

Then Kurdis let his gaze descend.

Before him he could see the village, the clay-built houses, weathered by storms, and the curved roofs weighted down by stones. Their rafters could be seen through the thatch like the boncs of some unknown animal. The houses were surrounded by small plots of land with a pitiable crop of green garlic, plus the criss-crossing of canes and the nets moving in the wind.

They were sad hearths, poor human habitations on the shore of the empty island among the emptiness of the shoreless sea!

The air was so clear Kurdis could almost see the knots in the nets and the autumn flies buzzing around them. Only what seemed to be a wall of glass separated him from the village by the bay.

Now and again, the sound of pipes could be heard over the rush of the wind on the beach. Today there would be a great feast, a great wedding—today was Kaspar the Red's wedding!

Ah, Kaspar the Red brought joy both to himself and to his people: let the wedding instruments play, the wedding song rise to the heavens! Let the players blow their pipes, the bagpipers press their doodle sacks, let the serpent resound and the music float over land and water!

Ah, Kaspar the Red! Who was more powerful, greater and prouder than Kaspar the Red? Who could oppose Kaspar the Red—who would have enough wealth, enough power, to do so? What would happen to the island if there were no Kaspar, what would the children do, the women, the old men? Oh, hunger, cold, misery and death!

Ah, Kaspar the Red! His house is like a castle in the village, his was the king of windmills. In his cellars stood reinforced chests and boxes, barrels and troughs—full of strong spirits, frog's meat, tobacco and salt. All he needed to do was give the order and men winched up iron trays with loaves of bread; he gave a wave of his hand and barrels of rum are rolled in. This house was full of victuals from cellar to ceiling! Out by the islands stood Kaspar the Red's three merchant vessels: one arrived with the salt, kegs of rum were loaded from the second into boats, on the third dried fish was being prepared for export.

Ah, Kaspar the Red! The gods in the church and the people in the country bowed down before him. He could eat and drink as much as he wished, and yet there was never a shortage of anything. He spat at the walls of the temple and no one would think the worse of it.

Kaspar the Red! Today he considered it a good time to celebrate yet another marriage.

The skirl of pipes carried across the holms. It rose and fell, as did the bellows under the arm of the piper. The flag unfurled to the same rhythm up on the high roof, then straightened out like a yellow snake.

Across the courtyard of the house, the brick-colored arms of servant women shone as they carried tureens of frog soup. Groups of people were standing in the courtyard, like flowering shrubs onto which the pale rays of the autumn sun shone between two clouds. At the door to the house stood a man, pouring the spirits and the beer.

By the portal, dogs gnawed at bones. The clash of their hungry teeth reached Kurdis' ears. They were stretched out on their high knees the bones glittered between their jaws.

"What a wedding!" thought Kurdis, full of wonder. "What a wedding. Where there is bread and meat so that everyone eats their fill and yet there is still some left over. The great largess of today has even reached the dogs."

And Kurdis grew sad again when thinking about the dogs. He understood them, and sympathized with their sad complaints, when they would suddenly howl with fear at the setting of the sun. That this was invisible, yet ever present, was something he himself had felt. He was close to the appalling secret that held back everyone.

The minds of dogs, the minds of frogs, the minds of crows—he understood them. Rarely, oh so rarely, did a dog curl its lip into a smile, and what a smile! The frog would wend its silent way, full of silence and secrecy. And the crow, that black bird with dung-splashed claws, was dear to his heart.

But people were incomprehensible to him. When other creatures would hum their quiet little songs of joy, an angry human being would turn up, seize the creature by the throat, beat it to death with a club and eat it up. People were abominable, fear was their handiwork, their breath was disgusting!

And Kurdis felt horror that he too had to be with them, that he had to take part, like everyone else on this hideous island, if they wanted to stay alive.

His work was not lofty: simply to sit at the frog pit of Kaspar the Red and lure the frogs into it by playing his *kannel*, his harp. He could play quite a number of tunes to lure the frogs. They were bleak tunes, full of the bleak whine of mosquitoes, distant and subtle, and rarely did the pitch drop to the brief bass of the horsefly, even more loveless and sorrowful. Frogs would flop like lumps of dough, crawl around his feet—and he would play and play!

What was he thinking about during those long nights sitting there at the pit? He was happy for the poor littoral folk who got board and a roof over their heads on account of the frogs. And his playing continued to lure many swarms of insects.

But he took pity on the luckless frogs too; he would stroke their cold skins in the darkness and lift them up onto the edge of the pit, where the stars and the seas's phosphorescence shone in the evening. He had sympathy for all creatures in his heart and this rendered him powerless.

It was a good year. There were plenty of mosquitoes, the frogs were well fed. In the spring they would swarm onto the shore. Their croaking echoed like clay pipes across the island. Then the waters whistled with tiny frogs, and the marshes splish-splashed with the larger ones. In the late autumn they were caught and salted in enormous numbers and loaded onto ships. And all of this was for the benefit of the island!

In the autumn, endless flocks of birds would fly over the island. The air was full of their colors and echoed with their cries. They would land, covering roofs and rocks, and their droppings rained down on the knolls. Then the islanders would take snares and bows and arrows and kill boundless numbers of birds, whose flesh and feathers were sent to the mainland in a like manner.

It was a good year. Dog teams pulled loads of grain from the ships to the shore; night and day, it was taken to the windmills. An oil lamp burned in every mud hut to honor Saint George, thanking him for the plenty around them.

And Kaspar the Red, the Only One, the Incomparable, was in a mild mood. He gave everyone a little more than they had earned. He granted the people almost everything they had earned in their free time. He did not punish as severely as usual.

This was because he had brought a good mood with him from the mainland. His son has reaped success in the wars in the south. The Emperor had thus been temperate with his father. And his home island seemed even more attractive to him.

He celebrated his own half-century and now felt he was at the height of his powers. The faces of his women pleased him once more and he felt it was time to have another wedding.

And now, thinking about Kaspar the Red, Kurdis was again swept along in a wave of enthusiasm. He was happy as a child.

Ah, Kaspar the Red—he was no longer a human being, he was a hero, a god. He no longer occupied a fixed place or had a fixed image. He could be in several places at once and changed guises like a red cloud in the evening sky.

In Kurdis' eyes, Kaspar became a mythical figure. He hardly remembered having ever seen him. He had heard of him far back during childhood.

Then foreign sailors were sitting there, becalmed, waiting for better weather by the light of oil lamps in their huts, drying out their pelts and telling yarns about the god of the distant islands, Kaspar the Red, against the background of the murmuring sea.

While daydreaming of all this, Kurdis suddenly spotted a man in a yellow suit leap out through the door of the wedding hall, beckon, and call out something.

Kurdis started to run down to the dune. He waded up to the tops of his boots in sand, grey wisps of hair streaming behind him as if he were riding a horse.

2.

People were swarming slowly out through the low door of the wedding hall.

Leading them was Kaspar the Red and his bride-to-be, after them the priest and the sorcerer, and behind them the people of thirteen villages.

Kaspar the Red was as proud as a pirate king. His countenance was splendid as steel, his body slender as a cedar. He wore a hat with red feathers. His neck was brown as leather. His red beard had been plaited in two, with gold thread woven into it. And the fringe of his yellow cloak trailed along the ground. He strode slowly forth in his beribboned red shoes with large gold rings through his ears.

Alongside walked his bride, the maiden Piret. She was snow white—her hair and face, her veil and clothes. She had no face, she was one stretch of pallor, one long veil, one goodness-knows-what.

Behind them stepped the island's priest. His purple chasuble reached only to his knees and his garters and nose were purple. He was muttering prayers, his leaden grey eyes raised to the heavens.

Around them swarmed the people, innumerable and of indistinct color.

The heads of the men were shorn and rings hung from their ears, their teeth were blackened by tobacco, the younger ones in knee-skirts, the older ones in mud-colored fur cloaks. The women's chests were bedecked with heavy brooches and their bellies protruded. And there were endless numbers of old women with sunken eyes and bat-like faces. Children ran on both sides, almost naked, their legs and faces smeared with red clay, and rings of brass through their navels.

The courtyard filled from end to end with the festive people's brightly-colored costumes.

When they were ready to depart, a miracle occurred in the sky: two grey walls of clouds parted and the bright sun shone forth, casting a sheen of gold over them all.

The bright yellow and red cloaks flamed up, the feathers on Kaspar the Red's hat blazed, and his bride's veils became pink like dawn clouds.

Then Kaspar the Red smirked with satisfaction and gave the sign that they could depart.

Kurdis put his hands to his *kannel*, the piper blew into his doodle sack and the assembled crowd moved across the courtyard. Now began the solemn procession to the seashore in order to cast the dragnet in honor of the bridal couple, as was a tradition in these parts.

Three groomsmen, Niil, Manglus and Tahve, walked in a triangle behind the couple, carrying the net like a veil.

The sea, blue and friendly, suddenly smiled at those approaching. It splashed onto the shore and bowed as if to a conqueror. Kaspar smiled at it, knowing his power extended over land and sea.

The sandy beach was filled with the noisy throng. They approached the waves, patting down the wet sand, and the dogs came and drank from the sea.

Niil and Tahve pushed the boat into the waves, Niil rowed and Tahve let down the net while Manglus, still standing on the shore, held its other end. The floats bobbed like ducks on the silent waters, cutting wide rings.

Now Niil and Tahve were back on shore, the priest raised his arms and blessed the catch.

"To you, our bride, this catch! As heavy a belly as this net is heavy. As many children as there are fish. May the pregnancy be light, lighter still the birth. Saint George, in your name, this catch—for the bride!"

Hardly had he uttered these words, when the wedding guests seized hold of the edge of the net. They ran in two lines up onto the dune, dragging the net behind them as they went. They were like two colored necklaces, glittering in the sun. Between the two necklaces stood the bride and groom, the priest and the musicians.

The floats soon approached the shore and the circle between them narrowed. Then it was all pulled together and the noose of the net and its wings came shuffling onto the shore, shimmering with the scales of small fish.

The lines of net-pullers had arrived at the top of the dune; their heads were now behind the ridge, only their shouts could be heard from afar. Then some waded back down through the sand onto the beach and grasped the wings of the net.

The rest of the net was drawn in. It frothed with foam and was green with sea grass. An incessant bustle and mix lay in it. It was full of creatures that could not yet been seen.

Then it was dragged noisily onto the pebbles and the pullers ran to the water's edge.

The net was full of fish. They tossed and turned in the foam. Their scales glittered. They pushed one another away and writhed in the air.

But a huge seashell, full of shiny pearls, shone in their midst. The fish swarmed around it, as if not seeing the danger.

Old Manglus stretched out his bony hands and picked up the shell.

It was a pearly blue and lilac inside, its edges curled like the calyx of a flower, its recesses like a horn of plenty under the curved fingers.

There were no limits to the wedding guests' astonishment!

"It's for you, young lady," said Manglus and presented the shell to the bride, "as a dish for your meal and cradle for your child!"

The bride stretched out her hand, but couldn't lift it and let it down on the sand instead. She knelt down next to the dish of the shell. She fingered the pearls, lifted them up into the air, then let tears of joy fall like a child's.

Meanwhile, the groomsmen collected the fish. They filled large baskets with them. They glittered in the sun like piles of scales. They overflowed over the edges of the baskets.

Then Niil and Tahve rowed out to sea again and threw out the net in a wider bow.

"For you, bridegroom, this catch! May you never sleep, as a fish never sleeps. Saint George may stay at your bedside anticipating your weariness. May your semen be as wet as that of a fish! For you, bridegroom, this catch, both small and large fish, especially the larger ones!"

Hardly had these words been uttered but that the wedding guests again seized the net. They ran uphill for a few brief moments, bare legs flashing. Then, suddenly, the net grew heavy as stone.

They pulled, dragged and cursed. The pebbles rolled under their feet, their arms strained, their legs interlocked like those of wrestlers. The sun shone golden on their floundering movements.

Then the net gradually eased. It was drawn up, silent and heavy. The eyes of those pulling were fixed on it until they vanished over the dune. Then one of them ran back to see what the heavy catch had been. But he stood petrified, arms raised, his silent mouth open in astonishment.

As the net was slowly drawn in, a creature was thrashing in the knots and the seaweed. It was in the foam, snowy white as the clouds. For a moment, a human head with long hair could be seen, then slender white limbs.

The small group of people on the shore stood frozen in their motley movements, full of amazement and wonder.

Then they all saw at once, desperately writhing in the net, the Mermaid.

The net would have been thrown back into the sea, but those pulling, who were now over the edge of the dune, did not see the wonder and continued their efforts.

The net reached the shore, devoid of fish, but with the Mermaid as its catch. She was naked; all that covered her were her light brown locks. A deep despair could be seen on her face, her grey eyes were screwed up and her red mouth stood open with pain amid her white face. Then she suddenly spotted the seashell with the pearls.

Her face changed, she made a movement towards it, as if to ask for it back. She looked at everyone, gesturing again with her hand. Tears sprang from her eyes.

By this time the pullers of the net had returned. They stood transfixed, some on the shore, some halfway down the dune, some still at the top, their legs still in a running position.

For countless ages, no mermaids had ever been seen in these parts!

Everyone stood there benumbed. There was a moment of helpless silence. Then, suddenly, Kaspar the Red's calm and commanding voice was heard:

"This is my catch."

On hearing this voice, everyone came to their senses. They ran to the water's edge and surrounded the net. Around it loomed a many-colored wall of human figures.

Amid this ring of red faces was the Mermaid. She wanted to flee, but could escape in no direction. She floundered this way and that, then covered her face with her hands and wept.

She was slender and beautiful. She had large breasts, but hardly any hips. Her skin was bright and delicate. Only her face was inhuman in its pallor, and her lips were intensely, intensely red.

"This is my catch," Kaspar repeated.

And all of a sudden, they had all grown accustomed to the fact that they had caught the Mermaid in the net. It seemed to them as if they had gone fishing for mermaids every day. That was the effect Kaspar the Red's voice had on them.

They crowded round the Mermaid's net, made a framework of oars, and got ready to carry her back.

Kaspar the Red walked in front. Behind him were carried the Mermaid and the seashell. The bagpipes played. The red and white cloaks were dazzling. The flags curled up and opened out. Dogs paced, snarling, on either side of the procession.

Kaspar the Red walked, his head held even higher. His eyes shone and, through his red beard, a smile flickered, first vanishing, then returning. He drew his shoulders back over his plaited beard and grinned.

Alongside him walked his silent bride in her snow-white veils. She rolled two pearls in her hand like a child, rolled them—and then burst into tears.

The sun was setting. Its rays descended over the dunes. The heavens turned grey. The colors of the procession faded and paled.

3.

An evening filled with a sea wind had come to the island, starless, moonless and black. The huts grew silent in the darkness. Only in Kaspar the Red's house were there still lights and the murmur of voices.

Kaspar the Red was holding his wedding.

His large hall had been decorated as a festival hall. From the ceiling hung square frames with earthenware oil lamps. The vault of the cedar wood ceiling was covered with the wings of birds, skins and fringed tapestries. The lamps burned as in a forest.

Only during Kaspar the Red's wedding were the islanders allowed to see the inside of his house. But Kaspar only held a wedding every third or fourth year. And in the meantime, they could do nothing but remember what they had seen, and recall with longing all they had eaten and drunk.

They wandered from room to room, they poked their hands everywhere, felt the walls, the furniture and furnishings. There were so many things here that had come from distant countries! And they mumbled their admiration of everything they saw.

The grim iron statue of the Emperor aroused fear in them. They saw the life-sized painting of Kaspar himself, wearing his robes and plumed crown. And that of his son on a giraffe's back in front of a troop of men in black.

The rooms were separated by rows of oaken pillars. And the guests wandered among the pillars, their coats a dark red from the distant lamps, their sleeves tasseled as if with drops of blood. The click of their sandals filled the rooms like the scratching of animals' claws.

Again they saw his hall, his drawing room, his workshop. They were struck with wonder.

But most wondrous of all was Kaspar's bedchamber. Here there were taps in the walls, so that he could drink without even having to get up. He could fill his gullet with sweet wine while lying in bed. Here there was a stone bathtub, there a table where he ate by the light of torches.

But the grandest thing of all was Kaspar the Red's bed itself. The posts were of cedar wood, the sides of stone oak, the base of iron oak. There were four feather pillows and seven smaller cushions. It was soft and warm. It was sinfully comfortable, as holy as an altar.

And the village women tiptoed up to it. They felt the pillows with reverence, touched the fabrics and sighed.

Half of them remembered that bed from when they had been young and pretty. And the older ones remembered Kaspar's father's days, and the even older ones those of his grandfather. They had all been here at some time, even the centenarians.

They sighed, their mouths open and their hands crossed over their chests; they sighed and remembered times past. Even the centenarians sighed.

Then they came back into the main hall. Here, the maidens set the table and brought the food. And what a table it was! It stretched from the hall to the kitchen, from the kitchen into the entrance hall, from the entrance hall to the mill, from the mill to the barn. Some strangers would have to eat with the pigs if Kaspar so decided.

On the table was a heap of tobacco, like hay on a large open farm wagon. And among the tobacco stood tubs of beer, dishes of frog meat, piles of griddle bread, jellied seal meat on platters, horns filled with wine, and countless other things to eat and drink.

Kaspar the Red's wedding—this was more than the islanders could even imagine. It exceeded their powers of wonder, however often they looked. They shook their heads and screwed up their faces and saliva flooded their tongues.

The torches in their holders, spanning the length of the walls, were lit, the lamps flared brightly, and the guests went to table.

This setting stretched like a giant manger from one room to the next, while reaching out to those sitting at the trough. Rows of yellow and ashen grey faces stretched long as a highway from the hills.

At one end of the table sat Kurdis with his dogs, at the other the blind and the lepers, crouched on straw.

Hardly had the priest blessed the food and drink, but thousands of hands stretched forth. They did so shyly and modestly, looking up and down the table to see what their neighbors were doing.

At the center of the table Kaspar presided over the banquet.

Opposite him sat his mother, whose face was like earth and hands like hooks. Her eyes moved like awls, there was but one tooth in her mouth, she was a hundred years old. Her name was Babylona.

On either side of Kaspar sat a woman. One was like the day, the other like a moonlit night. But both were Kaspar the Red's women.

Today, Kaspar the Red's loins had more strength than ever before.

On his right sat the Mermaid, in her nakedness and green veils. Her water-grey eyes were shut. Her fiery red mouth was open.

On his left sat the bride Piret. Her blue eyes were open. She was weeping. Tears fell into her goblet.

In Kaspar the Red's loins was more strength than ever before.

On his chest he wore the medal of Saint George—a spread-eagled frog. He raised his hand and showed everyone his new Order of the Green Frog. And he spoke, full of reverence, about himself:

"The Emperor has sent me this on the occasion of my seventh wedding. I have done much for the Emperor. My son is in command of the legions of war in the country of the blacks. The Emperor owes me half a realm."

And he cut himself a chunk of cheese made from human milk, which came from the land of the Negroes. It was black.

But no sooner had the first pitchers of wine been emptied, but the eating became a scoffing. Those present gobbled in competition with one another, despite one another, no longer even seeing one another.

They crammed food into their mouths with both hands. If they had had a third, they would have eaten with three hands, and a fourth with four. The one-armed man in the kitchen used his feet and the blind tore the food out of one another's jaws and would occasionally quarrel when the dumplings did not reach their stomachs as intended. Only the dogs gnawed, each at his own bone.

It was an exhibition of smacking and chewing jaws, biting their way through loaves, bolting down whole legs of pork and belching out clouds of garlic. It was like an eating-machine that consumed, ground, swallowed and digested to the point of exhaustion.

And the wine goblets were raised. The beer tubs made their rounds. The blind clashed foreheads, as they thrust their heads into the mead barrels in unison. Again the eaters would gulp, snort like horses, chew their cud like cattle.

But today Kaspar the Red was enjoying delicatessen. He was eating the paws of hippopotami, which had been roasted under a dunghill and on which a crocodile had breathed. Then he tasted nut porridge that had slowly fermented in human spittle. This suddenly went to his head.

The plumes on his head trembled, he leaned back in his chair and held an after-dinner speech for both himself and his guests:

"I am everything. I am the beginning and the end. After me there will be nothing. The Emperor is my friend.

"You are swine. Your snouts are not worthy of all you receive. You should live in a sty. You should gobble up your fodder from a trough. The Emperor is my friend.

"Today is my wedding. I wished to hold my wedding today. My wife is—which one it is, I do not know. One or the other.

"I've sent my previous wives off, whither I do not know. They are no doubt collecting bird dung by the sea. I don't know. I don't care. It's all the same to me. The Emperor is my friend.

"My son—I don't know from which of my wives—my boy is fighting against the Negroes. He has three million men. Every day he kills a hundred thousand and on Sundays, two hundred thousand. He can allow himself that. What is it to him?

"He has loads of women. He has Negro and Red Indian ones, he has ones from a country called Europe which is now deserted, he has ones from India and from the moon. He will marry none of them. All he does is hold weddings.

"I gained a wife today. She came from the sea. Is she human? I do not know. But she is a woman. Why should a woman have to be human?

"Oh yes—what was I going to say? Oh yes, you're all pigs. You've got strange snouts—huh-huh—such strange snouts! But I don't care. I don't care about anything.—The Emperor is my friend."

He now leaned into the back of his chair and stared at everyone with a glassy eye.

But the priest raised his hand, leaned across the table and said gently:

"You're so right: what are we? Nothing, nothing at all. We live by your charity; if you were gone we would die. You are here on the island, the Emperor out in the realm, and Saint George is in heaven –"

„George is manure!" Kaspar hiccupped meanwhile.

"Exactly so, manure, that was what I was trying to say. He is heavenly manure. He feeds us. So long live those who feed us! Long live our ruler Kaspar, long live the Emperor, long live Saint George!"

His words ceased and their echo reached the pigs' troughs. From there, the voices of the lepers rose in response.

Then the rows of yellow faces intervened, staggering to their feet, still gnawing bones and holding their lips to the rims of their pitchers. The babble of voices rose to become an exalted scream. And the dogs began to squabble noisily.

Then the music began to echo. And the ceremony began in the hall and the troughs.

The "Dance of the White Cat" was being danced, which was performed while squatting, then the "Motley Hound Dance," which was performed on all fours, and the "Black Pig Dance," which was danced with people's noses touching the ground. The blind, the lepers, and the dogs all had their own dance.

Then Kaspar the Red rose from the banquet table and went to bed with his wives.

Old crones led the wives, one of whom seemed lifeless, the other as if dead. The lifeless one was Piret, the dead one, the Mermaid.

She did not move from the time she was taken home. She did not open her eyes, only her mouth stood a little open, and this revealed a silent scream, a desperate cry for help. It was as if she were petrified with fear.

Kaspar the Red went to bed with his two wives.

His mother was waiting in the bedchamber. She had aired the pillows, was holding the corner of the covers like the sail of a windmill. Rows of large torches cast a mournful light.

Kurdis was standing behind a pillar, holding his kannel. For he was to play for Kaspar the Red on his wedding night. This was a custom of Kaspar's: he liked fiery music to accompany his joy! He wished for a mix of all the wines and the intoxicating hops of sound.

From afar, merry singing and reveling could be heard. From beyond the pig's bladder windows, the night sea could be heard moaning. The torch flames flickered.

Kaspar was now alone with his two brides. Suddenly Piret fell to her knees at his bedside and burst into tears:

"What am I to do now? Why am I here?"

Kaspar the Red, his chest bared, replied:

"You? You can play with the Mermaid's pearls at our feet. Come on child, play!"

Then, addressing Kurdis:

"Hey you, musician, start up the music!"

Kurdis strummed the strings and shuddered.

4.

At midnight, Kurdis fled from the wedding feast in despair. He ran into the darkness and the wind, as if pursued by a thousand devils.

His ears still rang with the shriek of the Mermaid, one long cry, but as hideous as if it had circled Earth and Heaven!

Kurdis was trembling all over. The wind snatched at his clothing and whirled around his head. From the valley the dull sound of the orchestra in the wedding hall could be heard, the grim chain of the island could faintly be seen in the night, the boundless sea moved in the distance. But Kurdis stood benumbed and helpless in the darkness, not even realizing where he was.

The moon or some stars hazily lit up the heavens.

A cloud arose from beyond the sea—blood red and misty. It split, grew misty, waned, waxed—it was warm.

Kurdis wiped his brow with both arms like a fly. Somewhere else, the sky grew leaden, lilac, deepened, ended—Kurdis felt this was cold and ghastly.

He had never before felt such moods, the limits and extent of suffering. His thoughts fogged and stretched, tangled like knots in string.

Kurdis began to untangle the net of his thoughts. It was long and brightly colored, he hid his head in it as if in a flag, as if he were stumbling through nocturnal empty fields in a cloak of thought. Along the windy sand dunes, ferns and spiders of thought were chasing.

Heavens above! he muttered quietly to himself: my sea! Give me succor, o wind; take me, night air; look with solace into my eyes, everlasting warmth. I am so cold, so boundlessly cold!

Has the whole country been turned into one huge grave? Is the world a cellar where the maggot gnaws and the toad crouches in the corner? Are the eyes of the whole world covered with potsherds, mouth wide open, dry teeth bared? Is the world simply one hideous grimace, facing the winking stars in the open heavens?

My bright heavens, my dear Sun, give me your warmth, give me warmth! If not, I will die, if not, I will die!

He was now stumbling along through the landmarks of clay that rose like anthills around him. These were the cairns. Beneath them lay untold generations of islanders—vaults of clay, generation pressed on generation, arms twined around knees, jaws pressed into knees, as if in eternal thought.

It was towards these dead thinkers that he now directed his despair:

You who sleep, do you dream? Are you not buried in a sitting posture so that your thoughts remain clear? Think now, dead people! Think, think, because the living are sinking into the thoughtlessness that holds sway above your clay hillocks.

Are not clay frogs placed before you so that you will always see an image of creatures jumping forwards? Dead people, move! The world above is petrified to the point of despair! The world has frozen in brutal horror! It is ghastly! Ghastly!

But all he heard was the drone of the hollow earth. It seemed as if the earth was so thin that he was walking over the bared heads of the dead.

But you do not answer, he said staggering hither and thither. You are dead! You too are dead! No one is alive any longer, not even the dead! The world has become one huge graveyard.

And Kurdis wandered from place to place. Everything had left his mind: aim, purpose and goal. Everything he had ever lived for was rent asunder that night. Everything he had ever adhered to had fallen away. His world had been turned upside-down, as had his thoughts about the pointless Earth.

What was life? What was Man? Why did people writhe in their cages, why did a meaningless void hem them in on all sides?

Among mankind there was nothing but wolf people and pig people. One group wallowed in their own might, the other in their powerlessness. Everything Man touched became terrible! The air he breathed became disgusting, as did the heavens to which he raised his rheumy eyes!

Kurdis staggered in the pitch darkness from one end of the island to the other. The winds and thoughts bore him along. He erred hither and thither, came back to where he had been before, but no longer recognized where he was. Only his legs and thoughts failed to grow weary.

How had he ended up in this horrible country? He all at once asked himself. And he knew nothing of it.

It was as if he had become lost, without family or friends. He had been found by the sea as a child, and had grown up as an animal in the company of animals. He had only loved animals, he had only understood animals. He kept warm by sleeping next to the dogs, as if among brothers.

Was he a human being at all? He suddenly asked himself. He did not know.

Not human? He was so taken aback that he stood stock still. Not human?

Yes, he did not understand them. He had learned their language, but it was a foreign language. He had learned to think as they did, but it was a foreign way of thinking.

But there had to be a second language, which those like him spoke. There had to be a land where he felt profoundly at home. Where was this homeland to be found, where he remembered having heard his mother tongue as a child as if through a fog?

He stood in wonder, but the clouds scudded along unceasingly above his head. They rolled open like a warm aurora borealis. Banks of cloud, with their pink hems and green rays, fell through the black carpet. And then it began to rain what looked like red butterflies of light...

Somewhere in a distant land had been his home, he remembered in this fire-lit darkness. He also remembered the soft caress of the water, the bright sunshine, playing with his brothers on warm reefs, he remembered trumpeting through seashells, the waves whose foam was tossed over their heads... When and where had this all been?

And then he remembered the dark clouds rising, the wind gusting over the waves, the rush of squalls as they fell over him, the crack of the thunder and the green waves of lightning as they rose to the surface of the waters, then rushed down again, howling and bellowing in a joy that could not be put into words. And their voice was like the roll of thunder, which circled the horizon... When and where had this been?

On what shore had his mother sat while rocking her baby, what sort of sparkle had her bright laughing eyes thrown out onto the air, on which threshold had she bared her full breast and put it to his mouth? And who would not remember his father, a large man with a red beard, a breastplate, and glittering armor, when he was lying in the grass of that unknown land, telling stories, then sitting up and laughing so hard that sky reverberated... Did he not remember all this as if through a thousand nights and a sea of mist?

This thought affected him so that he threw himself down on the sand, unable to get back to his feet. Above him, the sky bathed in light grew misty and the hazy island opened up. His mind grew tender and bubbled over like the fizzing of hops:

If only his mother was somewhere to be found! The people were dead, their gods were dead, everything that surrounded mankind was dead. If only his mother could be found!

Sitting thus in the sand like a child, he heard, as if from afar, the rush of the wind and the running of feet. They were approaching rapidly, and a moment later a white figure rushed past, its hair flying, its arms outstretched.

All that could be heard was the rush of the air, like a slight moan, and the splash of the waves. The wide ripple shone phosphorescent along the edge of the water.

Kurdis raised his head, but the vision was gone. Nonetheless he knew it had been the Mermaid, fleeing back into the sea. The air was still filled with the breeze of her running.

And as he grasped this fact, Kurdis suddenly heard the faint echo of an instrument playing. Now he noticed that he was still holding his kannel. The wind was playing on its strings, bringing with it the quiet thrum of music.

Now he touched the strings himself and listened. New sounds were rising from them, sounds he had never heard before. He struck the strings and a lay that was wondrously strange arose. He had never heard such music from a human instrument.

He arose with a shudder. He wanted to play, but dared not do so. He looked in wonder around him.

There before him lay the wide sea. It glittered like phosphor. The waves rolled glinting onto the sand. Everything was filled with a marvelous brilliance.

He struck the strings of the kannel again, and again came this mysterious lay. Now he began to play. He played as if he were possessed.

Before now, his playing had been soft and sad. Its purpose had been to soothe him amid the life that was all around. Now it was splendid and powerful. It was like the voice of nature itself.

Amid this playing he could hear someone singing back to him from the sea. The song approached and receded, grew faint and grew strong. It was as if the words of the waves had become music.

Still playing, Kurdis approached the water, the waves touching his legs. Now he saw, in the mysterious brilliance of the waves, how heads appeared from the sea, hair flowing, then arms beckoning.

He took his first steps into the water, and the playing of the kannel sounded louder, even louder the song of the sea. He walked steadily onwards, the water rose around him, his playing spread across the surface of the waters.

Ever deeper and deeper Kurdis waded, the water now touched the kannel, the water rose up to its strings, the water covered the strings, but his playing could still be heard through the water like the voice of the ocean itself.

And so he vanished from the world of Man and again found his brothers and sisters, his own mother—the Great Mother of all living creatures.

1919

The Air is Full of Passion

Lieutenant Lorens rode out that evening. Usually, he would have taken his batman. This was an enemy soldier he had once captured during a night attack and, against his usual practice, granted him his life so that he now followed his every step as a slave. But tonight Lorens wanted to go out alone.

He was too wrapped up in his own thoughts to be able to cope with anyone else now. He was happy and smiled in eager anticipation. And the dumb face of the slave would have gotten in the way.

The evening was warm, though the ground had cooled off. There was not the slightest breeze. The leafless trees of the forest stood watery grey under the misty sky.

Today Lorens did not wish to follow trodden paths. He let his horse wander through fields and meadows at will. He only had a league to ride, so he was not afraid of losing his way. Besides, he had often ridden this stretch of countryside.

He rode out of the village at a good speed, but where the way turned, he let his horse make its own way. The frosty ground broke crisply under the animal's hooves.

Then the rider turned off into the meadows.

Patches of black forest stood here and there in the dusk of the evening, the bushes bare as bundles of twigs. In the depressions in the meadow, smooth sheets of ice gleamed, doubling the trees and bushes. The whole landscape was like one large silent park.

At first, he could still hear muffled noises behind him; then they too faded away. The rider was now alone in a landscape silent as autumn.

He was no dreamer, yet his surroundings had an effect on him. He let the bridle hang on the horse's neck, placed his feet more firmly in the stirrups, and let the horse amble forward by itself, swaying with the rhythmic movements.

He was again overcome by sweet expectancy, as he had been back there on the road.

His hard, if handsome, face, enhanced even by the barely noticeable scar on the forehead, was smug. His upper lip, on which a clipped moustache grew, took on a somewhat cynical smile. And his grey, deeply cold eyes grew hazy with a violent, yet sweet, thought.

He had been looking forward to this ride for several days now. It gave him the same thrill as rushing headlong into the fray in fear of his life. He was a soldier and a man of the world at one and the same time.

He loved both callings with equal passion. All the more so when they afforded him great experiences to arouse his nerves. All the more when discipline and violence were inherent in them.

He knew the rules of upbringing practiced by the Samurai. Even as boys, the Samurai were confronted with the sight of blood. They were taken along to watch when people were executed, and they were not allowed to show pity. On arriving back home, they were given food that resembled clotted blood and that they had to eat without blinking.

Lorens experienced this as something close to himself. This was a discipline in preparation for bloody violence.

But he would have wanted to have the same stern discipline in another brand of violence—lovemaking.

This was also close to him personally. He understood this too as a bloody and sweetly appalling war.

For this too, one had to be trained, he thought. Not everyone, for not everyone was worthy of it, only individually chosen and passionate Samurai.

Every Don Juan had been a dilettante, was what he was thinking. Their imaginations had fed on dreams and poetry. But to have love as one's profession—that would be as ruthless and terrible as war.

And in this twofold war he recognized no boundaries save his own egotism. What was mankind to him, or mercy for the masses!

Riding through the scattered trees of the meadow, as between black towers, he was intoxicated by this austere emotion. A row of carnal bodies rose up and filled his being from top to toe. Cynicism and tenderness mixed like the alcohol in grape juice. He would have liked to shout for joy amid the dead silence of the nature around him!

He imagined the opportunities that would present themselves to him that day. He saw the alabaster shoulder of a woman with its delicate veil, her blue eyes melting into prayer before his gaze. Those eyes overflowed with love like springs, humility, prayer and invitation. He himself, however, was as heartless as the conqueror of a city!

Suddenly, he spurred his horse into a gallop. The trees flew past, the bushes flashed by, a stream twinkled to the left and right. Once again the branches of the scattered trees stretched before him in a vague wall.

Then the landscape grew hilly. Hillsides rose up with their sparse vegetation, giving way to small valleys. Night had already fallen and the wall of darkness was so close that he could hardly see more than a few dozen paces around him.

He now expected to see the main highway that had to cut through the forest, but it did not come. He halted, looked around, and turned to the right. He rode on for a while, but still he did not reach the highway. Then he turned to the left and dared his way forward.

Now the landscape grew even stranger. The land rose and fell in huge billows. Lorens shut his eyes from exhaustion. The rhythmical movements of his horse gave him the impression he was gliding over the intruding waves on a boat.

He opened his eyes again and saw that the landscape had changed yet again. The ground was completely blackened and hardly any grass grew there. Here and there, trees arose, but their branches were bare and they were just as black.

The earth droned on under the horse's hooves and a fine dust rose up, making the horse snort. It stumbled over stumps and seemed to fear the black silhouettes of the trees all around.

When Lorens surveyed the hideous landscape with astonishment, he all of a sudden saw a large bonfire atop a hill, as if it had been lit by herdsmen. It came into view and disappeared. Then it flared up for a moment, higher, bright yellow and daunting. Now Lorens saw that this was the rising full moon.

He looked around him, as if waking from sleep. Where was he?

As far as the eye could see, this black, branchless forest extended out into the bright moonlight. He now understood that this was where slash and burn land clearance had taken place.

The coal black silhouettes of the trees moved slowly across the bright backdrop of the moon, like skeletons with their stumps of branches. On some ridges they were hollowed out on one side, as if they had grown rigid in a storm.

This view deprived Lorens of every last vestige of recognition. He no longer knew whence and whither he was riding. He simply had the feeling he was rising higher and higher into the hills. Every moment new, unexpected vistas opened up, filling his thoughts with unease.

He slackened the bridle, allowing the horse to choose its own way forward.

But the horse interpreted this as indecision on the part of its rider and also began to vacillate. Heavily and reluctantly, it climbed the hills, and then descended into the dales cautiously and with fear.

This all took a long time. Lorens looked at his watch, but could not see the time, despite the bright moonlight. The air seemed full of some kind of yellow dust.

Then the rider eased himself onto his back, merely gripping the horse with his legs. He was used to riding like this. It was like the swaying you felt riding on the back of a camel in a caravan.

On both sides the black trunks loomed, then they too disappeared, and above him stretched the boundless heavens, yellowed by the rapidly rising moon. Lorens' eyes widened, when he saw this curious light: the huge orange-colored moon, surrounded by a hardly perceptible halo of light. His eyes were hypnotized by this ball of light, which seemed like the only living being in this realm of death.

A total silence prevailed all around. All that Lorens could hear was the tread of the horse's hooves. Even his heart seemed to have stopped.

A weariness seized Lorens. He had sat at the card table for two nights in a row, and the fatigue, which he had not noticed while involved in this activity, now overtook him like an enemy, in silence and loneliness.

Abruptly he made himself sit up again. He had to conquer this inertia and sleepiness. He had to do something to prevent him from riding like this till morning!

At that moment he spied a copse and a light beneath the trees on top of the hill before him. It seemed as if the horse had noticed before he had, because it quickened its step unbidden. Then under the trees, the black outline of a house, in whose windows lights winked, could be seen.

He steered his horse in that direction without hesitation.

The house was surrounded by a fence, but it was so rotten and broken down that the rider could pass over it into the yard. The house stood alone, black and silent. Its eaves stuck out in all directions like the brim of a hat over the walls, increasing the shadows around it. Only one single window was illuminated.

Lorens stopped at the window, wondering whether to call out to the occupants or jump down from his horse. He was bathed in moonlight and both he and the horse cast a black shadow in the grass. He tarried for a moment, marveling at the silence of the house. Then suddenly, he saw the figure of a man, who had clearly been standing motionlessly there under the eaves, right in front of the horse's muzzle.

"Hey, who's that?" he cried out, startled.

A couple of moments passed, then a low, barely audible voice replied:

"From the house, who else would I be?" The voice of the speaker was old, subservient and fearful. "But whence the stranger, if I may ask? Have you come from afar?"

Lorens did not reply to the old man's question, but inquired how far it was to the manor house, to which he was on his way.

"Oh, sir," replied the still muffled voice, "it is far, some twenty versts."

"Twenty versts!" said Lorens with astonishment.

"Yes, sir, even more. No one rides there at night. There are large pits and a forest in between. No one would ride there. Troubled times we have now."

Lorens stopped to think. He had obviously taken the wrong path early on. He turned his wrist to the light from the window and gazed at his watch. He had been underway for at least three hours. Then he asked, irritably:

"Is there any other house round here?"

"No," replied the voice, "there is no one. Just forest and pits. It is five versts to the village.—And the times are troubled."

Lorens shook his head in anger. It had grown late. He would never manage to get to the party now. Nor had he the energy to ride back from where he had come.

"I see," he said, "very well, I will have to stay here. I will rest out at your place."

And, without requesting lodging for the night, he jumped down from his horse. The old man heard the chink of his spurs and remained silent. Lorens reached for and adjusted his sword belt.

"Do you have stables?" he asked.

"No," replied the old man. "But the eaves are very deep here. The horse can be tied up under them. Let it feed and rest outside."

He took the horse and led it under the eaves, which stuck out straight from the walls of the house. Lorens stood and watched the black shadows of man and beast.

Then the old man returned to the front of the house.

"Well, please come in," he said and pushed open the door.

Suddenly an eye-searing flood of light shone through the doorway. Lorens stooped and entered the low door, his sword rattling against the threshold. Suddenly he saw several people whose presence he would never have imagined in such a small house.

On the table a lamp burned and around it sat three men and a woman, who seemed to be finishing their dinner.

The old man—Lorens now saw he really was old and grey—the old man said a few words about the stranger's arrival. Those sitting there lifted their heads in his direction, but without surprise, without a word, as if they had been expecting his arrival. They all huddled together on the bench under the window, leaving the table free for the new arrival. He sat down without any introduction, and asked:

"Could I have something to eat?"

He was brought milk and bread and began to eat with a hearty appetite. A few moments of silence passed. Lorens ate and his hosts, five in a row, watched him without turning their heads away.

Then the old man began to ask a few questions in order to break the silence. But Lorens was in no mood to enter into conversation. He replied in monosyllables words or simply left the question unanswered. And soon the old man was doing all the talking.

But as Lorens' hunger was sated, he began looking around him.

The room was spacious, but with a low ceiling and its corners were bathed in darkness. Then he began to feel constricted and despondent.

He began to let his eyes rest on the people before him. He didn't care for them, as is the case with people one has no dealings with. But once he had cast his eyes over the whole row, he could not help doing so again.

They aroused a feeling in him that something sinister was going on.

The three youngest men were of roughly the same age and of similar appearance, so they could have been brothers. They all wore the same ragged clothing, all had moustaches, only one had a red matted beard.

But when he regarded them for longer, he noticed the same expression on all of them. It was one of savagery—a savagery of an incomparably superhuman kind. It was impossible to say where this savagery lay, but it seemed to emanate from their silence, as they all looked at him at once.

These were somehow the faces of dogs, dogs' eyes, misshapen noses and battered brows. Their mouths, however, did not speak of the savagery their eyes radiated. They sat there motionless, their large veiny hands resting on the table like dogs' paws.

They were people whom work and isolation had turned into wild creatures, at a level to which Lorens would never want to stoop. He despised them with an inborn disregard, without even wanting to become aware of the feeling.

Only the old man seemed, by comparison, to reach out above their silent stasis. He wriggled on his chair and asked again and again, even when he received no answer.

But now Lorens noticed a strange paradox in the old man's behavior. His speech was faltering and simple, but his face was limitlessly crafty and his eyes as sharp as awls. The whole of his being seemed steeped in this mysterious spirit, which was so powerful that it affected Lorens physically.

Feeling disgust, Lorens now turned his eyes to the woman.

She was leaning back, her head resting against the plank wall, and was staring fixedly at him. She was wearing a red costume and her forearms were bare. Her feet were planted next to one another and her large hands were on her knees. The light fell from a low lamp onto her face, illuminating her jaw line more than the rest of the face. And her face looked strange in this light.

She was young and had a voluptuous figure. She had high cheekbones, her eyebrows were almost knit together, her forehead broad and smooth. But the weird aspect of her face was concentrated in her mouth. It was large, red and crying out with sensuality. Her thick lips, slightly ajar, spoke of the same natural savagery as did her brothers' eyes. They were slightly pursed, as if she were astonished at something she saw. And above them, beneath half-closed eyelids, shone moist and misty eyes, insensate as those of an animal.

Lorens had suddenly lost his appetite. He pushed away his dish and rose from the table.

"Could I take a rest somewhere?" he said, turning to the old man. "In the morning, I'll continue my journey."

"Mirandola—" the old man ordered, turning his face towards the woman.

She rose and wiggled her way across the room. Her hair was light brown and thick as a horse's mane. She opened a door near one corner and vanished into an adjoining room. But she soon returned and looked her father in the face.

"Would you be so kind," he said to the stranger, rising and taking the lamp.

Lorens stepped into a room that was so small you could hardly stretch out your arms without hitting the walls. Its narrowness and height gave it the appearance of a mineshaft. The window was covered with some thick material. A lamp burned on the table, lighting up the grim walls and the bed.

The old man wished him goodnight, his crafty eyes aglitter, then vanished.

Lorens was alone.

He was so tired that all he wanted to do was throw himself on the bed and sleep. But something kept him awake and alert. He looked around the room, tested the window—it was narrow with a thick frame—then the door, which was impossible to lock from the inside. He wavered.

Then he smiled to himself, shrugged his shoulders and began to undress. Then he thought better, merely loosened his collar, put his revolver under his pillow, put out the light and lay on the bed fully dressed. He even forgot his sword, which remained hanging at his hip.

He wanted to sleep, but as always, thoughts entered his head, thoughts from goodness-knew-where that rose for whatever reason. They were mostly of an erotic nature. He imagined several existing and non-existent situations and their physical prerequisites. These dreams were concrete and specific. He was thinking more with his body than with his mind, and therefore no one was spared his mental assaults.

Today he felt regret at not having taken advantage of his opportunities. No one could underestimate the losses incurred by the fact that he had lost his way. Maybe they would never be regained. Something that could never be recovered had been wasted!

And he analyzed these opportunities down to the last detail. The gentle presence of the young woman worked on his dreamy thoughts until she was there before him, unclothed, available. It was a still and silent violence against this delicate, virginal woman in full bloom, who was now somewhere beyond the dark forest, sleeping her innocent sleep, moaning at her violator through her very sleep.

Then Lorens began to imagine her face, her eyes, her hair, her lips. But the more in detail he imagined them, the more vigorously they began to change and multiply. And already the gentle, delicate facial traits were beginning to dissolve, turn crude and become more like an animal, and suddenly there they were pouting at him, thick, red, lustful lips...

Lorens started.

"Mirandola?" he asked, and was taken aback by his own words. "Wasn't the girl's name Mirandola? Wasn't that what the old man had called out? What an amazing coincidence! That one there and this one here!"

He tossed restlessly on the bed, tormented by the images in his head. But in the end he fell asleep. This was no restful sleep, and he did not remember having dreamt. It was more torpor than sleep. Pitch darkness covered his strong, young body with all its passions.

He did not know how long he had slept, but suddenly he started out of his sleep. He sat up.

Somewhere, from afar, from outside or from under the earth, came a strange voice, a smothered cry or whimper. He listened for several moments, then understood: it was his horse! It seemed that it was warning him or calling for help against some unknown danger!

Lorens rushed to the door, located it in his haste in the dark, hurried, stumbling over benches through the moonlit entrance hall and opened the front door.

But there he came to his senses, and a spirit of caution entered his head. He stepped outside quietly and stole over to the dark shadow of the eaves.

His horse was standing there in silence, but when Lorens stroked its flank, the creature was soaking wet, its body all a-quiver. Lorens soothed it and calmed it down as if it were a child, looking around him all the while as a precaution.

The moon had risen higher in the sky and the shadow of the house fell on the grass. Everything under the sky was bathed in a kind of silver silence. It felt as if it had grown warmer than it had been the previous evening.

Across the yard, the bare, black outlines of the trees in the copse could be seen. It stood alone on top of the hill, like a grove. A line of bushes linked the trees with the yard, and also cast their shadows on the ground.

When Lorens was gazing at this reassuring view, he suddenly saw on the whitened grass a strange shadow slipping across the yard. He raised his eyes to follow the shadow and saw there a silent, strange shape moving towards the trees. It was not a bird, he could detect no flapping of wings; it was so round that it did not seem to have any wings. All he saw in the moonlight was a dark streak in its wake. It vanished, a moment later, into the copse and was no longer to be seen.

At first, Lorens thought it was some ghost, but then it struck him that there was some intangible link between the whinnying of his horse and this strange vision. But what on earth could it all mean? Or was he still asleep and dreaming?

He looked up again at the treetops of the grove. And now he thought he could see some weird flying creature, black and solid. And everything was so horribly silent! Again, no one near this lone house, but he and his horse!

He uttered a few more soothing words to his horse and again walked by the eaves. He reached the line of bushes and behind it found a ditch, which ran parallel to them. He descended into the ditch and in the shadow of the bushes walked towards the copse.

He had not even got half way there, when he began to hear strange sounds coming from the woods. They were not the cries of animals, nor of human voices. They resembled the words of human beings, but had no resonance, like gurgling from deep down the throat. They were not coming from the earth. No, they sounded from the heavens!

Lorens was shaken by this. He became more watchful, at times wading through shallow water, sometime crawling on hands and knees along the ground. He was shaking from this horrible agitation.

Now he was nearly under the trees and looked around him. At that moment, he saw what looked like a black ball approach him with a whine, circle a bare tree and perch on a branch. And that instant he saw it was a human head, and that four such heads were perched in the tree.

It was like a bare palm tree with five coconuts!

Lorens felt his hair stand on end!

But he had still not awoken from the dream when the flying head began to speak:

"I was flying. I made a tour of the woods. I did not see anyone. The moon was shining and all was silent. All was silent."

Then another head replied—and now Lorens recognized the voice as that of the old man:

"We must be careful. They are crafty. They are ruthless. They are terrible. We must be careful!"

Another head croaked:

"He is rich. He has a lot of money. He has a nice horse. I would like to pull on his jacket and sit astride his horse. Oh, oh, how I would like to shake his money pouch!"

A third head erupted:

"Aa, he must be killed. Kill him immediately. Like a dog. Dogs deserve a dog's fate."

A fourth head replied:

"No, let's take him alive. I'd like to put him in a cage. In a cage like a duckling, with all his clothes and equipment. Fatten him like a pig, before slaughtering him."

The head laughed hoarsely and raucously, so that the branch below it shook.

"Hush! Hush!" coughed the old man. "This is a big fish, oh what a big fish. Did you not see how proud he was. Pride is a sign of greatness. He will pay whether alive or dead. He is worth his weight in gold. Take care! Take care!"

Lorens had sunk back into the bushes. He was not thinking of anything, but his survival instinct had been awoken. He groped for his revolver in his pocket, but he had left the weapon back at the house. All he had with him was his sword.

Then he heard the heads speaking:

"Did you see how fine his clothes were? Silk and velvet, while we shiver! Did you see the rings on his fingers? I'm telling you, I have never even seen such rings in my wildest dreams. Oh, if only I could pull the rings from the fingers of his corpse! The time has come. We too would like to be fine gentlemen—ho, ho, ho!"

"He is well fed," replied another head. "His cheeks are red and his hands lily white. He has slept on a feather pillow, while we have been slaving away. He has squandered his wealth, while we go hungry. Enough of the people's sweat has been spent on him! Now our time has come! Now we will get our revenge for all our sufferings! Now we will flay him alive like an eel!"

Suddenly a bare branch rustled, black hair hovered over half the tree and Mirandola's passionate cries were to be heard:

"Did you see his eyes—I'll rip them out of his face with my nails! His mouth is as red as a flower—I'll gnaw those lips to pieces with my teeth! Oh, I know him all right: he is unfaithful to women, rapes the innocent, defiles those who are upright—always so honorable and innocent himself! The hour has come to wreak revenge on behalf of all those who have been thrown out onto the street, hanged, drowned! Just hand him to me! Just hand him to me! I want to pay him back, and his father and his father's father, for all the tears that have been shed on their account, for what they have done. Just hand him to me! Just hand him to me!"

And the whole group of heads in the tree screamed and croaked hoarsely: "Revenge! Revenge!"

"Hush! Hush!" the old man admonished. "He's still alive. And he has ears. Yes, all of them have good ears.—Let one of us fly out and see what he is doing."

Whereupon one of the heads rose from the tree, circled it and glided off towards the house, with a hardly perceptible flap of its winged ears. It vanished like an arrow, and the rest waited silently on the branch as if taking a nap. But it returned a moment later, shrieking from afar:

"He's not there!"

The others were dismayed: "Not there?!"

"He's not there! His horse is feeding under the eaves, but he himself is gone. I was in his room, his bed is empty, his sword is gone, nothing of his is there. He's left!"

"What did I say," croaked another voice in accusation, "you've let him get away. It was nearly time to strike him down. Now he's gone! Now he's gone!"

Amid the babble of voices, the woman's voice could be heard all of a sudden:

"Look, there he is, in the bushes, our brave hero! Look, look, there his is lying on his stomach in the mud, the fine gentleman!"

All eyes turned to where Lorens lay—then they all stormed, howling, wailing and gnashing their teeth towards him, so that the branches rustled. Their eyes were aflame, their long teeth exposed, revealing their reddish-dark throats.

Lorens jumped up in fear of death and seized his sword. He waved it about in desperation, hither and thither, hemmed in on all sides by heads, hair and gulping faces.

The heads leapt up and down like rubber balls. There was no end to their howling rage. Every swish of the sword merely increased their wrath.

Suddenly, Lorens' sword became entangled in the woman's hair. A great shout of wordless joy came from the open jaws and they rushed like dragons at him.

With enormous effort, Lorens managed to free his sword—and cut a swathe of hair from the head, also removing the skin. The head somersaulted, screaming, into the bushes.

Now it was Lorens' turn to act. He swung the sword left and right, turned on his heels, retreated cautiously, so that he stood with his back to the trees, and swung his sword at one of the gaping mouths with all his might. The skull was cloven in two like a rock.

But the remaining heads continued the attack. They fell wounded to the ground, rolled in the grass like balls, crushing twigs and the cold earth in their desperate rage. One of them had an ear chopped off; the head somersaulted and rolled into the bushes, smacking its other ear against the ground like the tail of a fish. The ground and the bushes all around were bloody.

Then everything fell silent. Lorens was alone. He stopped and wiped the sweat of death from his brow. He breathed in deeply, as if rising from the grave.

Suddenly he felt a push in his side and nearly fell over. He jumped up and turned his eyes to the left. One of the wounded heads had come out of the bushes and jumped onto his sleeve, gripping it in its teeth.

Lorens tensed his arm, but couldn't reach the head with his sword. He shook his sleeve, smashed it against tree trunks and the ground, but in vain. The head would not budge, holding fast with its teeth.

And Lorens saw that it was the woman's head. It was ghastly. Black, bloody matted hair hung down from it. The bulging eyes gazed glassily, filled with trickling blood.

The head was dead, but even in death the brain was irreconcilable, everything still burned with ire.

Then Lorens began running towards the house, the head still clamped to his sleeve. The skull weighed him down and the bloody hair tripped him up, but he did not stop running. He untied the horse and brought it out from under the eaves. The horse snorted, whinnied and rose onto its hind legs. But Lorens finally managed to climb onto its back, hatless, sword in hand, and fled from the yard.

Lorens could afterwards remember nothing of the journey that followed. All he did remember was that he was lost in some realm of darkness. Whether this was a night forest, the embodiment of fear, or the darkness of an enfeebled mind—he just didn't know!

But he was under way a long time. He did not travel along roads, simply rode cross country. There were pits, thickets, black and blind woods, treeless knolls. And all the while darkness, black as pitch, which the moonbeams of consciousness could not manage to light up.

His appearance during this ride was ghastly: his face was contorted with fear, his hair stood on end, the skull still clung to his sleeve. It was no longer a human being that rode through the night and the woods. This was some spectral soldier.

All at once, Lorens awoke. Dawn was breaking. A pink mist was rising from the ground. The rider was at the edge of some wood. A misty moor with a cattle track stretched out before him. In the distance he caught sight of houses under the trees.

It was the village to which his detachment was billeted.

As he was looking at this view, dazed and numbed, he suddenly heard a voice behind him.

"Sir! Sir!"

Out of the bushes, leading his jade, which was frothy all over, came Lorens' slave. Even before he had come up to his master, he began to babble in a wretched sickly voice:

"Sir, I was beginning to worry about you in the night. I don't know where it came from. And there was someone who said: arise, arise, your master is in danger! So I saddled my horse and rode, rode, the whole night long, but I didn't find you, until..."

He stopped all of a sudden, his mouth open wide in astonishment.

"What are you looking at?" said Lorens dully, as if through a dream.

"Your hair has—turned white" stammered Lorens' batman.

"White?" asked Lorens and raised his arm in order to run his fingers through his hair. But the bloody head, which up to then had not been visible, rose along with it. Its hair hung down over his arm like the fringe of a shawl.

Indescribable fear could be seen on the face of the slave, who ran howling to the village.

Slowly, Lorens rode into the village alone. The people paled and retreated. He himself saw nothing. He left the froth-covered horse in the hands of his shaking slave and entered his dwelling.

He took off his coat, unbuckled his sword, and sat down at the table. All his movements were labored, like those of an automaton. Then he put the head in front of him and stared at it fixedly.

A couple of bloody wounds crossed the face, which had turned blue. The eyes were wide open, glowing with a yellow hatred, and the lips curled in a snarl, mouthing a withering curse. It was like the head of Medusa, the sight of which could freeze the blood in one's veins. And this sight gnawed through Lorens' life.

His thoughts came, slow and ponderous:

Life is a dream, a revolting, horrible dream. I am alive, but life ahead is meaningless. That head is dead, but carries its secret within it. I know nothing, and that head will say nothing. Was I asleep to life before, or am I asleep now?

Life has two faces. Before I knew the one face, now I know the other. For one it is I who am horrible. The other is horrible to me. I no longer wish to see either face. I want to see neither myself nor the world.

1920

The Poet and the Idiot

Ormusson was doing a couple of rounds of the park. Absorbed in thought, he approached the ruins, turned in the direction of the Angel Bridge, then strolled back towards the statue of Baer. Once there, he raised his head in surprise.

The old man of metal was sitting in his armchair, a book open on his lap, his hair flowing, and appeared to be reading. But then the wind blew a yellowed leaf onto the book, and the old man did not stir, as if reading the leaf. He seemed weirdly absent-minded.

Ormusson's eyes scanned the long avenue along which he had come. It was deserted, the bare trees stood motionless, an occasional yellow leaf fluttered to the ground, the odd stroller's silhouette could be seen in the distance. Everything was veiled by the wordless melancholy of autumn.

Ormusson took a few slow steps, then stopped at the brow of the hill and sank down on a park bench.

From there, his view was cut off by a row of clipped hedges, to the left a many-colored, exotic tower that had strayed here from far southern climes, but to the right was a row of leafless trees. Between their branches, the roofs of the city could be seen, the grey cinders of the yards, and, above it all, the leaden grey autumn sky.

From up here, he had always loved this city. The bench and the panorama were associated with a host of memories in his mind.

He had sat here on summer's mornings in his youth, when he had rarely gone to bed before sunrise. He had heard the nightingale in the gardens, breathed in the jasmine, and become intoxicated with the heroism of his people.

He had come here alone later on, after nights of passion, and looked out over how, across the river, a large wooden house was burning like a torch while the city was still asleep, and no one was ringing the alarm bell. (This was the time of classic city fires.) The black smoke rose vertically into space, the pillar of fire, alongside which the red wheel of the sun rose on the horizon, rose high, yet the city was still so silent... This scene was in blinding harmony with his own mood: burning, everything lost, yet consuming ever more—ever more insatiable, rich, squandering.

But this view had also seen him struggling with his art, his soul filled with a frightening asceticism. In those days he was like a monk whom the dark night had buried in the depths of his cell, his mind full of desperate visions.

Now he was looking down on the city in a mood of weariness and sadness.

There in the middle, the squat tower of Saint John's Church rose. Near the horizon was Saint Peter's slender silhouette, and, on the other side, the reddish roof of the madhouse. Between all of these were the grey shrubbery of the gardens and bricks and roofing tiles; the trays of sheet-iron roofs and of roofing felt heavy and hazy under the grey sky.

Even now, he still loved that nest of human life from above, at a distance, with space between. He forgot about the anger and the disgustingly muddy streets and the dull people. Everything receded into the distance, everything was viewed as if through a wall of glass. He simply felt that he had come from there and was linked with that city, as he was with the horizon.

If only he could avoid seeing those people, is what he was thinking. Not to have to feel their stupidity around him, which led to physical pain! Not to have to see the everyday toil, their newspapers and grocery shops, their fairs, meetings, celebrations and funerals! Not to have to meet those lawyers, shop assistants, students and society ladies! Not to have to go into the bookshops, where a sleepy fly crawls from the cover of an ABC book to the cover of a will with an idiot sitting in the other room writing an editorial! He was just gazing out over the city—and still loving it from here—with a painful, sad love.

Immediately, the same type of silent sadness arose in him as when viewing the Eternal City of Rome from Monte Pincio.

Ormusson did not notice how the figure of a man, meanwhile, was approaching under the bare branches of the trees. He was walking hurriedly, stooped slightly forward and flailing his arms about. He came nearer, stopped on the brow of the hill, muttering something to himself, turned around, saw Ormusson, raised his hat and continued on his way, at the same speed as before.

Ormusson hardly returned the greeting, as he did not know the man. He looked at him as he receded, absent-mindedly. The man was wearing a worn coat around his hunched body, his collar was turned up, one trouser cuff was tucked behind a torn spat and a worn peaked cap was pressed down on his head. His pockets were bulging so much that his coat was drawn tight around his skeleton.

But he had not gone more than twenty paces, when he turned round and approached Ormusson once more. Now Orumusson could see his face. It was pallid, with a thin growth of grey beard and blue lips, which seemed to be moving. His cap was pressed so far down over his eyes that both ears stuck out under it.

Under the upturned collar a soiled shirtfront could be seen, but the stranger was wearing neither collar nor tie.

His bursting pockets seemed almost swollen with their contents. His sleeves were so short that quite a length of his bony blue wrists could be seen.

No, Ormusson did not know this tramp. He assumed it was some beggar or other and reached into his pocket for his wallet. Then, however, he heard the man's curious, low voice:

"I see that you don't recognize me, Ormusson."

"No" replied Ormusson, hesitantly, struck by the stranger's familiar tone.

"But I know you well, though you have changed," the stranger continued. "Not surprising, not surprising," he said, shaking his head. "Fifteen, twenty years have passed—isn't that true? Or even more?"

He must be some former schoolmate of mine, thought Ormusson, a wry smile on his lips. But he had forgotten them all, down to the last man, as if making an effort to forget everything unpleasant from his past. He didn't remember one face or name. But now and again, he did bump into someone—a postal clerk, the owner of a shop, a farmer or a schoolteacher. Then he could simply not understand how he could once have shared all the joys and sorrows of such lifeless, blunt and dull people. He would see the odd one, pushing a pram out of town on Sunday morning with his fat wife, dripping with milk, a pack of food in her hand—such images made him retch.

"We used to sit next to each other," the stranger continued, as if reading Ormusson's thoughts. "We did so for two years."

"Kobras—?" asked Ormusson uncertainly.

"Yes, it's me!" the stranger brightened up in a grim sort of way.

Ormusson extended his hand involuntarily, which the stranger shook with his cold, bony, sweaty fingers.

"It's me," he repeated. "And if I'm not disturbing you, I'll sit here for a few minutes. I'm tired, and it's a long way from beyond the yeast factory.

Ormusson looked diffidently at the man sitting beside him, hardly turning his head.

So this is him; he was beginning to remember now. He had been a shock-headed, lively and joyful soul, with delicate features, as lithe as a willow wand. He had been one of those who somehow stuck in your memory, a bright flame against the dull pages of memories of school. How long ago that had all been!

Now and again, Kobras took off his cap and wiped his face with both hands like a fly. Ormusson could now see his entire head in all its wretchedness.

His hair had fallen out, a few grey wisps covered his decadent skull. Everything about him was dull and hazy, perhaps because of the yellowish light of the autumn evening. Only his sunken eyes glowed with restless life.

He wiped his face and continued:

"You've forgotten me—oh, I understand that. I understand it very well. Not worth remembering. But I have always followed what you've been doing in life. And that too is understandable. Quite understandable. I've read every line you've written. You might say that every comma is familiar to me. I'm a great admirer of yours."

He stopped the flow of words, then carried on:

"I have to admit that there have been passages I don't agree with, you'll have to forgive mc for saying so. You're a bit of an *aestheticizer*. And the world just isn't that beautiful. Mankind is disgusting! And you write so much about women, but don't you see that they're not that important? They're not important for *men*. You can get by without them."

This thought surprised Ormusson. He had had the same negative thoughts himself about his own writings. He looked at Kobras in astonishment.

"The world is much more guileful a place than you want to see," he continued. "It belongs to very crafty people,—belongs to *one* guileful being. And that is a *male* being, not a woman." He stressed the last sentences, placing special emphasis on them. "But that is kept secret. It's all in the shadows, that thought. Looks as if there's an agreement not to utter it aloud. But haven't you ever thought it? Tell me, you who've thought so much, has the thought never crossed your mind? That it's a guileful, intelligent and male being?"

Ormusson naturally edged away from the speaker. Next to him was a madman, an idiot, as if he hadn't seen it right away! But he did seem to be a calm and harmless madman, of whom you didn't need to be too afraid.

How many degenerates of every sort in this city, and those tempted by evil! There was probably nowhere else in the world where there were more than in this hole. Some days he thought that half the population of the madhouse had turned up, spread out across the city, sowing the seeds of their bleak and horrible affairs.

He had seen such people on the main streets every day— the prophets, geniuses, Ophelias with flowers, commanders-in-chief with their tin medals, proclaimers of thousand year Reichs, those who knelt before shop signs, those who prayed to the sun, the agoraphobics or the grand souls strutting with the steps of madmen, their hair flying, their eyes ablaze. They wrote hymns, got involved in politics, preached, ran countries, swallowed pills, mourned eternally, laughed their unending laugh, every one frozen in some pose or other, wearing the unchanging mien or costume of madness. And sometimes it struck Ormusson that this city was eternally cursed on account of those lunatics.

Now one of them was sitting next to him, a new one, whom he had never seen before, who had dragged himself into the park from some unknown lair beyond the yeast factory.

"Yes, I've pondered the question," said Ormusson with a wry smile. "But it's too profound a question for the likes of me.

"It *is* a profound question!" said Kobras, seizing on his words. "Profound! I've thought a lot about it. My head sometimes *aches* from the thought, my whole body aches. But now I've reached it. Now I've got it!" But now Kobras' jubilant voice turned into a meek whisper, and he bent his head towards Ormusson. "Sometimes it wants to slip out of my grasp. I keep hold of it with all my strength, but it wriggles and tries to escape. And so I lose it for a day or two. You understand what it means to lose it for a day or two? It's horrible. I wander around, I am ill, the whole of me aches, and I am searching for it. Everyone wants to take it away from me or hide it, so I can't say anything aloud. Its enemies are everywhere.—You imagine they can't hear, as I tell you these things?" he asked all of a sudden, pointing at the church tower. "They're listening. They know. They're like a lightning conductor, picking up my thoughts, so that this world doesn't burst. That would be a conflagration! But I always have to be on my guard and keep my thoughts under control."

He fell silent for a moment, and Ormusson had nothing to reply. He only looked at the man sitting next him with a sad introverted gaze.

At that moment, a longhaired student wearing a worn student cap passed by, a skeleton of some animal under his arm. The student had no coat on, despite the chilly autumn weather. The bones seemed even paler than they were against his dark jacket. The jaws of the skull were open in complaint.

"The skull is the symbol of death," said Kobras, waking to this scene. "We all carry such symbols within us. But no one thinks of the fact that there is a skeleton concealed within him. No one wants to know that, while they are eating, drinking and making love to women, who are themselves no more than hidden skeletons. The same with my idea. It is in everything, but no one wants to admit it. They do not understand it, for to do so they would have to forget all else. You have to become a monk, who fasts and kills the flesh. I have reached that far. I bow down to that in truth and in spirit."

"The guileful being—?" said Ormusson in a mocking tone.

"The very one. I've managed to catch up with him now. He no longer runs away from me. And even if he did before, that wasn't because I myself wasn't certain enough. I myself am not worthy of him. And since I'm still so far from being so, I need you."

"Me?" said Ormusson, expressing surprise.

"You, you, you!" cried Kobras, his eyes ablaze, which startled Ormusson. "You imagine, don't you, that I just chanced upon you. Not at all. I have been following you for a long time. I could have gotten hold of you on a couple of occasions, but then my idea happened to be in eclipse, had been hidden from me. And then what would I have said to you? What good am I without my idea in my head? Today I followed you for a good while, and my idea has managed to stay in my head. Today we are together, you, me and my train of thought!"

Ormusson felt a shudder pass through his whole body and looked around hesitantly.

"So what do you need me for?" he asked cautiously.

"I'll tell you my idea, then you will not refuse to help me!"

Kobras leaned against the back of the bench and looked Ormusson in the eye, breaking off as if something had already been agreed upon.

"But I don't actually yet know your—idea," muttered Ormusson.

"You soon will!" cried Kobras triumphantly. "But it's a long story. Not an easy matter. It involves history and philosophy, ethics and theology. Theology, if you like, turned on its head, but theology nonetheless.—I want to speak to you about a new belief," he whispered, bending towards Ormusson's ear.

"Belief? But you ought to know that I'm not in the slightest bit religious. In fact, religion disgusts me. I just can't bring myself to say anything on such topics."

"Ah yes, but there is belief and belief. I call it belief, because I can't find a better word for it. But it's something quite different. It's an idea! When it arose in me for the first time, I cried out like someone from under whose feet the earth had been torn away and whom the air could no longer support. And when you hear what I've got to say, you won't look at me like that any more."

Ormusson felt uneasy. He would have liked to free himself from this madness, but at the same time he was beginning to grow a bit curious about the whole matter.

He felt the constraint and suffocation of being too close to a madman, but he didn't want to rise abruptly and leave.

All the bitter and crazy experiences of the past few days seemed to be coming to a head here. It was necessary to voluntarily descend the vortex of madness and senselessness to the lower depths.

"Tell me then," said Ormusson submissively.

"You say 'tell me'. But how can you tell an idea? I want to convey thoughts—thoughts, feelings, experiences, not just words! But all that human beings utter is words. My thoughts are floundering inside me, but once they've been put into words, they are no longer mine any more."

He stopped again, as if collecting his faculties.

"Look," he said, "you saw that man going by just now with a skeleton. There is profound wisdom in bones. Bones are the threads that keep thoughts together. A mollusk does not think, even though it is alive. But, to my mind, an Egyptian mummy does think, even though it is dead. What kind of idea can stir in a bleached skull, where there is not the soft pulp of the brain for it to mingle with! It is not vodka that you drink from the chalice of the skull, but philosophy. I express myself more willingly, only when my flesh has been boiled off my bones in one of Genghis Khan's forty cauldrons."

"Well, then eloquence no longer exists," said Ormusson, smiling.

"Oh but it does! In the orbits of eyes, teeth, skulls."

"But in the end you no longer have any use for it."

"Yes, that's right, no use. But what use do I have for it now? Sometimes I think to myself: isn't this all in vain, all this gnawing at your soul? Then I think again: no, you must, you've been entrusted to do so, do not hide your light under a bushel. Yes," his voice sank to a whisper, "tonight it will appear to me again in person and say: come and belong to me, come, even if you are stoned to death!"

"Who?" asked Ormusson, shuddering.

"He Himself, Satan, Beelzebub, the Devil," said Kobras solemnly pronouncing every syllable. "Come and belong to me, he said, bind thy feet with the law which hitherto has been trampled upon, build sacrificial altars, which have been scattered, proclaim my name to all that live on the earth, under the earth, and flying through the air. My time has come, my realm is nigh'. The world is ripe, the world thirsts for me, it is time for me to come. From the great struggle in chaos, which tore down the false frontiers between light, right and virtue, where my Brother entered in triumph into the human consciousness, the world has not been as ready to accept me as now. Look to the bottom of the sea: there steel human beings with eyes of glass move, reconnoitering. Look into the air: there flies a winged human being, peering down. They are searching for me. Art, philosophy, even belief, yes, religious belief has served my purpose. The walls of ancient temples have been sapped. The great day will come when they crumble to dust. And that will be my day! Come and hear!—And there was nothing left for me to do but act as I had imagined for so long."

He wiped his forehead and continued more calmly, as if this were a performance:

"Now listen to what my idea is. I will approach it in a roundabout way. But it is clear as only truth alone can be.

Have you never thought about mankind and the difference between its Devil and its God? Have you not noticed that every nation and every person creates his own Devil or God, each according to his capacity for thought? The cruder the being, the cruder his Devil or God. The more complex the mind, the more complex these superior beings. In this way, as the human psyche changes, they too change, let us call them *gods* the way the ancients did: they evolve, materialize, become ideals and abstractions in such a way that they almost cease to exist. But this only affects their method of understanding, not their essential being. First of all, this affects the national manifestations of the Devil and God. And this is one of my fundamental premises.

We know that the characteristics of godliness appear in different forms, spread out over several gods. There are specialist gods for war, love, art and various other types of human activity. They work within their narrow discipline and can thus even come into conflict with other gods. So it was in Ancient Egypt, Greece, and Rome. As early as in Judaism did these gods unite to form a collective God. He was the great subordinator and unifier, a monarchist and centralist, the destroyer of the autonomy of the gods. According to legend, he threw his only remaining rival off the throne and down into the deep.

But this God, now arisen, was still only the God of one nation. His powers were confined by the bounds of that nation. His blessings only went out over one nation, beyond was only the God of Evil, Satan if you like.

But a couple of thousand years ago, the monotheistic belief of the Jews began to spread right across the world. It was like a germ, eating away at the bodies of the other gods. The national Jewish God became international, his psyche international. In this way he lost all the specifically national characteristics, he rose in the air, his character pure contour. He was no longer an individual, had become something without character, without a name. He tried, with much effort, to retain his national forms. In Syria women danced in Christian temples in his honor while in Abyssinia he fused with former shards of belief. Not until the total victory of Catholicism was his final featureless and formless essence determined.

This international God was reborn before the spirit of nations was born—and that was his misfortune. He lost an organic link to His worshippers. He was no longer a bone from among the nation's bones, flesh from the nation's flesh. Whole peoples could die out, without this God affecting the course of events. But how could the Jewish nation die, yet their God live! Nietzsche—read him, he is my precursor—already shows how, by becoming cosmopolitan, God necessarily degenerates. His pull weakens, his style grows dim, as many styles are mixed within Him. He is like translated literature—a God translated into many tongues and ways of thinking. His temperament slackens, his aggressive ways change to listlessness, because he no longer has rivals. He can no longer depend on any one people, as He lacks His own. How absurd when enemy nations pray to the same God for victory!

And yet, as soon as Roman culture and the assimilatory tendency of Catholicism lost their grip, the general God began to take on traits of particular peoples. National churches and schisms were the result. Great European nations each began to create their own versions of Christianity, which were only prevented from descending into the ultimate schism by the rock-firm tradition of the Bible. What is more, even in Catholicism, the deity was split up into a thousand saints, each with their own special task.

Only the smaller nations, those that had lacked political and cultural independence, had not managed to give a national semblance to their God. They had to borrow both their secular and heavenly leaders. They had no say in either quarter.

The acceptance of Christianity everywhere seemed inevitable. Paganism no longer had the strength to survive. The spirit of the times needed Christianity. Even we, the Estonians, could not let that chalice pass by. To a certain extent, to drink from it was a necessity. It is without a doubt that ancient Estonians voluntarily—that is to say, without the coercion of crusading knights—became Christians. They would even have done so later on. Maybe not before 1400, maybe even later. Under ideal circumstances it would have become some kind of compromise between paganism and Christianity, where the old myths and the new would be conflated to form a kind of pagan Christianity; under less favorable circumstances at least some kind of independent Christian church would have arisen, as happened in Abyssinia. At any rate, the national spirit would have been reflected in the belief in God.

But unfortunately our Christianity was forced upon us too vigorously and by force of arms. We received an inalienably foreign belief and God. Our society tried desperately, during the Middle Ages, to hold onto paganism, keep it separate from Christianity, but nothing came of this compromise. When, later on, the Germans made revisions with respect to their own God, changing his nature somewhat, they ultimately brought us their God in a transmogrified guise. That was the *petit bourgeois* German God of the Reformation, who has never developed further. Our Church has never been a national church, nor have the people been able to exercise any influence over the type of God worshipped. A church belonging to the overlords, an overlords' God.—Are you listening, Ormusson?" Kobras asked suddenly, as if waking from his own speech. "Do you understand what I'm telling you?"

"Yes," said Ormusson with a start. "It's all quite clear."

"But what didn't succeed on the one hand, succeeded on the other," continued Kobras, now in a lower tone of voice, a half-whisper. "This happened to God's opposite pole, the Devil. The creative spirit of the nation has remained distant from God, and God has remained distant from the nation. All the creative spiritual instincts of our people have turned towards the Devil. And here they have had a certain measure of success!

It is strange that the belief in the one God did not lead to a belief in the one Devil. Monodemonism has never been a condition for belief, although it has, in Christianity, been regarded as logical. Quite the contrary, the Church has accentuated the existence of the sheer number of devils and their differences. Did you know how many Satans live in Hell, according to the demonologist Bodinus? There are 72 princes of darkness and 7,405,926 lesser devils of all ranks. That is a pretty large number, against which the Church has had nothing to say. Nor did the Church want to circumscribe the imagination of the people in that area of knowledge. Quite the opposite. It encouraged every initiative in this field. The larger the number of devils and the more hideous they are, the better things stand! Then the help of the Church is needed all the more!

Our nation especially has gone in for research into the nature of the soul of the Devil. Unfortunately, such research took place during times when slavery was at its height, so that no subtlety could develop in the work undertaken. But it is not the results that count, but the direction in which thought moved. When examining devils during the Middle Ages, there is no doubt that ancient shamanism developed further. Only in that branch of knowledge was a compromise arrived at with regard to the former and the present belief, because in this area the Church was less watchful. Read our folk poetry and you will see for yourself! What a collection of stories about *vanapagans, tonts and kratts.* What had Christian folk poetry to offer as an alternative? The people had a dozen names for the Devil. Where was there such a variety of official names given to God by the Church? How the imagination of the nation has been captured by the person of the Devil! The people know that not only human beings suffer from being alone, but also the Devil. We can see in stories from the island of Saaremaa that the Devil has a wife. This madonna's name is Babylona. And that family has a son whose name is Kurit. We have created devils who are not necessary for the faith. We have varied them, discovered amusing, robust individuals among them that interest people. We have related to them psychologically, set them in local surroundings while our relations to God are cool and official, beyond tome and space. There is a burgeoning, never-ending imagination at play in our investigations into the nature of devilry. In its everyday life, the Estonian people need the name of the Devil ten times more than they need that of God. While we decide that we are Christians by God, we are Satanists in the light of the Devil. *And we must fully exploit our nation's imagination with regard to the Devil.*—Do you see what I'm driving at?" cried Kobras in a solemn whisper. "Do you see what I mean?—No, you don't, do you? But let me explain. I never tire of explaining. This is the whole tenor of my argument. And if someone does not understand, then they do not understand anything of me.

I'm not talking about that Devil we know from Christianity and rudimentary folk poetry. I'm simply talking about the tendency that has arisen of late. I have always had respect for that brilliant idea, even when I was blind and my eyes unseeing. Even as a child scripture and religion interested me more than anything else. I was like the woman who was fooled in church and saw how the Devil wrote the names of those dozing off on a horse's skin, stretched the skin with his teeth and stuck it up on the wall. Then I laughed, because I was still blind! By thinking about him, I cultivated my imagination later on, and devoted more time to intellectual pursuits. What horizons his genius have opened up to me! He has awoken an understanding of science and art in me, as every form of art is of the Devil. And I only realized this when I no longer thought *my own* thoughts. He had instilled in me a capacity for devilish meditation and to see the world and existence through quite different eyes. Over the years, my interest in him has turned into an intimate friendship. And I can say without exaggeration that I know the Devil personally in such and such a guise. Believe you me, these are my findings about him, from the horse's mouth! And now I know that everything within me originates with him, I live in him and will die in him. There's something for you to think about!

The important thing is that the Devil has not changed from being national to being international. Nor has he taken on the specific guise belonging to one particular nation. He is not a collective, but an individual phenomenon. His being has not become petrified in dogma, nor in any particular canon. There has been no Augsburg Confession to circumscribe him. Nor does he demand a catechism be followed. For him, a frame of mind suffices. Not the Christian's confession of faith, but a devilish reverence!

All that is written about him is more or less personal, even Mr. Milton's dreary tales or the pamphlets of the clergy, so lacking in spirit. You can even say that when people have described his qualities, they have made him too fantastic a figure. They have exaggerated the Devil in a mocking sort of way. And this is not surprising, since only his enemies have written about him! They have been biased, one-sided and unjust out of self-interest and submissiveness to God. He, who has been portrayed as a pitiful and evil being, has not received his fair share of love and justice. Listen, I'm asking you now, has any love of one's neighbor ever been shown with regard to the Devil? And yet he is more than an acquaintance of ours. Perhaps only the Cainites of the Caucasus have prayed to God for his soul, something that is very humiliating. What manner of disgusting wrongs have been attributed to the Devil, what has he not been accused of! He has been exploited to justify the lowest of sins. He has been regarded as a sinner when in fact he is no other than Man himself. As if it would interest the Devil to tempt *everyone*! No, mankind is of little interest to him. He has enough to do looking after himself. His taste is too good for him to be running after every evildoer. When he does, on occasions, take a loving interest in someone, it is only to the extent that Goethe meant when he said:

> *Und hätt' er sich dem Teufel nicht ergeben,*
> *Er müße doch zu Grunde geh'n"*

Kobras seized Ormusson's hand. His hand was glowing, his eyes sparkled in the growing dusk, as he whispered:

"But all the wrongs he suffers don't mean a thing to the Devil. He has simply ignored them. He has paid them little attention. While God has defined the borders around him with clarity, and punished anyone who would wish to change them, the Devil is tolerant and well meaning. He never dismisses any form of imagination. He resigns himself to it as a human weakness. He does not jealously guard his own guises. He accepts whatever guise allows him to offer all manner of imagination. He is glad at every genuine attempt and act of good will. He is loving and forbearing. He does not thrust his person forward. He waits patiently. He does not seek public fame. He rarely receives credit as the genius of the people! He knows that mankind is weak and dreamy. He therefore knows mankind well, so that there is a lot that is human in him. He knows people's weaknesses and evil aspects, but he doesn't make so big a thing of it as does God. He even supports and succors people in their weakness. He does not keep aloof from blessedness, virtue and goodness. Oh, they can manage without him. But he understands those who are burdened and tempted very well. For he too has had to suffer the same fate. He has not pushed his personal problems onto mankind. He accepts the fact that people bow down to him in thousands of variations, that he is in the same situation as were the Greek gods in the public consciousness. But he does not suffer, does not struggle, does not have the intolerant egotism of the Christian God. It's not important to him! No, he doesn't even get angry at the fact that people tend not to believe in his existence. Oh, he knows the all-consuming poison of doubt only too well. He leaves mankind free to think that such a possibility exists. And in the end, it doesn't affect his absolute existence. And what's more, it is possible that he is only a figment of his own imagination! And that would be one of his most remarkable qualities. What reverence a power of the will evokes, that is created by the one who himself wills! Not the world as idea and will, but the world as will. That mad old philosopher whose bitter gaze encompassed the world began to realize the true value of things. He realized, he realized, but dared not speak..."

It had grown dark. A chill breeze stirred the bare branches of the trees. The branches swayed, creaking. A few black leaves whirled before the feet of the two sitting men, then lay motionless on the ground.

But Kobras talked on. He was intoxicated with himself. He spoke as if in a dream. On occasion, he would seize Ormusson's arm, stare at him with his insane eyes, and whisper breathlessly.

Now Ormusson was under the influence of the flow of words. He no longer tried to escape. He felt only physical and mental pressure. He was hemmed in on all sides by this madman's frenzy. It rose up from the bare trees, the seemingly misty labyrinth of the city, and the gloomy horizon. And the idiot's voice continued to ring in his ears, like a faint instrument in an orchestra of madness.

"A great lie has held sway over the world for millennia," said Kobras hoarsely. "This is a false way of treating the Devil. Conditions for the right way have been poor. Art and philosophy have idealized and refined

God, making Him more profound. No one has cared about the Devil! Medieval man was too crude to regard the refined being of the Devil. He was a savage who smacked of the Inquisition and the rack. And he imagined the Devil to be equally savage. Luther, who made some attempts to reform religion, found nothing more intelligent to do than throw a vulgar inkwell at him. What naïveté! The Devil has only reached the Middle Ages until now. He is still Dante's Inferno and the fresco of the Campo Santo in Pisa. In such circumstances, he was unable to develop. It was not his epoch. He maintained his individuality and, with it, his spiritual being, while God became international and general, and became regarded as blessed. The Devil bided his time, waiting for better, more beautiful, more hopeful times! Now philosophical thought concerns him as well. He shall free scholasticism. A Reformation truly worthy of our epoch will take place on his behalf. And when he finally becomes universal, we will have a truly cosmopolitan human being in a cosmopolitan psyche. Only then will the golden age of pan-demonism begin!

You need a refined and subtle soul to understand this. God is the God of the crowd, His realm is that of the poor of heart. Among His followers the Devil cannot find true believers and admirers for himself! The Devil's congregation includes thinkers, scientists, inventors. They are near to him, and he to them. They embody that poisonous thirst, longing, and the flame of doubt, which never reaches those who spend three hours in church every week. The Devil is too spiritual and elastic a concept to be able to be tolerated by the present *petit bourgeois* materialistic way of thinking. His tragic pose is an aristocratic one. If you've grasped that, you will understand what I am thinking!

The Devil's deep, undisturbed meditation continues, in space and silence. God created a world and fell asleep. The Devil created a world and carried on thinking. His attitude toward his many personifications, the attitude of his being to being—that is what he thinks about. Finding a resonance between his own being and being as a whole, that is what he has been striving for from time immemorial. Yes, he has yearned for a final form like God has. He has thirsted for the absolute, but in and of itself, not in Man's image, as God has done. He has had countless opportunities to change his mind, to sit once more at the right hand of God as His brother. But this is where his own independence as a being begins, the mystery of his great fall! His noble desire for respect grows larger. His dream is, in shedding his individual being, to become universal, an indivisible devilish absolute. But this would have to be something more perfect than God is. He would have to encapsulate all sides of good and evil, embody all tendencies toward evil and blessedness in one fell swoop. His symbol has always been the tree of good and evil. And one day this synthesis will be at hand!

In dealing with all this, let us ignore the idea as to what would have happened had the Devil remained in heaven as an angel or vassal of God. The thought is a false one. From personal experience I can only confirm that it *is* a falsehood. The Devil has never waged war against God. It never struck him to take God seriously.

He has had enough to do, looking after himself! He has seen everything as if through a veil, and so God has often seemed to him a mere dream. And in this nebula of doubt his thought has thickened, its misty spirals have come together, ever denser than the yolk of the firmament, from which a sun will one day be born. And at length, when his tautness of thought has risen to its pinnacle, a glittering ocean of light will be born, like a sea of electric fire from a thundercloud. Do not forget what the name Lucifer means: the Bringer of Light! And do not forget how the Jesites of Syria picture the Devil—the sun being the symbol of the peacock!"

Kobras was gasping with enthusiasm. He had risen from the bench and was bowing in front of Ormusson. He hissed:

"Now I will tell you my idea: we shall found a new belief, a new religion, a new Church. That shall be the Church of Satan. Do you want to do so? Do you?"

"Me?" stammered Ormusson, waking from his dreams. "What could I do in this matter?"

"You? You are the prophet. You are the man that cries words over the world like fire. You will perform miracles so that they believe. They will listen to you. To you, if they listen to anyone."

"No," said Ormusson, shaking his head. "That's for you to do. You have arrived at this idea, you also should put it into practice."

"Oh no, I cannot speak in front of crowds!" said Kobras aghast.

"Then write it all down."

"Do you imagine that I haven't already done so? Look, look!" he cried, pulling bunches of papers from all his pockets. "Look here, it's all written down, all my thoughts over weeks, months, years. I have begun over and over again, broken off halfway, started all over again. This is my work, entitled "Apologia for the Devil." The only reason I have not forgotten all of my idea is because I have committed it to paper—But that's not how it's meant to be!" he sighed. "It's not all meant to be writing. What is needed are words of flame! Letters of lightning are needed! But I don't possess them. I am but a poor man. My words do not take wing. That's what you will have to do. And you can. You will be believed. You are not mad, as they accuse me of being."

"Mad! Have they said that about you?"

Kobras nodded sadly.

"They have—but I'm not actually mad. It's just that my idea makes me desperate. But what an idea it is! My reason darkens when you think of it!—Do you want to help me?"

"No," said Ormusson as if freeing himself from something.

"You don't want to! You don't want to!" groaned Kobras in despair. He slumped down onto the bench again and was silent for a while. He then grasped Ormusson's hand again and continued passionately: "Listen, those are not the outer limits of my idea. They extend further. Even I cannot detect the furthest frontier. It disappears before me into an infinity I run towards, but never catch up with. But listen, listen to what I have to say about as far as I *can* see!

You remember that I mentioned God's evolution from a multiplicity of gods, via the god of one nation to becoming an international God? This is also the triumphal route of my God-Devil! In the same way as Yahweh was the monotheistic God of the Jews, so the Devil will one day become the god of Estonia. It is he who gives us our strength and who makes our arms and thoughts invincible. Can you grasp this dream? But then, when he has taken hold of our souls, when he has become an individual, when he has passed through this stage of his development, as Yahweh did for the People of Israel—then he will begin to penetrate the world beyond the frontiers of our nation. Do you see now what I'm driving at? Can your thoughts range across the whole panorama? Think, before us lies the world, we are guided by a pillar of flame in the desert, we are the messianic people, among us the new God will be born, one that shall inherit the Earth! My mind is melting in the heat of the very thought!

You remember how we, in the same place as we are now, used to muse so often, as small boys, about the future of our nation. We were enthused, aflame, our plans knew no bounds, we looked down over the city and thought to ourselves: this is *our* city, around it stretches *our* country, where *our* people live. *Our people*! How that thought filled our hearts! But we were like the Jews in bondage in Egypt, under foreign rule, because we did not have the power and lacked a unifying idea. Now, I have found it. Think, it is our culture that spreads like wildfire across the globe. This little country was once like tiny Palestine, with its holy places. The river down there is like the Jordan, which people come to view from afar. To people of the future, the past history of the Estonian people could be like the Old Testament. Never since the Jews has the destiny of a single people been like ours!

But only if you wish it to be so! If you wish it! I bow down to you. I do not wish to be at your side. I am like a humble John the Baptist or, if you like, Judas the Baptist. I could be like a shadow at your side, only you and I would be nothing.—Do you want to?"

"No!" cried Ormusson and jumped up abruptly. "If I have to go mad, please allow me to do so on my own terms! And why are you tempting me? Why don't you turn to someone else, who is more interested in such things?"

"Have I not tried!" whispered Kobras sadly. "But what's the use? I tried myself at first to promote my idea. I appeared at all sorts of meetings and spoke, admittedly in veiled terms, about my idea. I have attended the annual general meeting of the literary society, but five members present voted that my proposal be examined by a seven-man committee that never met. I spoke at a gathering of farmers, but they suspected I was a Socialist, and at a property-owners' meeting where no one had even heard of Christianity. Then I wanted to publish my "Apologia for the Devil"; I advertised that it would appear in three years' time, but nevertheless did not publish it. So I turned to the editor of a major newspaper in order to explain the importance of my idea for the nation and to ask his help, but he didn't hear me out, and simply said: listen, young man, could you not apply your efforts to some genuine work? Then I went to see a doctor who was interested in religion, but he answered me with the explanation: yes, if you want an explanation as to Lembit's beliefs... That is how I was treated. You are my last hope. What am I going to do?"

Kobras' voice had grown melancholy and broken. He had grown tired of expounding his great idea and of the physical effort involved. His thoughts began to grow muddled and he had begun to stammer. Finally, he fell completely silent.

They stood there alone in the darkness under the trees. The city below them was black. Lamps were being lit. It was as if they were standing before an abyss in whose depths fireflies were glimmering. It was ghastly and detached.

Ormusson was trembling from sheer nerves. He had run out of curiosity and had satisfied his need to experience strangeness. Now he just wanted to go into the light, among people—even those people who were walking down there. It was so suffocating, so sickening, so stifling to be in the presence of this madman!

But he didn't go anywhere. He knew that, as soon as he began to go, the madman would resume his diatribe. Only by running away could he possibly still escape.

But as they remained there, a window in the tower across from them lit up, casting a broad swathe of pale light across the brow of the hill. At the same moment, they saw the student was approaching with slow step, the skeleton under his arm just as before. He raised his student cap and said to Ormusson:

"Comrade, would you like to buy a monkey's bones from me?"

"A monkey's bones?" asked an astonished Ormusson.

"Good bones," the man explained. "A full-blooded *Pithecia Satanas*. I can assure you, the skeleton is complete. All that is missing is a small vertebrae in the tail."

"But what would I do with the bones?" asked Ormusson in astonishment.

"You're not a zoologist? What a pity. But it's a damned good skeleton. I'm reluctant to sell it, but I need the money."

"Sorry—don't need one."

"But maybe you could buy it, after all? Give it to a friend, or keep it yourself as a momento? Eh?"

"No."

Suddenly Kobras whispered:

"Buy it anyway."

"But what for, for heaven's sake?"

"Give—it—to me," the idiot muttered. "I would hang it on the wall as a crucifix. I have the cross already, but not the Christ."

Ormusson grabbed his wallet and paid the necessary sum. But the moment that Kobras took the skeleton from the student, Ormusson vanished into the darkness of the park.

It was a gloomy autumn evening, depthless and void as primeval chaos. Shadows rose on every side like fantastic materializations of madness. In them the last logical fragments of human thought seemed to scatter.

2.

Ormusson ran up the stairs to his quarters panting. There was no hall on the second floor, the steps ended at the door. It looked as if they continued beyond. The door was merely a partition in a continuous flight of stairs. Ahead of him lay another run to take his breath away, up the endless stairs, through further locked doors.

Ormusson pulled the key out of his pocket, fumbled his way to the lock, opened the door, and pushed his way in. He then turned, thrust the key in the keyhole on the inside and locked the door. The link to the disgusting madness outside had been broken. It yawned like a chasm behind him.

He threw his coat, wet with autumn, onto a coat hanger and lit the lamp. The dim light from the table lamp shone like dawn over the dark furniture, the books and pictures. Then Ormusson drew the curtains, so that at least one cube was separated from the sense of autumnal night and filled with protective light.

Ormusson stopped in the middle of the room. After all that had happened, it was marvelous to do something, move to the right or left, stand or sit. All he could do was be, and to marvel in horror.

For a moment, everything seemed futile. Something great had rolled away from him, even if only great madness. Half the city was in flames—could he now go back to his stamp collection? Every once in a while, he experienced someone's great passion, and although this time it came from the madhouse—it really was a great idea and a passion. What was a trivial stamp collection by comparison!

Ormusson threw himself on the sofa, his head against one armrest, his patent leather shoes resting on the floor at the other end. His body lay aslant along the length of this blood-red piece of furniture, heavy and abrupt. In front of him the lamp burned, surrounded by a halo of yellow light.

For a while he was entirely thoughtless. He just felt the glowing of his nerves, worked up in him by the madman. His fear abated inside the locked door, now he was on his own. All that remained was the blaze of the ideas rushing through his sizzling nerves. He enjoyed this for a brief moment, like an opium smoker.

Inverted paradises opened out in front of him—those of madmen, hunchbacks, dwarfs. Pandemonium reigned, at whose portal stood two black papposilenes, supporting the weight of the new values on their shoulders like caryatids. There were the figures of shamans at the door of a tent—twenty-humped camels passed by. It was pleasant to see their train—without thought, and without longing.

The tedium that had smoldered as spleen until then now burst into flame. It had not burned openly for such a long time. It had seemed as if everything had been extinguished under the ashes of his blasé middle-aged mind. Now the weariness exploded, becoming filled with pathos, like tragedy.

So what if the ideas were but negative ones, if the ideology was turned on its head, carrying within it the pathos of *à rebours*? These ideas were still powerful, causing people to pale like birch bark, and causing the hairs on their heads to stand up. In this state of mind, it didn't matter whether the mood emanated from the hollow reed of Prometheus or the brain of a madman.

All of a sudden, Ormusson jumped up from the sofa and strode over to the bookshelves in two strides. He snatched a volume from the silent row of books and tossed it onto the table. The book had nearly six-hundred pages and was entitled:

HISTOIRE DU DIABLE. Tome premier. Contenant un Détail des circonstances, où s'est trouvé, depuis son Bannissement du Ciel, jusqu'à la Création de l'Homme... Tome second, qui traite de la Conduite qu'il a tenue jusqu'à-present & des moïens don't il se fert pour venir à bout de ses Desseins... Amsterdam, MDCCXXIX.

Didn't Ormusson know all this already! Hadn't he read a little about demonology and what the Gnostics had to say about the matter? Only recently had he read Saint Augustine's polemic with old Manes, who was interested in a strict dualism. He had furnished his life with books filled with sick thoughts, just as you would furnish a room with furniture.

But now there was a surfeit of such furniture. His library had become a whirling wilderness of sand, without plants, without animals. There was no link to the recently uttered thoughts of a living soul. A cloud of sand whirled up into your eyes from the lines of the folio editions!

– No, a true blaze of thought can only be ignited by a living person, seeking words for his passion, however fumbling or warty and racked by birth pangs they might be. By suffering these thoughts once again, at that very moment, he is digging a well in the desert and planting palms. He is giving birth to oases just as a woman does to children, themselves crying out with pain.

– But when the coconuts have ripened, caravans of merchants arrive and take them off to the markets of the world. In some university department someone is sawing through the shell of a coconut, weighing the flesh and giving the coconut milk to thirsty children. At the same time, the strong, hot, sand-laden wind drives through the desert, wind whirling up the sand over the oasis, and the nomad is felling the palm trunks for his camp fire.

Ormusson burst into bitter laughter. Once again a whirlwind of reassessment was blowing within him. It blew the waste paper of his life hither and thither—and swept the books from the table with its hand. They landed on the floor with a thump, like the severed heads of dwarfs falling from the scaffold.

He was now thinking more calmly: no thought was any longer really a thought once it had been removed from its context. Thought evaporates like spirits and turns into dry literature. Only at the meridian point of time and space did thought ignite and become fire. One step to the left or the right—and all you had was a tepid lie!

He again thought of Kobras. In these madman's thoughts lay something from their time and place. Who could guarantee that they were not based on truth? But you then had to ask yourself who in their thoughts was mad, and who sane. Madness, sheer madness! But today it was all painfully true as far as his nervous system was concerned.

Ormusson put out the lamp and threw himself onto the sofa once more. He lay there in an uncomfortable position, motionless. He didn't even want to think. He seemed to have had enough of everything. He seemed only to be somehow, to feel throughout his whole body the weariness that follows an attack of nerves.

At first his eyes could make out nothing in the darkness. Then he saw a thin strip of light between the curtains. People's footsteps could be heard from the pavement outside, the clatter of a cart in the distance. It was strange to feel the presence of others around him. But then the strip of light faded and the voices on the street fell silent. The loneliness and silence continued.

His thoughts kept treading their old paths. However much he tried, he couldn't free himself from the world of Kobras' ideas. He was already a partner to them, he had to cultivate the plantation of burdocks and dog-roses. A portion of these ideas were already his own and he began to reshape them to suit his mind.

In the approaching whirl of sleep he thought thoughts distilled from the mind. This same idea continued to take on an ever-changing hue, weight and temperature, according to what mind it was thought by. Some minds would cleanse the ideas, as you would a piece of coal from muddy water, others simply defiled them. Not one single idea, however idiotic, failed to pass through without leaving traces. Thoughts change, but so do minds. Each thought becomes a criterion for your life, your world of thought and feeling. In letting each thought pass through your head, you provide an inkling of the power of your own thought.

Then he gave a start: am I already under the influence of this insanity? This is sheer madness!

– When Goethe's philosophical cogitations were once disturbed by the barking of a dog, he stuck his head out of the window and yelled: "Shadow, you will never entangle me in your nets!" and then said to his conversation partner: "In our little planetary corner of existence, we are obliged to live alongside completely monadic garbage; if they got to know about this on other planets, such company would not do us any credit..."

– But it is still a good question whether shadow has indeed managed to entangle us in its net. A shadow passes over and changes colors, even the shadow of a dog. What happens when a shadow falls is far from absurd. The Earth, which is already a shady little planet, has its own shady little satellite—the Moon. And how the colors change on Earth when the Moon gets in front of the Sun! People's faces become yellow and blue, like those of drowned people, the birds stop singing and the temperature drops. Why then should not the face of God change when it is overshadowed by the shadow of an idiot? And why should I not admit to this change in color?

– People's minds are secret worlds—full of cellars, caves and cells, which conceal dust and spiders' webs, but also surprising thoughts. Today, I have peered down into one vault of the cellar, which is filled with weeds, parasitic shoots and picked Potentilla blooms, but also in one corner a bracken is flowering, its flower aflame.

– And this bearer of flame is now whirling around on the horizon, searching for me—from the yeast factory to the Tivoli, from the madhouse to the slaughterhouse—always to and fro, to and fro, the skeleton of a monkey under his arm. It is searching out of longing, it is searching out of despair, in order to proclaim me the Prophet and Messiah. All around stand dark houses, flames throb, the corners of the town sink in poverty and mud and beyond them begins the countryside clothed as if in eternal night. The city is asleep, the countryside is asleep, only an insane individual wanders abroad without growing weary, guarding his morsel of throbbing thought. This image is so full of pain and horrific beauty. But in the end, this insane man, wearied by his fruitless search, staggers home through the autumn drizzle.

Home?—said Ormusson, stupefied,—whose home?

The blood flowing into his fevered brain on account of the fever of thought filled his whole head with a flight of sparks like an electrical storm. The light spread to his body in concentric circles, its core dense, tightened into a ball of fire, from which burst protuberances like those on the Sun's surface. There was blinding colored pain in this vision.

Then the light grew more even, the colors merged, filling the whole room with a misty red glow. It was the same room, only the ceiling was higher, bowing above like Gothic vaults. The spines of the books in the bookcase and the picture frames lost their relief, merged with the wall, changed to form arabesques and tapestry letters. There was an oaken table with cruciform legs in the middle of the room, around which stood high-backed chairs. On the table a seven-branched candelabra with black candles was burning. There was a halo around each candle, black tears of wax running slowly down them.

Then resonant steps could be heard on the stairs. Someone was trudging up the stairs, dragging something with him. The door opened with a muffled thump and in stepped Kobras, over his shoulder the monkey's skeleton. He was bare headed, his wispy damp hair stood on end, each hair covered with microscopic drops.

He walked blindly over to the window, whose frame Ormusson saw as a cross. With a sudden movement, Kobras spread the skeleton out to form a cross. It remained hanging there; the head was fixed to the upper strut of the window, hanging grimly down. The monkey man's skeleton glowed like an innocent lamb, absolving the sins of the human race's development.

Kobras stood in the middle of the room before his crucifix and sighed deeply. Primeval reverence and a longing for eternity were expressed in that sigh. His eyes glowed with a phosphorescent light, looking up at the teeth of the monkey's open mouth. Then he slowly turned, sat down at the oaken table, rested his head on his hands and huddled up. His collar was still turned up, his pockets bulging with papers, the tails of his coat trailing on the floor, opened like wings.

Ormusson watched this spectacle, unable to move. A kind of throbbing pain was tormenting him, as if his limbs were dying. Thoughts swarmed in his head, contorting themselves into images and figures with the same kind of inspirational logic as when he was creating a work of art. He was suffering, but could not rein in the flight of thought. A row of torches, one after the other, seemed to light up, lighting an abyss.

Then suddenly he heard swift, abrupt steps running down the stairs to the door. At the same time other staggering steps ascended, until they reached the threshold. Who else could be arriving? thought Ormusson with a shudder, but also with sickly curiosity. Who else? The door opened and in stepped two men, approached the table, one stepping briskly, the other staggering. They sat down next to one another on the chairs.

One of the men was tall and thin, with short coal-black hair and the same colored stubble. His commanding yet suffering lips were pressed together in pain. His eyes flashed hither and thither under his black eyebrows, as if seeing that orders were being carried out. A row of medals and ribbons could be seen under his open overcoat.

Ormusson knew this man. He was the Chairman of the Royal Defense League, the Incorporator of the Member States, the Master of Ceremonies and the first Ruler of Europe. He was the President of the World, the Prince, Knight and Margrave of the World Government. This was the Owner of the most important inventions in the world and the Sole World Champion. He was the Artist, the Poet, the Composer and the Sage. Only yesterday, Ormusson had seen him rushing along the street, his brows knit on account of the clouds in the political heavens. His pockets were filled with mandates, certificates and diplomas, plus the medals that would not fit on his chest.

His companion was fat and flushed. Fair hair covered his low brow. His cheeks glowed with health and an abundance of blood. Under his yellow moustache, his lips moved unceasingly.

Ormusson knew this man too. He had also seen him yesterday swaying along through the park with his slow, ambling gait. He had the task of amusing two foreign guests, whose views differed considerably. They were arguing vehemently with one another, both in a different voice, and he had been forced to wave his hands at them. When they stopped quarrelling for a moment, he had laughed generously: ho-ho-ho! Because, to his mind, the whole business had been childish. Constantly supervising others had caused the tolerance within him to grow. As if smoothing over their childish differences of opinion with his well-meaning laugh.

Ormusson marveled at the appearance of the two strangers. They were both governed by their own realm of ideas. They did not represent the first, second or third dimension, but the fourth, fifth or sixth. The borders of their realms never met. What did they have to do with Kobras?

Then the following thought entered Ormusson's buzzing mind: what joined together their ways was their passion of thought. It was the conflagration of feeling that made them part of the same family. With sickly curiosity, he began to follow his flight of fancy.

As if in answer to these thoughts, he again heard footsteps on the stairs. But one of those approaching trod with so light a step that he was already at the door when the other was still halfway up. The door opened abruptly, but nevertheless with tempered force. On the threshold stood a tall monk in a habit that reached the floor, his hood drawn tightly round his head. Out of this black frame, a bony, chalk-white face could be seen. The eyes in this bloodless face slid over those already in the room, and were ultimately drawn to the crucifix. He frowned sternly.

At the same time, a short, gasping man reached the door. Around his rotund body he also wore a black habit that reached the floor, above his fat stomach the bowsprit of a white ship: an ancient brig in full sail and with flags flying. His face was a yellowish white like the Moon. Only his thick red lips stood out against this yellow circle. His head was bare and bald.

The strangers entered the room and took their places at the table, the monk introvertedly aloof from the rest. Ormusson watched them for a time, pondering as to where he had seen them before. Then a flash of memory.

Was it not years ago in Paris, at the founding meeting of the International Order of the Puerile Genius? The men were sitting on a podium in Alcázar Hall, surrounded by religious women. Before them pupils with oiled hair from a seminary were singing hymns from a Latin liturgy in harmony and in high voices. The Dominican was speaking with grim pathos. His coal black eyes glowed in his chalk white face.

He had noted the titles on the program: The Provocator-General of the International Order of Puerile Genius, Leader of the East and West European Geniuses, Deputy to Don Quixote de la Mancha, Tonika the Genius of the First Golden Galleon. He was speaking about the subject of provocation: art and life, but this was not a speech about art or life. The Provocator-General was setting out a thesis: 1) We do not recognize limitless time in space; 2) The state of puerility needs no proof; and 3) No proof convinces a genius.

Then the monk's companion spoke—an artist—the sculptor of the black Venus. He apathetically praised his Nubian Venus—the new Madonna, humpbacked, gibbous, scabby. There was a superior beauty in ugliness, stuntedness, huge chunks of stone, a greater aesthetic value and ethical perfection, senselessness, childishness, the creases of laughter on the face on an idiot. He stamped from one foot to the other, spread his arms wide, beat his belly with his fists, swore in the name of Roman galley slaves.

It was a dark autumn evening and raining outside. The air in the hall grew heavy like humid heat. Madness grew under the ceiling among the misty electric light bulbs. The voices of the singers grew muffled. In an instant the question arose: why this Catholic ritual here, why a real Dominican, why was this happening under the auspices of the Church? But then logical thought melted like candle wax...

Suddenly Ormusson heard soft footsteps on the stairs, hardly audible, like the wings of a bat. It seemed as if someone were leaping upwards, two steps up and one down. The door opened soundlessly and slightly, and a small head on a thin neck peered inside. He looked in both directions, slid into the room, shut the door behind him and sidled up to the table, as if hovering.

Everything about him seemed pliant and lithe. He did not seem to have any fixed height. He could draw in his arms and legs at will, then stretch them out like antennae. His darting eyes glided from one person to the other, both looking in a different direction and it seemed as if he could turn his head in two directions at once, so fanciful was his neck.

Ormusson had known this man a long time, since his schooldays. Was this not the one who could fold his fingers into the palms of his hands so that they looked as if they belonged to someone else—and then offer them for sale? And who held others' fingers in his hand as if they were his own, then offering them for sale to their true owners? But more importantly than that: he had invented a device for looking around corners, had taken out a patent on it and marketed it. He was planning to invent a pair of radio spectacles and an extendable arm. He himself was like a chameleon: he could change his hair color at will and his nails would grow as you watched. He could wiggle his ears and belonged to every group.

He bowed nicely in all directions, hunched up, and sat down at the table. But although he now had a place, he spread himself: his spring-like legs stretched under the table over to the other side, his pliant arms lay like whiplashes across the table, his delicate fingers moving like the tentacles of a polyp towards the table's edge.

The presence of this man gave rise to a surge of anger in Ormusson. He was the only guileful and shady character in this family of noble dreamers and sufferers! He was a compromise of ideas, a mixture of dimensions, the wrong embryo of good and evil! And Ormusson felt pain in his mind, and a flight of sparks arose, alternating with the pain.

When he came to, a lively conversation had started around the table. A symposium had begun—an intoxicated passion of thought, the broken words of exchanges of words, brought forth with painful pathos. The six sitters together formed a fantastical group, their bodies became distorted, their faces halved, their arms waved like the bare branches of trees in the black winds of autumn. The debate could be heard as if from afar through a mist. There were no logical words, only flying thought!

Kobras: The time is ripe! The time to bow down to the works of the Master! Drive all feelings of evil to a greater logic, drive passion to become clearer thought! The world is waiting! The nations are waiting like the woods for a wildfire.

Round-the-Corner (his voice high and deceitful: he shifted backwards and forwards nimbly as he spoke; he wet his thin lips as with a serpent's tongue): But the Gravedigger is not here, the great Burier of God, ha, ha... The digger of graves for all reality, so that ideas would hold sway... The demolisher of straight lines, the executioner of geometry, the murderer of logic, the great master of dreams... heh, heh, heh...

Kobras: Time is passing. We are growing old from thinking. Every year that passes is a thousand. Years are full of thought like quarries. They are charged as if with dynamite. Time to light the fuse! The fuse!

Dominican (gruffly, not moving a muscle of his face): That is not the way for Evil to gain control. Only through the Catholic Church can that be achieved. The Church holds all possibilities within it. It can also develop supreme Evil once the time is ripe. It can bring it to victory, all that is needed is a sense of purpose!

Round-the-Corner: Heh, heh, heh! This has been going on for two thousand years! The odd Borgia as Pope, the odd woman Pope like John, who gave birth on the street, the odd Torquemada... heh, heh, heh...

Kobras: You cannot lead Evil to victory only by way of vice, when no ideology exists. Evil is a virtue! Thought is needed!

Sculptor of the Black Venus (mumbling): Ideology—none needed. Just someone with hairy, scabby. Black. A female. Decline. Reaction. Nubia. The ship sails off. Forward, Burbuhti.

World President (loudly): That would lead to anarchy. It is against nature. It is not allowed. It was not foreseen when the statutes were drawn up.

Trinity Man (reprimanding): I can't understand, what with everyone talking through one another. Hold on! One at a time. The rest should wait their turn. One at a time!

Kobras: There is life on other planets too. Sometimes at another level of development, but life nonetheless. Abstract thought arises there as well. The idea of a god and a devil is developing there too. But worlds are born and die, and for that reason the move from the creation of a world to its doomsday should form a continuous process. But the first and last points cannot be continuous. We cannot therefore link our idea of the devil's works with our local descent into sin, or our doomsday.

And for that reason our brother the Dominican is in error when he thinks the question can be solved only via our earthly church.

– You have to think in greater, broader terms—in interplanetary ones. Our local mystery is only a small detail within the universal mystery, among the dust of the cosmos. If we only make decisions on that basis, we are like children who do not know what is happening beyond the walls of their playroom.

– How narrow the idea of Christianity is! Can you go and preach on distant planets, those that exist and those to come, about one miracle worker in an obscure Jewish province who solved the problem of salvation for the entire universe? Childishness! Sheer childishness!

– Or must the same mystery of Christ's suffering repeat itself on every planet as it has occurred here on Earth? But in that case God would need to have many sons—myriads! And his invitation would be to the crucifixion of His sons!

– Or would the same Christ have to appear on each different planet? But that would be interplanetary theatre, finished a thousand times, begun again a thousand times. Christ would have to be a professional miracle worker and perisher on the Cross. Judas would have to sell himself myriads of times and hang himself likewise. Who can say whether we have had the première here? Maybe it was the thousand-and-first time, here on Earth. Could it not have happened tens of millions of years before in the Golgotha of the Moon?—At the craters of Alpetragius or Regiomontanus? But who would be saved by theatre?

– Whole peoples have been tricked! They have taken this performance for real! The reverence of peoples has been trampled underfoot! The Crusades have been in vain, the Inquisition likewise, and the violent deeds of missionaries! Believers have been dragged to the stake for nothing! This has all been nothing more than endless repetition, a thousandth reprint, unwitting plagiarism, from other planets!

Dominican: If Christ has appeared before, then first and foremost as plagiarism of the Devil. Why not? He knew of Christ's coming, right from the time of his falling into sin. Buddha too followed Christ with his life, as he came later. He lived like Christ, performed his miracles and taught like Christ, but was nevertheless not Christ! What happened on other planets could be plagiarism, the only true mystery occurring here.

Kobras: You are therefore trying to say that the inhabitants of other planets will become "blessed" on account of the plagiarism of the Devil or they will die out? Very well! But then it is clear that God is only interested in the Earth, while the whole universe is the inheritance of the Devil! Christianity's idea of God is too narrow. The idea of evil, however, is beyond space and time. And for that reason let us bear our new faith beyond our miserable Earth, into the solar system and the Milky Way. Let us embrace the whole universe, whose history had not been repeated in any local occurrence, with our reverence, falling into sin, salvation or latter day! Let us recognize broader ideas!

Round-the Corner: And let us not limit ourselves to mankind. Is not a larger part of life beyond Man—in animals and plants. The Jew Christ said: let little children come unto me. The Jew Heine could, however, imagine a time when monkeys and kangaroos would have converted to Christianity! Quite true! Go on from there! Animals rising from the dead, snails going to heaven, primeval slime becoming blessed... heh, heh, heh... Already there are Negro bishops, why couldn't baboons hold that office?

Dominican: Brother apologist for the Devil, you are mixing things up. The principle of God is as universal as that of the Devil. It's the same pure concept...

Round-the-Corner: Is that the principle of pure good?

Dominican: It is.

Round-the-Corner: Well, tell me then, brother Dominican, how good can be evil? How can absolute good be vicious, vengeful, destructive? Is this not taking bread from the Devil? Explain this paradox to me, heh, heh, heh...

Dominican: Are you thus an advocate of the Devil, in that you are defending his interests? There is but one logic: God has created the Devil to tempt people and then punish those who fall...

Round-the-Corner: Is then the Devil nothing more than a servant to God? Heh, heh, heh...

Dominican: Yes, that principle is what the salvational church is based on, when it resists the Devil's work and is therefore no more than the servant of another god.

Round-the-Corner: A grand plan: to appoint servants for the struggle and then pass judgment yourself! Grand indeed! But why does God judge at all, if He could have made mankind infallible in the first place? Does everything depend solely on Him? Or on someone else after all? Some servant? Ha, ha, ha!

– But He himself is not absolutely good and infallible either. So ditto His handiwork—and that is where the whole problem lies. He has a mixture of the principles of good and evil within him, but in unequal proportions. He is secretive and inquisitive. I can't say I know whether the Devil is any more perfect, as our comrade here, Kobras opines, but it seems to me that they are very similar. But what I would like to know is: which of them created the world as it is? Which of them has created which of them? That for me is the million-dollar question. Heh, heh, heh...

– God is the beginning and the end, beyond Him there is no will. Where then did the Devil's world come from? A revolt among angels? A revolt against an almighty, omniscient, absolute being, who, by the way, also created those angels as they are? And among these, the Devil himself, about whom God *must* have known, when He created him, that he was going to revolt? This for me is the million-dollar question: can God be naïve and do what He Himself does not know anything about?

– To sum up: absolute good creates angels, about whom He already knew that they would stage a revolt; creates human beings, about whom He knew that the Fall was coming to them; and finally, as if that all weren't enough, He kills His own son in order to continue to experiment on mankind... And furthermore: the "free will" of human beings to choose between two masters, heh, heh, heh...Isn't this all a bit of a tale, thin on logic, brother Dominican?

Dominican: Yes, human logic cannot penetrate here. That is the greatest mystery of faith.

Kobras: What is clearer is that the compromise Manes made was one between the teachings of Zoroaster and Christianity. Two similar points of departure: Ormuzd and Ahriman, good and evil, light and darkness. The good God created Adam—the bad one, Eve. Their children carry two souls in their breast: a light soul and a dark soul. There exists a primeval evil deity and that is why mankind is innocent of evildoing. Man dangles between the two fundamental principles...

Round-the-Corner (laughing up his sleeve): Just like Jesus between the two robbers on the Cross... hee, hee, hee!

Kobras: Only Greenlanders think logically: good is not worth bothering about, because if something is intrinsically good it therefore *cannot* be evil. It cannot do evil or even want to do so. It is against its nature, like burning is to water. Yes, if God is omnipotent, one thing would be impossible for Him to do: renounce his godliness. That would amount to suicide. Not even God has a choice—isn't that strange? For that reason, human beings have no reason at all to take God's wishes into account, as He cannot punish them for transgressions. The only being people should pray to, and come to terms with, is the Devil. That is what Gediminas, the pagan Prince of Lithuania, thought when he said: "If I want to get myself crucified, then it must be by the Devil!"—The only logical thinkers of mankind! But such a thought will open up the whole enormous system of philosophy of the shamans of the polar region and bog Lithuanians.

Sculptor: Shamans. Black night. Tents of skins. Drums. Dancing in bear pelts, around and around in one direction, until all is darkness, before them a coal black chasm. The ultimate descent into the depths. Burbuhti!

Kobras: Ideas are needed!

Round-the-Corner: Heh, heh, heh—ideas! Who needs them? (In a whisper:) Exploit the stupidity of Man—that is a stroke of genius. Not wisdom—that doesn't carry far. Napoleon owes his success to human stupidity, prejudice, cupidity, puerility. Find the golden mean of human spiritual benightedness—and you will have achieved all.

– Ideas? Heh, heh, heh... No faith is built upon ingenious ideas. Ideas are for the chosen ones, but those chosen do not need a belief. The herd does not need anything ingenious or new. It is conservative and mistrustful. It only moves forward by way of old ideas, which have changed little. Use the moods that hold sway with the masses right now. No faith is built on wholly new foundations: they are old ideas warmed up. No leader of a faith can be shown to have founded it. They've just mixed a bit of water in old vessels. Later on the storm breaks, in which they merely drown.

– Which is why I am entirely in agreement with our brother the Dominican: the belief in evil must also be developed under the protection of the Church. At least initially, and apparently so. Gather old women around you and announce to them that henceforth Sunday will no longer be the holy day of the week but, say, Friday. No other renewals! Then they will run after you, so you can do anything you like with them. Then poison them, gradually and without their knowledge. If you carry out your new idea you will shock them to death. If you carry out your new idea, you won't get the world moving. Your new idea will not crucify anyone, simply send them to the madhouse!

– Looking askance, looking askew—that encapsulates the whole of the philosophy of life. Reveal your cards only one by one, say about everything else: this is a mystery. Look askance! Otherwise your business will fail...

Kobras: Business! Is our dream business? It is the straightening out for the first time in history of Promethean Man, head in the clouds, mind in space. It is the first true world revolution, the throwing off of all burdens, the crushing of dogmas, the stepping out of belief as such. For the first time mankind will become like God!

Kobras' pathos changed into the flight of a shower of sparks. Under the illumination of this pathos, time changed. Words fell like gleaming meteors. Thoughts were transformed to become fire and light. They lasted forever.

Then suddenly, amid the ensuing silence, a heavy, even tread was heard, approaching steadily and with the sureness of the strokes of a bell. Ever louder, ever nearer, but no quicker. Now they were at the door. It opened slowly and heavily and just as slowly the stranger stepped inside.

"The Grand Gravedigger has arrived!" intoned Kobras solemnly, and rose to his feet. The stranger took a seat in the remaining empty chair and sat there without looking at anyone. The silence continued. The candles burned. Seven black shadows fell on the walls, large and fantastic.

Ormusson looked at the stranger with horrified curiosity. There was something so foreign yet so familiar about him. His back was bowed as if on account of the weight of his head. His hair was parted into white strands and he seemed to be engrossed in boundless thought. He had aged, becoming a thousand years old with all the thinking. Only yesterday, Ormusson had seen him, yet a millennium had passed between. Thought had taken him beyond time and space, into the nameless absolute. He was—absolute phantasm.

Suddenly the stranger raised his hand as if wanting to speak. Ormusson saw a strange ring on his finger, whose stone depicted Leda as she merged with the swan. Then, as if in a flash, he understood whose face he had. This thought became blinding, his head became a ball of fire that could explode at any moment. This endless light was blended with the endless pain of feeling. It was blazing tribulation.

Cold sweat covered Ormusson's brow. "Save me, save me!" he whispered, his lips distorted with fear. It seemed to him that he had been dreaming. But the dream had taken hold of him. It pressed its will, the only will possible in the dream. His limbs became like barbed wire, struggling with this phantasm.

He jumped to his feet as if electrocuted and only woke up when he found himself sitting on the edge of the sofa. His whole body ached from the uncomfortable position. There was sharp drilling in his head. A pale light filled the room.

Ormusson looked around him, his eyes still mixed with dreams. There Kobras was sitting, there the Dominican, there the figure—so foreign yet so familiar. But who was responsible for the fact that they were still sitting where they were—? The thought was a heavy one, making him feel faint, as if the dream were continuing.

Then his attention was caught by the illumination, still so strange. There was something dreamlike in it, it could not be real. A cold, bright grey, shifting light.

And Ormusson rose to go to look at the window. When he had managed to stumble across the room, he saw diagonal lines swish across the window. At the same time he heard a rhythmic rumble coming from the windows and the roof, so dense that it became a roar. A hailstorm was lashing the street outside. Large hailstones were jumping off the telegraph wires, the posts, the windowpanes, and fell bouncing to the ground like white peas.

The street was deserted, every living being had fled to their burrow. At the street corner there was only the tranter's wagon, against whose hood the hailstones were thrashing. The horse was snorting sadly, its head drooping down to its shanks, its ears hanging down. Under the hood the shafts of the tranter's boots could be seen. The scene was as dead as a still life.

Suddenly Kobras came into view on the opposite pavement. He was forging ahead, bent forwards. His face was blue in the grey light of the hail, only his pink ears stuck out like gills. The idiot was trotting along past the closed windows and doors and disappeared into the hailstorm, which lashed his bare pate like the egg of an ostrich.

1924

The Day of the Androgyne

For Elo Tuglas

1.

And so: a summer's morning, sunrise! In the gardens the clumps of trees were stretching towards the radiant clouds. The rosebushes were bending to the ground, spreading their dew, their cool fragrance. The twitter of the tiniest birds could be heard in the trees and rosebushes.

The Androgyne stirred at the warbling of a lark that was circling above the pavilion. One moment birdsong could be heard from one side, and then from the other, through the open windows, like a tiny wake-up call.

But the Androgyne did not open its eyes. It was still sleeping, unborn, still only an inkling of life, the first chord of being. All that it could hear was the twittering of the bird and all it could perceive was a quivering of light through its eyelids.

Through its sleep, it marveled at the fact that it was waking here today in this room, this bed. *Who* had it been yesterday, *where* had it been yesterday? It had forgotten. What was the past?—pollen dispersed on the wind.

Only the lark trilled.

Who to wake up as today? The thought was dreamed. To be a young hunter clothed in green, a grey-headed old man or a wandering gypsy with his bells—? To be a shepherdess in green pastures, a swarthy Moor in a palm forest, or a soldier in a distant desert—?

All possibilities were open to the not-yet-awakened, unborn Androgyne.

Whether even to be at all this day—? To remain in a state of non-existence like an embryo in its sweet dreams—? To see visions, compared with which ordinary dreams were worldly and real—?

To doze in non-existence for a day, several days—centuries, and wake up in another era—or even on another planet—?

Someone asleep and unborn has more opportunities than ever!

A thought shadow arose and fell. Only the billowing. Only the trill of the lark.

A pink light quivered through the eyelids of the Androgyne, spreading in oval rings, mixed with the song of the lark. An inkling of light and sound awoke in an apprehension of being.

The moist fragrance of the soil wafted in, along with the smell of roses. From this sensation of soil a branch formed, leaves, then a bud, then the bud opened up into a bloom. A bumblebee flew around the bloom, landed on it, entered the calyx. It was a sweet thought of the earth!

An instant of deep sleep followed—dark, devoid of sensations, like pitch-black night. Then the Androgyne suddenly awoke and opened its eyes. It was in a new world, in which all previous ones were forgotten.

In the centre of the apricot-colored bedroom, the bed rose like an altar. Indented screens that resembled the wings of butterflies surrounded it. Between them lay a little princess with laughing eyes, looking up at the ceiling.

Then her gaze turned to the windows. Beyond them, a breeze was stirring the waters of the ponds. Bright yellow, pink and green flashes of color played on the silk of the curtains.

The Princess' forget-me-not eyes blinked to the flashes in time. Her rosy ears smiled forth from the depths of the pillow. Somewhere in the sea of covers was the laughter of tiny toes.

Then suddenly from beneath the covers delicate fingers appeared. Hands rose in the air and made finger hares, finger kangaroos, finger giraffes against the light. This zoo ran and leapt, and the Princess laughed herself to distraction.

Because she was only ten years old.

Her awakening was like the first page of a picture book. The day lay ahead, full of marvelous games. She wanted to experience thousands of images before nightfall.

But all of a sudden she grew tired of this game. She gave a deep sigh, a smile still on her lips. She closed her eyes and clapped her hands three times.

At that very moment, the door opened and Madame Pimpa appeared on the threshold in a dress the color of raspberry. Her grey hair had been combed into a thousand curls, her face creased with hundreds of wrinkles of a smile.

Pimpa was followed in by Silvia, carrying a gilded potty. They curtseyed, stretching their arms up high. From between the curtains, a sunbeam penetrated, lighting up the rim of the vessel.

Behind Silvia stood Dorina, with a china cup of steaming chocolate on a tiny tray and microscopic biscuits, between which carnations had been placed.

Madame Pimpa, Silvia and Dorina approached the middle of the room. But the Princess acted as if she were still asleep, her hand under her cheek.

"Princess, Princess!" said Pimpa in her kindly bass voice and came up to the bed. "Princess!"

The lips of the Androgyne and the corners of its lips quivered. Then she could not stand it any longer, bursting into laughter like the tinkling of a bell. She sat bolt upright and clapped her hands. Pimpa's several chins also trembled from laughing, and the black hairs on her jaw quivered.

With mock anger she took the struggling Androgyne in her arms. It was as light as a wisp of mist. Her nightgown stretched to the floor like the tail of a snow-white swan.

Pimpa lifted the edge of her nightgown, revealing her pink bottom. She put the child on the potty.

The Princess wriggled her pink toes out from under the front of the nightgown and looked at the women standing around her. There she was, a tiny figure, hunched over her potty, the folds of her nightgown piled up around her.

The moment a slight tinkle was heard, a *viola d'amore* started up delicately in the adjoining room. The music imitated sighs of love in a pavilion in the rain.

When the music stopped, the Princess jumped back into bed. She began to eat her breakfast, all the while swaying back and forth on her pillow. Pimpa sat on the edge of the bed, her fleshy hands on her raspberry-colored stomach, her face full of motherly love.

They talked for a while seriously about how dreams of angels and bundles of twigs appear to little girls. Hardly had the Princess finished eating, when she slid back under the covers. There, she kicked with her legs and laughed brightly. The entire alcove was filled with frolic and naughtiness.

Meanwhile, Silvia had drawn back the curtain to the bathroom. The Princess hid under the covers, still laughing. Madame Pimpa picked her up and took her into the bathroom.

The walls of this Moorish-style bathroom glittered in gold, lapis lazuli and sapphire in the pink and green light that was flowing in through the round windows up high beneath the ceiling.

In the middle of the room stood a bathtub shaped like snail's shell, on the edge of which a wreath of putti danced. Curved shower taps, like down-turned lotus blooms, descended from the forest of stalactites on the ceiling.

The reflection of the bare body of the Princess trembled in the water. Covering her loins and breasts with her hands, she stepped into the bath. Her resting limbs could be seen in the fragrant water. She was now fifteen years old.

She lay there motionless, eyes closed, neck resting on the hands of Silvia and Dorina. Her earrings tinkled with the beating of her heart against the side of the bath. Her breasts were multiplied by the ripples in the water, so that it looked as if she had two, even three pairs.

A moment of silence that seemed like sleep followed. When the Princess again opened her eyes, the first visitor had arrived.

This was His Grace Benedictissimus, whose custom it was to be given an audience before worldly cares impinged upon the consciousness of the Princess.

The priest was wearing a lilac cloak, which fell in folds around his stout frame. His broad fingers were full of rings. His eyes spoke of great spiritual love. His red nose was ringed by a halo.

The priest sat down on a stool next to the bath and let his blessed gaze fall over the water.

He spoke of the night that had just passed in a quiet voice, and of how it was sister of eternal night. What is beyond we do not know. All we hear is its sound, realize that night is approaching, and shudder.

Hearing this, the eyes of the Princess grew wide with fear.

Then the priest spoke of the temptations of the flesh and the soul. Young princesses were the embodiment of angels. Heavenly blessings fell straight on them as into a chalice. Their souls were beauty, their bodies a mystery.

The Princess laughed lightly on hearing this. The bath echoed the sound like the vault of a temple reflected the sound of the altar bells.

When His Grace left, the Princess rose from the bath. A trickle of water emerged from the stalactites, colored blue, pink and green. The trickle passed over the body of the Princess like misty rainbows, giving only an inkling of their presence.

Then Pimpa wrapped the Princess in a towel and put her on the divan. Quiet music, at which the eyes of the Princess closed, could be heard from somewhere. When she opened them again, Dorina had drawn the curtains aside from the door to the boudoir.

This was an oval hall, whose walls were covered with golden yellow tapestries. Along the walls stood small Rococo tables with bottles of eau de cologne, whose glass fragmented the sunbeams like prisms. The powder boxes were stacked in piles of color, only to be rivaled by the most complex bouquets of flowers.

Between the windows were several of Aubrey Beardsley's sketches of the dressing of Venus from *Under the Hill*, full of godly anachronisms.

The Princess appeared on the threshold, her feet clad in red Moroccan slippers and wearing a lemon yellow mantle, which nevertheless did not mask the beauty of her body.

On either side of the dressing table stood Fantesca and Smeraldina, next to them a row of mannequins all dressed in costumes never seen before.

Here were the underclothes, pink as pimpinella, whose flimsiness made them seem held together by sheer magic. Here were miraculously delicate stockings made from fibers of glass, ending at the top with a kind of chalice of flowers. Here were shoes, whose embroidery had been worked out with a greater degree of imagination than had ever been granted the human mind.

Dressing began, full of inner passion and outward grace.

Both dressers were glowing with enthusiasm. The inspiration was conveyed to their nimble fingers, as they turned the most amazing ideas into reality. Given their wealth of knowledge, the counterpoint of creation and dressing was more perfect than ever before.

Dressing itself lasted three hours and by the end of it the Princess was twenty years old, and one or two details of her toilet had to be changed to take account of her age.

At the very moment that Truffaldino stepped forward to begin the complex process of coiffure, two strangers emerged from another door: the scientist Plusquamdottore and the poet Lelian.

Plusquamdottore was wearing a flowing periwig and spectacles with large black frames. He pointed at himself without interruption with the long nail of the index finger of his right hand as he spoke.

Lelian was a short old man, with wispy hair surrounding his bald pate like a laurel wreath. In his hand he held a thick, gnarled walking stick.

He partly reminded one of the bard who died a thousand years before in the Yellow River, partly of the one that wrote the godly *Sagesse.* His nose, presumably like theirs, was red.

The Princess nodded to the guests in a friendly way, her hair now in a bun like a white dandelion bud.

The guests took their places on small gilded stools by the window and entered into conversation.

The poet was as lost for words as ever. He could not find the right expressions, he stumbled and bumbled through his sentences like someone unacquainted with prose. Then he stopped helplessly, simply knocking rhythmically on the floor with his stick, as if parsing a line of verse.

Plusquamdottore, on the other hand, was loquacious. He spoke with much clamor and grand gestures of great knowledge, generously spicing his tale with quotes from dead languages. He held all the secrets of astrology in his hand, and his entire being was steeped in alchemy. He was ready to draw up horoscopes for all of mankind, to make gold from lead and, if anyone so wished, lead from gold.

But today he was amusing the Princess with much mockery of his enemy Spaccastrummolo. He had come to ask whether she couldn't have this rogue and charlatan burned at the stake, or at least have him knocked to the ground. He had even drawn up a horoscope for Spaccastrummolo that pointed clearly to the stake.

The Princess laughed herself silly, so that Truffaldino had to dance a gig around her head with his curling tongs.

But the Princess didn't grant the scientist his wish. Instead, she allowed the poet to hand over a purse filled with coins to pay for his debts at the tavern. The poet had in fact intended to cancel this debt by reading some of his poetry.

The coiffure, which took an endless time to complete, turned the Princess' head into something ever more fantastic. Her hair rose like flames in the wind, was plucked into a ball, and sprouted horns on both sides of her head. And yet the result of all this combing was both light of touch and tasteful.

Her locks fell in gentle spirals along both her cheeks, enhanced by a couple of natural blooms whose fragrance was discreetly supplemented with eau-de-cologne.

When, at length, the Princess rose to her feet to dress, her underclothing was fluffy with lace all over, like a lilac bush.

Lelian produced a sonnet suitable to the occasion, but was unable to utter it out loud. Maybe he didn't dare, as, despite his age, he was rather flippant, as writers, even prose authors, had always been.

Soon the formlessness of the Princess' underclothing was covered by a costume whose collar rose behind her head, but whose décolleté reached her waist in a narrow strip. In the middle of the back of the costume was a heart-shaped hole. Truffaldino adorned it with a tiny amourette.

By the end of her toilet, the Princess was perfect. Even the most mendacious mirror could not refute this truth. Even Madame Pimpa had to admit this, since Lelian had grown even more tongue-tied at the Princess' beauty.

At the very end of the dressing session, the heavy footsteps of the Chancellor of the Court, Trastullo, could be heard, as well as the thump of his staff as it hit the marble floor.

Trastullo stopped on the threshold, fat and flushed, and leaned his head against the doorpost. His profuse moustache had been twirled, he was wearing a broad-brimmed hat with huge plumes, and was carrying a silver staff. He reminded one partly of the Jack of Hearts, partly of the King of Diamonds.

In a booming voice he announced that the Cabinet was awaiting the arrival of Her Majesty. And Madame Pimpa fastened the cinnabar buttons of the Princess' silver-colored gloves.

2.

Trastullo strode forth, striking his staff against the marble floor at every step so that the rooms resounded. The Princess followed in his footsteps, an expression of boredom on her face. Ardelia, Lucinda and Amaryllis, who appeared more beautiful than ever, walked behind her, brandishing their fans.

Right at the door some Moors joined the company. Today, their bodies were burnished especially black and their fingernails were gilded. They were leading a small monkey with golden earrings that was eating sweets.

The creature was called Joujou.

It was the only living being in the whole company to which the Princess paid any attention. She threatened it with a loving finger, pinched its tiny ear, which was delicate as a withered petal. Then the monkey offered the Princess a half-eaten sweet.

An endless succession of rooms followed.

Bright glassed galleries, in which the sun's rays were split in the colored windows, opened up, alternating with gloomy halls whose walls were covered with horrible frescoes.

Matt white candelabra hung from the ceilings of other halls and the walls were covered with crystals and shells. The light fluttered around the candelabra and crystals like a trapped butterfly.

In some of the rooms huge globes with the contours of unexplored worlds loomed. Ancient toys stood against the back wall of the hall like a forest of bamboo. Items of furniture maintained a mysterious silence, standing on their outstretched legs like fauns whose hooves had trodden centuries.

Then the halls of weaponry opened out with their suits of knights' armor, their visors closed and swords in their hands. An entire embassy of stuffed elephants appeared, their eyes aglitter, along with Indians whose turbans were as red as blood.

Heavy walls, vaults and stairways crisscrossed hither and thither, carving out a wordless epic. The occasional open small room in between whispered with veiled irony.

Then the chaos of rooms opened out into the giant coronation hall. This could only be likened, in fantasy and scope, to other works by its creator, the godlike Piranesi. Here his fantasies of dungeons had reached its pinnacle, as if it were an allegory of the captivity of government.

A broad flagged staircase led up to the throne in tiers. The baldachin over it broke through to the third floor of the palace. Its purple ropes descended like shafts.

Eight-and-twenty iron chandeliers hung from the ceiling of the hall. Their chains could have supported the loads of the most powerful cranes.

The hall itself resembled a primeval forest with all its towering pillars, vaulted balconies, mazes of small bridges and crisscross of arches. Its huge caryatids, Atlases, bowed under the weight of the vaults, their open mouths crying out their stoney anguish, so that the hall looked like more of a mythical stone quarry than a work of architecture.

The fathom-wide cushion of the throne was covered with a thick layer of dust. Never had the Princess sat on that seat of government!

She rushed across the hall without looking around. Only the monkey turned aside, and suddenly climbed up the cords of the baldachin. There he leapt onto the forest of chandeliers from where he jumped onto a prominent abutment. He greeted the Princess at the top of the stair, his snout and paws covered with the dust of history.

The company ascended the stairs, crossed a couple of rooms, and came to a sudden halt in the blindingly bright sunshine.

All around rose the turrets of the Balli de Sfessania, below it was the muddle of the roofs of houses, around it land and sea up to the horizon.

The terrace atop the palace was circumscribed by a crenellated Saracen wall. Here and there one or two parts of the building rose higher, rounding into cupolas or becoming pointed as spires.

The trees were burgeoning, taking over entire parks in places. Vines wreathed between the towers. Fountains played, watering curved palm trees. Red awnings shone brightly beside the ponds like tents in the sun.

It was a palace that had been built in monumental style by the Princess' grandfather, the King Jacopo Carvane, and which had been refined by her uncle, the Prince Regent, Leandro Malaspina.

Her grandfather had built a grim Saracen castle, surrounded by a moat and defended by drawbridges. It stood like an eagle's nest at the top of a cliff, looming over city and land.

Her uncle broke up the sweep of the grim walls, constructing countless ancillary edifices. He turned the moat into ponds and the drawbridges into trellises for vines.

He built hanging gardens in terraces from the walls of the palace down to the sea. He positioned airy pavilions in the parks, created new vistas through the foliage and mysterious groves.

He set up libraries, galleries for paintings and gardens with giraffes. He gave the grottoes their echo, the fountains fragrance, and colored the waters of the ponds.

He commissioned musicians from across the sea, jugglers and firework-makers. In his time, the godly Gozzi built theatres and the master engraver Callot held sway.

Ernst Theodor Amadeus had been his guest, and it was indeed here that Lord Beckford sketched out what would become his grandiose *Vathek*. (It is a lie when they say it was based on Fonthill Abbey!)

While pursuing such amusing and serious pastimes he had turned his own life into a fairytale.

His heir had changed nothing. He agreed to himself to become part of the tale.

The Princess stopped for a moment at the opening in the roof to gaze out over the environs.

Below on three sides lay the red roofs of the city, and the narrow streets wound around. The river meandered like a ribbon among the houses, intersected by bridges, and ran into the sea.

In the west, the city walls could be seen, and beyond the shore and the low sands, which rose up to a red desert. Behind this rose ridges of hills, like a line of teeth on the horizon.

To the north vineyards rose like the breasts of the landscape. They disappeared into the distance, interspersed with snowy mountains and by extensive forests to the east.

But the further south you looked, the punier the forests became. There began the shoreless marems, whose woods were at times like bamboo. Above the eternally sleeping pools, russet mists could be seen. Against the mist, the silhouettes of flamingos.

The marshes came to an end at a black strip of coast, as if filled in with Indian ink. The sea opened out, veiled in a milky haze, through which the sapphire surface beckoned sweetly.

Far away on the horizon, half sea, half sky, an island stood, blue with the cupolas of a palace, looking transparent in the sun. That was the royal sea palace, more marvelous than a fairytale.

The bay cut a triangle into the city. Across the bay was the arch of a tower bridge. On the nearside was the port full of the pennons of ships, gilded galleons with red baldachins, and, over the sterns of light fisherman's boats, nets hung out to dry.

In the port, crowds of people from the four corners of the globe bustled about: Moors in their large turbans, Asians with their beards dyed red, and grim Melanchlenes where only ice fell instead of snow.

In the distance of the bay, three ships with unfurled sails were plying towards the horizon. They grew smaller gradually, vanishing altogether in the end.

The Princess watched them; her eyes seemed to reveal yet unfulfilled desires.

Ah, to sail in one of those ships, disappear at the horizon, sailing towards uncharted territories, and in the end vanish into non-existence... Maybe that desire would come true as soon as tomorrow...

At that instant, the Princess heard the thud of Trastullo's staff against the stone flags, like a pitiless command. She obeyed, stepping into the Council Chamber that lay at the end of the terrace.

This was a somber room, left over from the days of her grandfather. The arches vaulted black above her, a yellow fusty light shone through the narrow windows.

Only the portraits of statesmen, sketched by Callot, brightened up this grim chamber. The master had expressed all of his genius in here. Never had he been so inventive with his series of *commedia dell'arte* figures!

What faces and poses, hidden behind masks and purple mantles! One face was like an entire military campaign and some eyes looked like coups d'état. The master had used more poison and blood than paint. Some portraits had even been painted with the bile of intrigue.

The ministers and the military commanders sat as the Princess arrived at the council table, passing a snuffbox around.

The company parted, only Joujou leapt onto an easy chair in order to take part in the meeting. This was his favorite sleeping place.

The Princess let her eye rove over the Cabinet, which she had largely inherited from her grandfather.

At her right sat the Minister of the Interior, Count Moncrif. He was an old man with a bitter countenance, a sharply cut jaw, and a long narrow goatee. On his belt he wore five pistols. His lace collar stood around his neck like the walls of a city.

To the left of the Princess, the Minister of Foreign Affairs, Count Balletti, a man of indeterminate age, had taken his seat. He was clothed in a tight-fitting suit, on his belt a dagger and poison bottle. He wore a black mask from behind which an indeterminate voice could be heard.

At the two sides of the table sat Marshal Tabacchino, his nose in the snuffbox, and Admiral Bravo, his close-fitting plumed hat singed by gunpowder. Their faces were like grapes ripened in sun and storm.

Straight across the table from the Princess, Lord Byron was leaning back in his chair—the Secretary of State. He was the only member of the Cabinet, whom the Princess had appointed herself. Locks of his dark hair curled in a lighthearted way around his cheeks. He was dressed in the most modern of fashions, beyond time and space. In his large décolleté the order of the Holy Amor, awarded for services rendered, could be seen.

The Princess opened the meeting and her box of chocolates at one fell swoop.

"And so, gentlemen," she pronounced, pushing a chocolate into the mouth of the monkey, "all is quiet in the realm, I'm afraid to say."

"All is indeed quiet in the realm!" Count Moncrif blurted out, banging his fist on the table. "I am responsible for that!"

"Oh really?" sniggered Count Balletti, surprised behind his mask. "In that case, please excuse me for not having been aware of this. The information I receive is so inadequate!"

"What are you trying to say with that, Count Balletti?" thundered Count Moncrif in a challenging tone of voice.

"Nothing, nothing at all," said Count Balletti smoothly, turning in his chair. "It's just that I have heard that beyond the Black Isles pirate vessels have been spotted, and beyond the White Mountains, Bedouins are on the prowl. But I'm not trying to imply anything."

"Pirates and Bedouins?" said Moncrif in astonishment. "But those are matters for Foreign Affairs, my dear Count Balletti!"

"That they are, that they are," tittered Balletti, "but they threaten to become internal affairs, my dear Count Moncrif—heh, heh, heh!"

Right at the start of this dialogue, a most difficult question had been broached. And now Admiral Bravo and Marshal Tabacchino entered the fray.

They were as different as chalk and cheese. Their military sarcasm was poisonous and abrupt. And their services to the realm in holding it together were greater than the realm itself.

The Marshal suggested trying to conquer the desert with the fleet; the Admiral wanted to tackle the pirates by means of cavalry. It looked as if they wanted to begin the battle right across the table.

There was by now so much gunpowder smoke in the air that the monkey in the easy chair sneezed.

The Princess was in the best of moods. Right from the start, the meeting had proved more interesting than she could ever have imagined. Politics was not, after all, so lacking in imagination! And the Princess immersed herself in it with gleeful seriousness.

Especially from the moment that Count Moncrif accused Count Balletti of siding with the pirates and Count Balletti accused Count Moncrif of taking bribes from the Bedouins.

As a pastime, the Princess was daydreaming about which of them she would have hanged, her Minister of the Interior or her Minister of Foreign Affairs. This was important, with regard to the ceremony involved. In the former case, she would have to make her request in an honorably diplomatic manner, in the latter by way of a detachment of gendarmes.

Of course this was but a flight of fancy. For she was indifferent as to which one of them stole the most.

Soon, it became hard to distinguish the faces of the antagonists. They fused into one bout of impetuosity. In this, at least, the Cabinet was united.

All that could be heard now was Moncrif's hoarse roar: "My dear Count, you have forgotten the fact that I am your elder!"

Whereupon Balletti replied in a slithery whisper: "My dear Count, you have forgotten that I have been a Minister longer than you!"

"Gentlemen," interrupted the Princess laughing, "abandon this topic. Your imagination is becoming too realistic. And what is more, you are frightening my monkey.—There, there, little Joujou, politics is a gloomy affair. You are happy—you cannot even control yourself, let alone others!"

But to the Cabinet, not even the boundaries of the realm were clear. It seemed as if some minister or other had sold a portion of the realm without the prior knowledge of the others.

Fantastic maps of even more fantastic continents and oceans were brought in. They were on papyrus and parchment and dated back to the days of the geographer Ptolemy. The maps were unfurled with a rustle and the ministers stuck their noses into them.

The Princess suddenly grew bored with it all. Lord Byron yawned, like a man who thought it sufficient if only the tiniest of states would manage to survive. The Princess leaned across the table towards him.

"They can even make buffoonery boring!" she whispered with a sigh. "During their tussle, I have aged five years!"

Then she put her finger to her lips, took Lord Byron by the hand, and they tiptoed out together. The monkey awoke and tripped after them.

The ministers' suffocating squabbling could be heard over the maps. The pile of maps grew over their heads. They probably died beneath them.

3.

On the great terrace Lucinda, Amaryllis and Ardelia, along with Leandro, Lelio and Florimond, were waiting.

The ladies were wearing hyacinth mantles and gilded shoes. Under veiled hats their heads seemed like the buds of flowers, their hair hung in golden spirals.

The curly heads of the men were topped by red plumed berets. Their pink waistcoats were covered with enameled buttons. Lelio's hose was green on one leg, white on the other. Leandro's left leg was covered with black and white horizontal bands, his right leg was bare. Florimond's trouser cuffs were pink.

The company passed the time watching parrots fighting. The parrots called one another hideous names. Leandro whispered quite dubious jokes into Ardelia's ear. Lelio was watching Amaryllis and sighing.

The Moors baited the parrots, bending down over them, their fingers touching the ground. They looked like toys made of black wood in the sunshine. And the sun itself flared up in the glass cupolas, with a vehemence only to be found in ancient times and fairy tales.

The Princess was glad at seeing everything as it was, so that she took on a more youthful appearance. Only the presence of Lord Byron obliged her to remain in what were her best years as a woman.

But she clapped her hands, laughed loudly and cried out the nicknames of her favorites, so that even the monkey grew jealous.

Filled with this merry laughter and lively fun, the company left the great terrace. A wide staircase led down over the walls, borne on the strongest of arches. The Moors followed the company, carrying bright red parasols decorated with bells and fringes.

On each side of the terrace, pools mirrored the feet of the marble pillars and the cypresses, which had been clipped to form cubes and pyramids. Behind them began the long avenues of the park, full of secrets and surprises, like a labyrinth.

The company disappeared from view in this realm of green mystery and surprise.

How gay was the *Avenue des Ah Ah Ha*! How forlornly sweet the Path of Mischievous Thoughts! How deep and anonymous the *allées* whose darkness could be compared only to alcoves!

In the shade of the trees, gentle quartets, which ceased their playing as the company passed by, were playing, then striking up again once it had passed. Fountains bubbled their terse frenzy onto an unguarded world. And lovers sighed into the grottoes so that the echoes might reach their partners.

One of the statues of Venus in a grotto was at the same time a fountain, as if alive. A Black Neptune cast sideward glances at her, as if nurturing plans of fishing in his mind.

The pools were stagnant in front of the grottoes, and gave off a cloyingly soporific smell. The opus magnum of the landscape architects of Leandro Malaspina was thus all the more charming. With his forgetfulness, he added the melancholy of the ephemeral to the joy all around.

Like a bright mirage, the royal rose garden emerged out of the rose-colored marble colonnade. Sphinxes at the edge of the avenues smiled enigmatically. A sunbeam ran like a living being down one path. A number of tame fauns and nymphs were shrieking shrilly in the shadows of the trees.

Through the portals cut into the walls of the park, endless vistas with watercourses and landscapes where giraffes roamed could be seen.

Then sunlit meadows opened out before the company. Silver and lilac flower bushes were scattered over these meadows. Hillsides of magnolias, liriodendrons and rhododendrons flowered, their blooms exhibiting a surprising asymmetry.

Straight ahead, artificial lakes glittered like silver with their even more artificial islets. At the water's edge, gondolas rocked like black swans with golden wings.

The Princess stepped into a gondola, leaning lightly on Lord Byron's shoulder. The ringlets on his cheek were a bluish black.

Leandro plucked the strings of a mandolin and Lelio played a minuet on the lute. The gondoliers with their red sashes rocked in the high prows like black shadows. The baldachins' golden fringes billowed. The fleet of boats sailed away from the shore.

The lake was as still as a mirror, and silver glittered in its depths.

Ardelia, Amaryllis and Lucinda began to sing quietly, and were joined by Lelio and Florimond. The lay carried from one gondola to the next, billowing like waves. It was a bittersweet song:

To the land of joy, the land of joy,
The Isle of Cythera,—
Gondolier, gondolier,
Take me away,—
To the land of joy, the land of joy,
The Isle of Cythera...

This song expressed a longing, awakening a nameless pain in the heart. From the shore, the voices of the nymphs replied like the faintest of echoes.

The eyes of the ladies grew moist. Even the voice of the Princess broke, as if searching for something more perfect, as it was not so, even in a dream!

The fleet of gondolas arrived silently at the shore.

The lonely copses and water meadows of the Île d'Amour seemed to submit to the mood of those arriving. They were immovably silent in the bright sunshine. Even the birds of paradise draggled their tails silently through the grass.

Old Pan, the pensioned-off god, was the commandant of the island, and greeted the visitors on the shore with a toothless smile. Today he was wearing his best uniform. Then he withdrew, starting up an old tune about pirates on his pipes.

The picturesque company approached the Temple of Amor, chattering away. Amid the greenery, golden, hyacinth and Negro-black flashes of color winked out. Above the asymmetrical groups, the red parasols blazed.

The façade of the temple contained a row of the most frivolous pillars. Among these a door opened up like an Arabian ghazel. One bas relief depicted Leda in the embrace of the swan, as candid as on the doors of the basilica at Frivoli.

Let us here leave thc contents of the pavilion unnamed! Let us not speak of its intimate rooms and the alcove hall, a grotto of ambiguous fragrance, built by the Moor Al-Gever. Let us not utter a word about the fine collection of shields, of prints, and the library of erotica in which the most complete erotic manual plus the most exact version of the Kama Sutra in translation, along with magnificent Japanese drawings, were to be found.

Let us simply mention the fact that this pavilion housed the intimate secretariat of the Minister of Internal Affairs, Lord Byron. The Rococo style of its furnishings was a marvel to behold.

But today the Princess neither entered the alcove hall nor the secretariat. Perhaps she still heard the morning trill of the lark in her ear, but in any case she looked upon nature here with favor.

She sat down unexpectedly on the lawn, accentuating the green around her by the magnificence of her own costume. All of a sudden everyone appreciated nature. Even Leandro and Ardelia, who now preferred the shade of the trees to the intimacy of the pavilion.

In an instant, the open space in front of the temple was transformed into a camp filled with cushions, rugs and parasols. The Moors set up screens on either side, as Prince Vathek had done when protecting his idyllic beauty, Nouronihar.

Directly in front of the Princess, a meadow descended to the iris-bedecked shore. In the middle of the lawn stood one lone sculpture—a hermaphrodite figure, leaning perversely backwards as if in despair as to which of its natures to give preference to.

It was surrounded by a number of giant amorphophalluses: red calyxes from which poked yellow tongues. The water of the fountain before the statue rose without spray, dancing like a quiet flower, falling almost without sound.

Dwarfs appeared in red coats. Some of them served lyrical chocolate, grapes and waffles on salvers. Others made the grove fragrant with oils. Peacocks strutted slowly around the encampment, fanning out their tails.

The Princess rested, leaning on her cushions. At her feet lay Lord Byron, whose locks were stirred by the fans of the Moors. Her long white fingers played with the tufts of his robe.

The Princess conversed with her Minister about politics, especially internal affairs. Diplomacy rippled in their dreamy eyes. The conversation was conducted more with the eyes than through the lips.

The shadows of the Princess' eyelashes fell on her cheeks. Her carmine red lips twitched, as if in a kiss. Their ironic twist was accentuated by a tiny beauty mark in the corner of her mouth.

From time to time the Lord bowed his head. His fingers trembled. Then he raised his face again and the sweet ironic dialogue of glances continued. It was like a flame flickering in the breeze.

Back and forth the ball of emotion was tossed. It was tossed into the eyes of the opponents, onto their lips, above their heads. It rolled in the grass, disappeared, was found anew. It grew hotter from all this movement, so that eyes could no longer tolerate it. All that was left was the emotion—fracturing under its burden with its weight!

The sweet pain of fracture!

The Princess was now thirty years old, the volume of her body had increased, her upper lip was covered with a misty down. Her rouged face worked, her painted lips trembled. She was a middle-aged woman, with incomparable experience.

She leaned her head back and shut her eyes. Her voluptuous throat was alluringly exposed. Then, without a glance, she offered Lord Byron her two fingers.

The sun was at its zenith, it was hot, it was deathly quiet.

Suddenly, the Princess opened her eyes as if not sure where she was. Her wandering gaze passed over herself.

The blue sky was dazzling, the lawn blindingly blue-green. The fountain no longer purled, the water had remained hanging in the air. The peacocks stood motionless as if made of Indian porcelain.

Everything was frozen in stasis, everything had reached its zenith.

Lucinda and Amaryllis had been picking violets on the hillside. They had bent down, their backs towards those resting on the grass, their hands extended like the throats of birds. Their legs were bare to the knee, their embroidered stockings indicated the way upwards.

The Princess saw no more than their calves. How lithe, how slender, how sweet they were! Her nostrils quivered.

All at once, she felt hot. The swan's legs of the maidens had cut into her brain like a sword. The position of their bodies burned like fire. A dazzling thirst for violence arose in her.

Then the maidens' legs began to tremble like bulrushes. Their faces expressed fear and shame. They quaked like small birds before the hypnotic gaze of a serpent, not daring to move.

A stab of pain went through the body of the Princess and she would have liked to cry out. The embroidered bees of her mantle stung through her clothing, bringing a birth-like grief. She felt the sap flowing within her, her blood pressing through her arteries, her body metamorphosing.

She burst into laughter and jumped up like a panther. Treading carelessly over the cushions, the tea service, and the Moors, she went off in the direction of the pavilion. Her movements were abrupt and manly, the outlines of her face hard as that of an eagle. She vanished into the dark of the pavilion.

Presently, Lord Byron rose. He watched the hermaphroditic figure and on his lips a cynical smile formed.

At the same moment, through the pillars of the Temple of Amor, the sound of a dulcian, a clarino and a theorbo could be heard. At that same moment Pantalone emerged, accompanied by Brighella, dressed like a shepherdess.

Pantalone danced with boundless enticement, while Brighella was unstoppable. She fled dancing through the pâcquerette rosebushes, an expression of true love on her face.

Simultaneously, life had returned to all the rest.

Flavio, Cinthio and Prospero came out dancing, along with Narzissa, Ironetta and Brambilla, some in masks, some without. Daphnis and Chloë were dancing with Arcadian grace and Lovelace and Clarissa were dancing with one another, an epistolary distance apart. From the cool of the trees came Leandro and Ardelia, dancing languidly, each on their own.

The turbans of the Turks were like winding instruments, serpents and rankets. The Moors leapt about, striking huge gongs, fans and parasols in their hands. Even Pan joined in the dance, oblivious of his age and formal attire.

The whole area was transformed into a dance floor. The groups came together in pantomime around Pantalone and Brighella while developing their own individual themes. Here, a majestic sarabande was worked out, there, a solemn chaconne, elsewhere a subtle musette or a stormy bourrée. Even the music varied, covering various themes, coming from different places.

Only Pantalone was self-assured and unyielding. The tempo of his dancing increased to a level of insanity. He brought all his material and manly charms into play, showing off his money pouch and other pouches. All in vain! This drove him into a frenzy; there was sheer madness in his dancing.

He harried Brighella from one edge of the lawn to the other and danced with the most fantastic leaps. Brighella fled with nimble pirouettes, feigning fear and despair.

Pantalone became ever more insistent, ever more obsessive in his movements. And Brighella fled in the direction of the temple of Amor—not knowing whether to submit or seek sanctuary.

At that instant, the Androgyne appeared on the threshold of the temple portal, radiant as the young Apollo, surrounded by shouting and hand-clapping Moors.

He was wearing a short purple cloak and a Spanish hat with feathers. His carmine coat had a golden belt and his silver hose had been knit in such a wonderful way as to afford his legs a godly slenderness.

Brighella dropped to her knees before the temple steps. But he lifted the lady up and kissed her neck. Then they began to dance a gracious dance down to the shore.

Pantalone was green with envy. He danced desperately down the hill, scattering his unspent ducats, which were snatched up by the dancing Moors.

The music, dancing and cries accompanied the company to the gondolas. Pantalone danced until the last gondola was about to leave, then took a huge step and tumbled into the boat, shattering his mask.

It transpired that this had been no one else than Flaminio himself.

The fleet drew away from the shore, but the dwarfs and Moors stayed on land. They danced the despair of being left behind a while longer, then threw themselves one by one into the lake and began to swim. Even in the water their limbs described a dance.

The Moors swam with one arm, holding the parasol with the tinkling bells aloft in the other. Some held fans with which they cooled their perspiring brows as they swam. The yellow and red humps of the dwarfs bobbed in the water like the backs of dolphins.

Prince Androgyne was in the gondola with Amaryllis, Lucinda and Brighella. He was a peerless figure, paying the ladies ambiguous compliments.

His face was young and masculine. His self-willed brow had something of a god about it and his coal black eyes held an incomparable charm, so that Lucinda, who was sitting on his left, was trembling.

The group of gondolas was in the middle of the lake, ringing with music and laughter. Behind swam a motley array of Moors, decorating the surface of the water with their parasols like giant water lilies. Before them were the green hills of the park, behind the blue, gold and white azulejos-tiled cupolas of the palace.

The Prince suddenly felt the need to make broader gestures and enter into more stirring adventures. Everything in him boiled and seethed. He wished to throw himself like a rocket into space, illuminating worlds with an unknown splendor.

4.

The company rode out through the palace portal to the blowing of horns and the barking of dogs.

The Prince was mounted on a black stallion whose mane was braided, spangled with small red roses, its head adorned with large plumes. The saddlecloth had been embellished with small silver bells.

The Prince himself was wearing a short black cloak with golden filigree thrown over one shoulder. His blue satin sleeves were puffed like clouds. He had a red feathered beret on his head and held a snow white Scythian hawk in his hand.

One could almost imagine that he had been painted by Benozzo Gozzoli.

Behind him rode Florimond, Leandro and Lelio. The first of these was costumed like a fop, the other as a page.

They were in turn followed by hunters and boys with dogs, the older hunters clad as Turks, the younger ones as Nubians. The boys with dogs, mounted and on foot, tended to the hawks and kept the dogs under control.

Russet white-flecked Breton dogs were panting with thirst as they thundered ahead. Shaggy gryphons snarled as if rattling chains. And the light grey Berber greyhounds whined and whimpered like moist-eyed children.

The company rushed though the city. The horses were at full gallop; the dog boys ran as hard as they could, accompanied by the baying hounds; plumes fluttered.

On either side, the ancient streets of the city wound away. Sometimes the houses seemed as if they were from toy town, with fantastically painted façades; now and again they passed grim stone buildings, with neither doors nor windows. The streets dipped into dales and rose uphill.

Over the streets, balconies and galleries could be seen. There were large signs with grapes, jugs and wild animals reaching out to the middle of the street. Through the open doorways, goldsmiths, coopers and tanners could be seen working. In the taverns, men sat around, idling at their pitchers.

The bridge over the river was bound on two sides by a variety of small buildings, grouped like swallows' nests. Here, weapons, precious stones and bearskins were sold. Riding over the bridge, they had no inkling of the leaden waters below.

In the middle of the city stood an octagonal tower with a gilded cupola, up which a dark spiral staircase led. The weight of the entrance doorway was supported by stooping giants of stone.

The City Elder had appeared on the steps of the Town Hall to greet the Prince. He was an old man in a russet cloak. As the company passed, wisps of hair floated around his bald pate in the breeze.

Beggars lay under the rows of pillars, stretching their broken arms like tendrils into the light. Curly-haired boys ate melons in the sunlight, scratching mangy dogs. Flocks of pigeons rose from the attics and wheeled fearfully in the air, sensing the proximity of the hawks.

Then the houses grew lower and ended at the city wall. It was a somber scene, with a crenellated top and thin arrow slits.

At the gate stood guards with wide-brimmed hats and funnel-shaped jackboots. They took the toll money for the farmers' loads and chucked their daughters under the chin. As the Prince passed, they clicked their heels with enthusiasm and raised their halberds.

Beyond the ramparts were still a number of thatched houses, but then the fields commenced. There were fields of swaying crops on both sides, irrigated by sluggish channels. The sky was blue, the wind stirred the corn, raising the fresh of the field into the air.

Some large covered wagons passed the hunting party, drawn by slow oxen. On the wagons, men dozed in camel-skin cloaks.

To the left beyond the fields, the vineyards rose blue; to the right, an endless forest. Into these the party went, blowing their horns, their horses neighing, their dogs barking.

The forest grew denser, ever shadier under the trees. The rank foliage was like a roof that hardly a ray of sunshine penetrated. The ancient trees had hunched together, breaking through one another's branches, enclosed in wild growth.

Giant ferns stretched up to the chests of the horses. The dogs pushed through them passionately, and only from the swaying of the ferns could their location be seen.

Clearings came, meadows with high grass, knolls with oak groves, then forest and more forest.

In the clearings, the hunting birds were released and shot like arrows into the clouds, only to appear again with their prey, whose hearts were still beating, moments later. The air around them was filled with flying down and feathers.

The hegolites fled with a shriek, but the dogs drove them back towards the hunters. The Prince killed a trembling gazelle with his pistol. Antelopes shed bitter tears as they lay dying.

In a hillside a fox was stalking a pheasant. But both lost their lives, both the fox and the pheasant.

Then the gryphon dogs growled and out of the bushes emerged an enormous wild boar, clashing its tusks. The dogs pounced on it, but it fled, snorting angrily.

The Prince spurred on his horse and chased the animal. He could see its path through the flattened ferns. In the rush, he lost his hat and ripped his sleeve on a brier bush.

In one of the densest thickets, the dogs cornered the terrified creature. It rose up, its muzzle frothing. But the Prince ended its life with his dagger, his sleeve covered with the boar's blood.

The Prince raised his horn to his lips and blew. The echo of the horn reverberated through the entire forest. A few moments later, the hunters reached the Prince.

The sun was now beginning to set. The hunting party turned in the direction of the hunting lodge. The Turks were carrying the boar, the Nubians blew trumpets. The dogs were bustling about and licking their wounds in the grass.

At the edge of the clearing under the trees stood the hunting lodge. The dining hall was dusky and felt damp. All that penetrated the gloom was the greenish light of the trees. The stove blazed brightly, casting a red glow on the walls, which were covered with dimly discernible paintings.

Here fauns and the centaurs played with nymphs and silenes in love scenes. Amazons rushed around, their hair flying, their bows drawn, with deer fleeing ahead of them. A drunken silene was sleeping next to a wine crater and a passionate centaur was accosting a nymph.

Hardly had the hunters arrived, when kitchen boys dressed as fauns brought freshly baked pastries to the table. Dark red wine gleamed in green goblets. A blazing bonfire threw its glow over everyone.

While the members of the hunting party were eating and drinking, the dog handlers were roasting the wild boar. It rotated in the fire, shining and dripping with fat. The dogs watched, their eyes ablaze.

At the drinking table, the conversation was flowing freely, as it does when only men are present. Leandro told stories whose wit and cynicism knew no bounds. The Amazons on the walls fairly blushed, and the nymphs covered their faces and loins. The centaurs neighed with pleasure.

The Prince laughed loudly and raised his glass. He had grown old, his features had coarsened, his black hair lay matted on his forehead. He exhibited that kind of greatness and manliness that can be acquired only by killing.

Just as they had eaten, the Prince jumped into the saddle. As the others were still resting, he rode alone into the forest.

He was spurred on to go ever deeper in order to find something that would outstrip his previous experiences. His entourage had chained him to reality. Somewhere the frontier must begin, where everything was as impossible as hc himself!

The Prince galloped haphazardly, neither caring about direction nor choosing any route.

Rounded knolls followed, covered in luxurious deciduous trees. The copses rose to the sky like giant haystacks. Streams flowed between the knolls, swelling into lakes. The trees on the hillsides threw their shadows over them.

There was a yellowish gloom in the pillared hall of the somber coniferous forest. All at once, a wall of rock with the traits of a human face rose before the rider. The eye sockets were black under the grim eyebrows of the polypody fronds, the ferns were like a moustache. From its mouth ran a rusty stream like blood. The rider paused for a moment to look. It was as if the monster were winking at him, and his horse snorted with fear.

Then the Prince reached the bank of a wide river. It flowed rapidly and muddily through the forest. The trees had fallen down from their hollows in the bank, their crowns drooping into the water; new bunches of shoots had sprouted from their upright roots. Some of the branches bobbed in the current like black crocodiles.

The rider entered the forest anew. He had managed to completely lose his way. But it was all the same to him.

A winding path led along a sunny slope amid exotic foliage. A number of topaz humming birds flew in the tops of the bushes like butterflies. The Prince drew to a halt and watched this display of color between light and shade.

Then the countryside opened out and the woods receded. Stunted trees rose from the boggy ground. From one side the low sun shone, from the other a narrow sliver of moon could be seen. Evening was approaching.

The horse trod slowly, pressing its hooves into the black friable earth. A strong sickly odor rose, filling the Prince's breast with sweet distress.

The rosy sky above, the silver moon, the black earth and the mawkish smell aroused shades of longing in the Prince.

It was as if he were doing penance. The endless space of the sky opened out above, but the odors of the earth dragged him downwards. He almost wanted to be a human being with all his fetters: ageing, suffering and death.

But this was only a moment of weakness. A second later the Prince smiled a human, yet not human smile and spurred on his horse.

The forest had now come to an end and the boggy lowlands began. The muddy bows of the river wound their way lazily towards the sea. Here and there leaden pools gleamed, covered with milky streaks of mist. Over his head a bank of bulrushes rose. The heads swayed like parasols of papyrus. Beyond them there was the silhouette of the city on the horizon.

A barely discernable path led through the secret world of the marem, The Prince rode unhurriedly through this, scaring off the ibises, red from the sunset, that stood among the bulrushes.

Then the thicket grew so dense it became almost impenetrable. The horse pushed its way forward with its chest. Suddenly the Prince stopped in front of a low mud cabin with a reed roof. The sight of a cabin was so unexpected that the Prince was startled for a brief second.

Then he jumped from the saddle and gave a whistle. At that moment three pistols and a trumpet protruded from the open door.

The Prince burst into laughter: "My dear cavaliers, gunpowder is expensive. I am your friend Prince Androgyne, if you so please."

The brigands leapt out removed their broad-brimmed hats from their heads and described a bow: "Termigisto, Matamoros and Spavento dell'Inferno, your majesty's humble servants!"

The brigands were wearing black cloaks, under which red coats could be seen. Their belts looked like arsenals and the size of their spurs was overwhelming.

This was a grand encounter, rich in feeling and free of prejudice. Here so much beautiful irony and mutual understanding was expressed, that the meeting could even be described as one of sheer diplomacy.

The leader of the brigands, Termigisto, bowed gallantly, raising his hat, whose plumes reached down to the ground, and invited the Prince into the humble abode of the honorable brigands.

Bowing towards one another and uttering phrases of utmost courtesy, they entered the low cabin. In the middle of the table stood an earthenware jug of wine, next to it a roast pig with a dagger stuck into it. The feast was given a good start by the arrival of the Prince.

The banquet could commence!

The hosts looked after their guest as only brigands can. A large bowl of dark red wine went around. Every draught blew through their heads like a waft of fire. And the Prince quaffed his share more eagerly than all the rest.

They drank to one another's health. They held speeches in praise of one another's honor. Their voices swelled. At length the conversation became like the rumbling of thunder, full of praise for one another and threats to outsiders.

It would be impossible to describe the topics and tenor of this conversation—so varied and changeable had it become. It touched upon politics and women, art and philosophy—everything between heaven and earth.

Sad confessions were made, covering delicate matters of the heart. Spavento dell'Inferno wept loudly, exposing his bared chest, which was tattooed with the faces of pretty girls. His soft heart had been dealt a bloody blow by them. But for all that, he was an irrepressible beau. And anyone who doubted this would have their skull crushed!

Matamoros talked of his own deeds of violence on land and at sea. He had, all by himself, captured a hundred gendarmes and robbed three caravans in front of their very eyes. He had taken the virginity of the Queen of Sheba, even though the lady had been guarded by three hundred and three eunuchs. At the same time he had also cavorted with fifty of the Queen's maidservants, like that well-known sportsman Hercules.

His strength was so great that even he himself was afraid of it. He bade the company to hold him by the arms. Otherwise he did not know what he might do with his strength.

The interests and powers of Termigisto were greater still. He took a broad view of everything, being the local leader. He was not even devoid of higher interests.

For that reason, he assured the Prince, Count Moncrif had sentenced him to the gallows. But he had other views on the matter. And these were shared by the Prince. He was of the opinion that if only Termigisto could get hold of Moncrif, it was he that should be hanged.

This pact brought them closer together in an indescribable manner. They drank toasts to friendship and exchanged jackets, without either side making demands on the other. They hugged one another and banged their fists on the table, swearing eternal brotherhood.

This was all so moving that the conversation turned into a feast of song. The room had grown dark, only the flush of the wine still gave off light. In this glow they burst into song, a song still sung by individuals and whole classes, as history proves.

At the height of the feast the sound of a horn came from without. The merrymakers jumped to their feet, and a moment later three pistols and a trumpet were poked out around the door.

Out from the bulrushes emerged Leandro and Lelio, having followed the trail of the Prince. This was a surprising encounter, whose courtly stiffness was softened by the strong wine. After that, all they wanted to do was live—grandly and mind-blindingly!

5.

A Prince, two courtiers and three brigands were rushing towards the city. The moon had risen over the misty marems, casting its silvery light. In this light, the cloaks of the riders flew up like wings.

They followed the path, galloping at full speed. The reeds rustled, the puddle rippled and the hooves of the horses scattered the mud. They rode across the marems like ghosts!

They reached the edge of the mists and rose onto dry land. Beneath their feet the road threw up dust and all around the fields breathed.

Ahead was the dark outlinc of the cily, as grim as an Egyptian mummy. But above the city, between the marshes and the port, the sky glowed red from the bonfires.

Here the houses huddled against the city wall. Every starveling that had not found shelter in the city was here; every evildoer who had no place next to the church had sought refuge here. Here there were taverns, the booths of strolling players and houses of ill repute. For the city swarmed here too, grown tired of the holiness of the church.

Large lanterns hung on tall poles, shedding their light over the crowds of people and the huddle of houses, so that even the gloomy crenellations of the city wall glowed red. The buzz of voices, the loud joyous singing of songs, the blare of musical instruments and the skirl of pipes filled the evening with deafening noise. The voices and the light rose like an afterglow into the sky.

The Prince, the courtiers and the brigands entered this mass of light and voices like the sea. They mixed with sailors, bawds, clerks from the guilds, and groups of beggars in one big celebration. They breathed in the mass of people with quivering nostrils and tasted it with all their bodies.

From the port strange smells wafted: sailors from far countries, multilingual, multicolored, faces from all four corners of the globe. They came, exchanged their gold, apes and ordinary stones for precious ones or wines. They were as slow as history in their enjoyment, as parsimonious as the moment.

From the land, countryside fumes wafted: herds of goats from the distant hills, laborers preparing the corn, with wine pouches on their backs. They were voracious and raw, making do with their hands instead of drinking vessels, a stairwell instead of a bed. They encountered their own wives and sisters and enjoyed themselves.

Between sea and countryside the city sweated, selling itself in a thousand ways. It gobbled up money from all sides, bargained, begged and robbed. Amidst this hunt for Mammon, it enjoyed itself as both king and beggar.

The masks in the crowds were of a thousand kinds, even more expressive than human faces. Next to fake

Negroes were real ones, among feigned devils were the righteous. Evil was hidden behind innocence, but innocence itself was more evil still.

The true devils wore monks' habits, held rosaries in their hands. In a moment they would turn into tiny horned beings and scurry away between the feet of the crowd, climbing up onto the chests of women. They sat there between their breasts, dangling their hooves over the edge of the décolleté, warm and comfortable.

The doors to the booths were wide open, like the gates to Hell. Clowns whooped at the entrance, jingled bells and blew trumpets. Others ran to and fro among the bustle of people, inviting in customers and swearing horribly amongst themselves.

Mimics and histrionic actors gave performances. An acrobat was walking on a tightrope spanned across the street, his legs a fiery red in the light of the bonfires. Jugglers danced between spears, whistling like birds. Indian fakirs had their heads chopped off, but put them back on their shoulders and walked away. Fire-eaters swallowed flames and exhaled smoke.

To one side, Doctor Faust was performing even greater miracles. He appeared along with a Devil called Mephistopheles and had him changed first into a poodle, then into a beautiful woman. The poodle was called Prestigiari, the woman—Beautiful Helen.

A little further off, the captains Cocodrillo, Cucurucu and Bonbardon were bragging. They wore enormously wide-brimmed hats and their swords were so long they were hampered by them while walking. Their macaronic dialogues were bawdy and their voices crashed like thunder. But they fled in desperation when Doctor Bucephalus targeted them with an unbelievably huge enema syringe.

The people breathed heavily and sweatily, clutching their pouches and laughing easily. People flocked around the booths where they were selling sausage, macaroni and beer. They gobbled everything up with their eyes and mouths.

Watchmen chased thieves, making their way forward with their fists. Women squealed in the hands of soldiers, their breasts pressed together like dough in the crush. Beggars were vying with one another as to who could shout the loudest, advertising their ailments and sores like the most expensive of wares.

Gentlemen and robbers walked together for the time being. They drank wines that tasted of poison. They joined scuffles that were mere fantasy fights. And they became intoxicated, one and the other.

Lelio and Spavento dell'Inferno had found each other. They sat yoked together at the tavern table and lamented being cuckolded. Lelio bewailed the fact that a trickster had robbed him of his beloved Amaryllis. And Spavento dell'Inferno cursed his Rosa, who was as mendacious as an epitaph. But then in the tavern they met a couple of sutlers. Their breasts were like Towers of Babel. And the unhappy lovers were consoled.

Leandro and Matamoros took to foolhardy jousting. They had taken over the whole brothel. When they attacked one another they pelted each other with pillows, wine barrels and naked women. The feathers from the burst pillows flew around them like the smoke of battle. They vanished into this mist.

The Prince and Termigisto wandered between the dives of the port. Among the darkness and bonfires, the waft of tar, cinnamon and saffron welled forth. Suddenly, a stretch of black water opened up before them. In the darkness a knife glinted, someone fell into the waves, and someone droned a song. The sound of music and dance could be heard from the ships at anchor in the port.

They turned back towards the taverns. The flames of torches lit up their ghastly faces. The Prince's countenance had changed beyond recognition. The gaps of his missing teeth were black when he smiled broadly. His beard was a matted mass of black tufts.

He incessantly kept changing his costumes and mask in the crowd. He was a gypsy and a Moor, a sailor and an executioner. He wandered from one band to the next. His friendships and animosities knew no bounds.

In one harbor tavern they met friends.

Here was a Pater Benedictissimus, in a mask and garment that concealed his whole face and body. Lord Byron was here to carry out his official duties, his face hidden by two masks—one for his eyes, the other for his jaw, while the poet Lelian had disguised himself merely by having a gypsy girl sit on his knee.

It was a joyful reunion, where government and church met, poetry and an embassy of brigands!

The conversation, in as much as the drinking, embracing and brawling allowed it, was spirited and uplifting. Holding a wine beaker in one hand, a girl in the other,

Lelian declaimed one of his sonnets, which had gone unsaid that morning, about the underwear of the Princess.

It was a magnificent piece of poesy! Especially the last two lines, where it reached its apotheosis in the description of the hermaphrodite's trousers, in whose free verse was hidden such a degree of perversity, but at the same time deeply moral convictions.

The surroundings and situation grew even more miraculous. The Prince seemed to be in several places at once. His thirsting spirit gulped down faces, moods and movements. Naturalism burst out around him and within him.

In one tavern a fight had started, whose cause no one knew. They brandished their swords and bar stools flew through the air. Red wine and blood were blent together.

Termigisto, who had seized hold of a Pierrot that was scratching like a cat and was whirling it by its gaiters as if it were a sling, bawled in a terrible voice:

"I am Ter-r-rmigisto! I am the cripple-maker, the son of earthquake and lightning, the brother of death, the leader of every band of beggars!—Keep your distance if you value your life!

The sailors rolled up their sleeves and hissed through their teeth: "Porca Madonna!" But when Termigisto had whirled so long that all he was holding were the legs of the Pierrot, the enemy fled in panic.

In another tavern, the leader of the brigands, as he took a seat, announced:

"I am Ter-r-rmigisto! I have been raised up to become a Turk and a devil! Every day I shall eat ten Jews and other caricatures! Tomorrow I shall hang on the gallows on the city square Count Moncrif!—Flee, if you value your life!"

An instant later, the room was deserted. The Prince and Termigisto were sitting among the upturned tables. All was still. It was a moment for sadness and introspection. The eyes of the men, now bloodshot, were dreamy. The two of them continued on their way.

Once back in the port, they ended up in a tavern full of Negroes. The torches threw light on their sweating faces. Their earrings glittered and their white teeth shone.

Among the Negroes sat a woman whose black hair had been tied up in a bun, revealing her wrinkled throat. Her browless face was fat as a bag. She was so fleshy that she was spread like dough across three stools. Her costume consisted of a ring in her nose and a red ribbon around her body.

She emitted a terrible smell. The Negroes around her were drunk.

A sudden blinding passion arose in the Prince. Somewhere within him something had balled up, then exploded. He was like Apis, who had broken down the walls of the temple and could see the cattle grazing in the sunlit meadow.

He charged at the Negroes, with Termigisto at his side. The Negroes were livid with rage. The whites of their eyes rolled and trembled, their lips became even redder. They bellowed like stuck pigs at the slaughter:

"Ahii! Margodami! Shambara! Korana—ahii!"

The ensuing battle was a dazzling display, with angry fists and flashing knives. The Negroes bit with their teeth and butted the enemy, their heads like battering rams.

But they were defeated without mercy. They vanished howling into the darkness, and Termigisto rushed after them, howling in the same way.

The woman sat there, a broad smile on her lips, watching the battle. She took a few more swigs of wine. As the battle came to an end, she rose and waddled out of the back door of the tavern.

The Prince followed.

Everything was whirling in his eyes. The beauty of the Negress's body could be seen in glimpses. Her desirability was boundless. The Prince's desire erupted like a crater.

Amid the mud out in the yard stood a small house. By the light of a sliver of moon a huge bed could be seen standing in the middle of the muddy floor like a scaffold.

Nothing more in that house, just as in the world!

The Negress lay down on the bed, the Prince with her. They were animals, their love that of animals. They stayed there a long while.

On rising, the Prince had a strange feeling, as if there was something he had not yet done that day. Something that would be the culmination of the entire meaning of his existence. He reeled out, leaving the Negress-mountain-of-flesh lying there motionless.

All was still. All was dark.

Hardly had the Prince reached the street, but that three stark naked Negroes fell upon him. He only managed to see them on account of their flashing teeth. He killed two of his attackers with his dagger, but one disappeared into the darkness, howling.

The Prince staggered along the street alone. The people had vanished down to the last man and the Moon had begun to set. All that shone in the sky were a few bright stars. The Prince's hands were dripping with the Negroes' blood.

He vanished into the darkness, crawled through muddy marches, got to his feet. Above his head rose the crenellations of the city wall.

He leaned against the wall. Even in the darkness, his face was loathsome and full of fear. He was old and disgusting like a half-putrefied carcass.

But, standing there, his legs began to slip slowly away from the wall. His hairless skull scraped against its stones. He slumped to a sitting posture, then stretched out on the ground like a log.

With a gurgle, he fell asleep, to wake up the next morning—whether as the daughter of a king, a stoker, a shepherdess or a sailor on the open sea—who knows!

– I have grown weary of following his exploits.

1925

Author's Notes

FREEDOM AND DEATH

This is the first story that I began writing in the autumn of 1914 while staying with the Ålander family in their new summer home in Oulunkylä (Åggelby), outside Helsinki, Finland. The idea had ripened from an idea I had when I was a prisoner in the Toompea Gaol in Tallinn back in 1905. I even entered the firewood store there. A rumor was circulating among the prisoners that you could hide in the cellar, then escape. I even saw the door of the escape route, which was supposed to lead into the depths of Toompea Hill. But the prison governor had also heard these tales and thus sealed off the firewood store. It took me a long time before I wrote the first draft of the story. Meanwhile, my task became ever more difficult. I wanted to express the hardships of hiding through the form alone. I wanted the reader to feel the dull, dusty stone.

A long while passed before I went beyond the draft stage. The task grew more difficult as time passed. This gave rise to the paragraphs towards the end, laid upon one another like cyclopean blocks of stone. The idea fermented in my mind for a further ten years. I tried to write it several times in Paris, but got no further than the first page. I remember how I wrote one part in Naples in 1910 in the park of the Villa Nazionale, on a night when I had already been on the streets for a few days and was suffering from hunger and a lack of sleep. Now, in the autumn of 1914, I again had a go at completing it—and succeeded within a couple of weeks. It finally appeared in the fifth Noor-Eesti album, produced by the literary movement of that name.

THE GOLDEN HOOP

My quiet writing life at the Ålanders' house in Oulunkylä did not last long. In 1915 I was forced to flee again. As it was impossible to remain in Finland, I managed to borrow the passport of the artist Ilmari Aalto and left for Petrograd—now as a Finn. I lived on Vassily Island on the 15th Line, with a Latvian family. Life in Petrograd under war conditions was very hard; the winter was cold and damp. My room was only a few paces wide. On one occasion, I was poisoned by the fumes and the paint from the stove. I was very fuzzy in the head for several days and remember nothing from that time.

I could only stand living conditions in Petrograd for a month, then I went back to Finland and established myself in Tampere again in January 1916. I lived on the main street, Hämeenkatu, still using the Finnish surname Aalto, which was especially stressful. Here too, life was grim, the city was suffering a typhus epidemic, so I couldn't stand living there for more than a month either. But it was there nevertheless that I managed to write my story "The Golden Hoop."

The idea had arisen some years before while I was reading some German author (Heinrich Mann, Wassermann?). Although in the end my work had nothing to do with this author. The middle section is based on a folk motif (from Jakob Hurt's "The Songs of the Setu People") and didn't originally belong there, but was added later for the sake of the composition.

Once I returned to Helsinki, I sent the manuscript of "The Golden Hoop" to the Estonian daily "Päevaleht," although our newspapers seemed, over the space of two years of war, to have become entirely estranged from literature. But the story appeared immediately—and from there on, I began an intensive period of writing for Päevaleht, right up to the end of my period in exile.

ARTHUR VALDES

So in late winter 1916 I was in Helsinki again—still as a Finn. The war had entered its third year. I did not initially intend the story to be as broad in scope as it finally turned out. I simply wanted to write a review—except that the work in question did not exist. But things began to open up. I had to create the person of the non-existent writer, present his biography and aesthetic views, think about his work and finally write a criticism of it all. For it to be topical, I linked the work with what was currently taking place—the war. In writing this, I also managed to take myself to task for what was by then a surfeit of aestheticism. But, as regards his oeuvre, I had plenty of sketches for short stories purportedly written by Valdes, works I knew I would never complete. I now found a use for that material. And that is how my critical short-story "Arthur Valdes" came about.

I had intended the story as a joke, but it became something more serious. I began to treat him as someone who had actually lived, and mourned his passing.

The story was published in four consecutive issues of "Päevaleht." It was well received by the readership at large, especially by those people interested in literature. Few people realized that they were dealing with a hoax. I even met people who talked with great piety about the "author who had died young." There were people who really "remembered" Valdes. So it is hardly surprising that M. Kampmann wrestled with the fact of how to describe the author in the final volume of his five-volume history of Estonian literature, when he had not read a line he had written!

During the German occupation, I tried to publish "Arthur Valdes" as a separate work. The habit of the time in Tartu was that authors were personally asked to present their manuscripts to the censor and undergo a personal interview. It was clear to me, however, that the censor, who was a clergyman, would not see the joke and would imagine there to be some ulterior political motive behind the story. I therefore had to keep a straight face and speak of the "memoirs of a victim of the war." But there was one major problem: at the end of the story, there was mention of Valdes having fought on the British side as a volunteer! When I had published the story in the newspaper, I had suppressed the word "British," but this omission drew the attention of the censor, who consequently refused permission for the story to appear as a monograph.

Luckily, the occupation was soon over and Konrad Mägi drew the illustration, complete with mask, for the story, using as his model a photo of a deceased Finnish—Swedish scientist. I wrote a very "heart-rending" foreword which suggested that further works by Valdes remained unpublished on account of the religious beliefs of his relatives, after which the real-life Dr Albert Valdes expressed the opinion in a letter to the press that he would have nothing against the work of his "brother" Arthur appearing!

The myth began to live a life of its own. Aleksander Tassa and August Gailit both embroidered the theme in stories, introducing their own temperaments.

I will add that the works of Valdes presented are in fact those I had been working on for a long while but had not managed to complete. So, "Night Hours" was already written in 1909, first in Paris, but I felt that the verse form did not suit the story. "The Shadow of a Hill" was also originally intended to be written in verse, and I wrote several drafts. "Antoninus" was intended as a work of drama, begun in 1908. "The Island God" arose from my intensive reading of Nietzsche. As regards "The Golem," the theme had come up earlier, when Meyrink's novel (1915) had become so popular; although the German author's work could not yet, in those war years, have reached me.

Valdesiana was added to later. So, for instance, the Finnish author T. Vaaskivi wrote a couple of large feuilletons in the daily "Uusi Suomi" in 1937: "Arthur Valdes eli keinotekoinen kirjailija" (Arthur Valdes, or a Non-Existent Writer). And, later on, a couple of Estonian newspapers kept the myth alive as well. I myself have used Valdes' name as signature to several of my own works. Some jokes don't die easily. *[Translator's note: the contemporary Estonian authors Toomas Vint and Jaan Kross, also spun this tale further during the 1980s and 1990s.]*

CANNIBALS

In the summer of 1916 I was living under very trying circumstances in Ikaala in western Finland, then for a time in Helsinki, from where I made a secret journey back home, then returned to Helsinki. I lived on Kasarminkatu Street under the name of Gustav Suits. It was there that I wrote the story "Cannibals" in its final form.

In the autumn of 1907 some children in the Helsinki suburb of Oulunkylä had found the body of a hanged man while playing in the woods. This incident, which I happened to hear about, began to ferment in my imagination. I wrote the first draft of the story in summer 1908 while living in Tartu. I had already located the story in the surroundings of my childhood home near Ahja Manor. But that version was burnt in the fire at the Ålanders' house that same autumn, along with other manuscripts that I had intended for a collection called

"Hunger." Later on, I made several attempts to rewrite it, but I only succeeded in 1916 in Helsinki. The story appeared immediately in the Estonian daily "Päevaleht."

THE MERMAID

The idea arose in early 1908 when I saw a picture in "Stuudio." This depicted a man in a boat, around whose neck a siren had thrown her arms, so that the man was about to fall into the sea. The picture itself was of no particular value and I do not remember who the artist was, but it gave me the theme for my short story. I sketched out the first variant in Oulunkylä during February of that year. When I was living in Gölby on the Åland Isles in June, I wrote, among other things, the monologue Kaspar the Red held at table during the wedding banquet, after that also wedding songs and an episode in the island church, both of which I left out of the final version. But the work was not making any progress, like all my drafts at the time. Later, I collected material for it in the ethnographical museums in Munich, Berlin and Paris. I wanted to get a clear picture of the culture I was depicting, against whose background the characters appeared. I wanted to vivify a realist-fantasy world, whose culture and society was, to a certain extent, believable. I fused prehistoric Indians with the littoral culture of southern Europe. This story fermented in me for a long time, but I did not finish writing the story itself until ten years later, in December of 1919 in Tartu. It first appeared in "Ilo" in 1920.

Friedebert Tuglas

THE AIR IS FULL OF PASSION

While once reading Lafcadio Hearn's collection of stories, "Kwaidan" (1904), I was surprised by the horrible myth of the flying enraged heads—"Rokuro-kubi." The myth made me start thinking about writing a short story on this theme, and finally, in early 1920, I began writing it down. I tried deliberately to retain an element of Japan about it, although the story is set in a time and place far removed from that country. In Hearn's myth, it is told how a lone rider arrives at a bewitched place, where hideous heads are flying around. I tried, with the help of this myth, to write an allegory on the hatred and thirst for revenge in our society of the time. Although by 1920 our various wars (WWI, Russian Revolution, Estonian War of Independence) had come to an end, their aftershocks were still being felt. In the spring of that same year, I had resumed my literary readings. In the "Säde" hall in the southern Estonian town of Valga, were a number of officers and soldiers, some drunk, all brutalized by war. I read them my short story "The Air is Full of Passion." When I had got to the passage where Lorens fights the heads, one officer sitting in the front row drew a revolver and aimed it at me, so that I was forced to hear: "Well, if you're going to shoot, shoot!" I continued reading, but it was not particularly easy to do so. The story appeared that same year in "Ilo."

THE WANDERER

These three discrete scenes were joined together in time to become a triptych. The first thing I thought of, one warm October evening in 1907 in Oulunkylä, was the idea of three sections as I heard the sound of a musical instrument from behind the circus tent. I wrote the first longer draft at the Solbacken summer house in March 1909. Allan's living quarters were my own room in the Ålander's house, which subsequently burned down. And at that point, I broke off writing the story.

The sketch of the first section first came to me somewhat later—on a rainy day in 1910 in the Luxembourg Museum in Paris. And at that time, all I wrote was a short draft. I did not fill out the story until 1919 at Sarghaua Manor in Vändra, Estonia, (only a verst from C.R. Jakobson's Kurgja). Those were unquiet times, the war was raging in the south, the mood was grim. Pillaging detachments of soldiers were moving about in the woods. One stormy August evening, when the wind blew around the abandoned house, I wrote that fragment. I had imagined my own room on rue Monsieur le Prince in Paris, where I had lived in the late spring of 1914, as Allan's room there. I wrote this part off the cuff and in a way that differed significantly from the original draft, which had been going around in my mind for many years. I also had to rewrite the last section, a sketch for which I had produced earlier, completely from scratch. So in June 1921, while staying at the Puiga Manor in Kasaritsa, I wrote it in a small summer house near the millstream. At the same time, I cobbled together the middle section, and joined it to the two others.

The first chapter of "The Wanderer" appeared in "Ilo" in late 1919, the third in the same publication in 1921, and the whole story in my collection of short stories, "The Wandering of Souls," in 1925.

THE POET AND THE IDIOT

I had the original idea for this story back in 1908 while I was writing a dissertation on the gates of hell. The part of this entitled "And Apologia for the Devil" contained information on the fundamental paradox, but the reasoning did not fit the dissertation. Later I decided to use the episode for the third part of my novel, "Felix Ormusson." But it did not fit in here either, both by way of style and length.. So I decided to publish it separately. I wrote the first part in 1921, the second in 1924, both in Tartu. So sixteen years had passed between the original idea and the final story. The first chapter was published in "Ilo" in 1921, the whole work as a monograph in 1924. Almost all the "idiots" that appear in the story are people I knew personally.

THE DAY OF THE ANDROGYNE

As is the case with several of my stories, I owe its birth to chance. The first impulse came during a writers' meeting in 1918, when someone cracked a joke about a collection of my stories called "The Hermaphrodite's Trousers," to be published in the near future. I had not really thought of writing anything like that, let alone having anything of that nature ready to print. As a continuation of the joke, it was announced that the collection would appear under the somewhat more polite title, "The Hermaphrodite's Day."

But the story did not end there. The title of this non-existent book began to intrigue me. "The Hermaphrodite's Day"—what could this title conceal? What exotic landscapes, grotesque figures, fantasy occurrences? I began taking more and more notes. And the result was, seven years later, a novella entitled "The Day of the Androgyne."

As I cultivated my story, I used what might be termed a system of crop rotation. I have sometimes, over the years, tried to produce works of quite different types and their differing moods, while keeping their creation strictly separate. At about the same time as this story, I was writing "The Shadow of a Man" *(English translation by Oleg Mutt in the story collection "Riders in the Sky," Perioodika publishers, Tallinn, 1972)* in a more tragic vein. By contrast I was also writing such a spoof as "The Day of the Androgyne." Each separate theme is a magnet pulling towards it certain tendencies of feeling, even of style. I am interested in immersing myself in different kinds of literature and not repeating myself too much with regard to style. This has only been possible because I have tended to bury a text for years at a stretch, while the characters are consciously ripened and chance occurrences and comparisons occur. Even at the level of language, I have shared forms between the various literary subjects I have dealt with.

This conscious work has only, of course, been possible during the pre-writing stage. Once I have started committing a text to paper, I have immersed myself in the mood of the topic at hand, forgetting all else. And the result has often been that, while the inspiration has been carried forward from previous drafts, the end result has been quite different, so that only the subject matter and the outlines of the composition remain. This has meant that, when writing the final version, I have often not looked at sections I had already finished.

"The Day of the Androgyne" likewise lived through a series of developments. From a hardly perceptible original concept, the idea grew, first as a serious romantic story, then in the direction of irony, taking on firmer contours all the while. But only when I harnessed the genre of *commedia dell'arte* did I realize how to combine what were intrinsically decorative and grotesque ideas with certain elements of realism. I had now found the backdrop and the tone and I then began to bring together the various parts, without, however, sticking to any particular epoch, specificity of place or logic. A large number of stylistic elements and the names of the characters are borrowed from the world of *commedia dell'arte*, but other elements from quite different areas have been inserted. The grotesque subject matter demanded this. And the main comic thrust and interest was not to be displayed openly in the story, but was to be alluded to in asides, names, hints, almost as if from behind a curtain.

I hardly succeeded in achieving what I had set out to do on every occasion. But I do think it wrong to seek things here that did not interest me at the time. In that case there can be no contact between reviewer and author. But Estonian reviewers tend to only understand deadly serious matters or those for belly laughs, hardly ever things to be smiled at. They will criticize any attempt to aestheticize in a didactic kind of way, while the author has had no other intention but to perhaps make fun of exactly that kind of aestheticizing.

But I now feel I am defending my points of view in too serious a manner. And one should not do so, given the subject matter of the story in question!

Continuing *the* Central European Classics Series

The Central European Classics series, initiated by Timothy Garton Ash, was one of the first large undertakings of CEU Press. Garton Ash, who acted as the general editor of the series, aimed at taking these works of nineteenth- and early twentieth-century classic fiction "out of the ghetto," and onto the shelves of Western booksellers, into the consciousness of Western readers.

The ongoing success of the series, producing seven books between 1993 and 2002, prompted the CEU Press to re-commence and bring out further classics from eastern and central Europe, presenting Friedebert Tuglas' collection of stories under the title *The Poet and the Idiot.*

Forthcoming title:

Stefan Żeromski: *The Coming Spring* (*Przedwiośnie*)

ISSN 1418-0162